In the Amber Chamber

In the Amber Chamber

Stories

Carrie Messenger

BRIGHT
HORSE
BOOKS

Brighthorse Books
13202 N River Drive
Omaha, NE 68112
brighthorsebooks.com

ISBN: 978-1-944467-13-5

Some of the stories in this collection originally appeared in the following publications: "Children in the Time of Dust," *Fairy Tale Review*; "Children Left to Be Raised by Wolves," *Post Road*; "Edgewater," *Crab Orchard Review*; "How the Romanians Ruined Christmas," *Chicago Quarterly Review*; "The Inn of the Former Rural Farm Workers," *Pinball*; "In the Amber Chamber," *The Literary Review*; "In the Pines," *Witness*; "Old Maids," *Beloit Fiction Journal*; "The Poetess Writes Unanswered Letters," *Redivider*; "Reports from the Village of C," *Pleiades*; "South 1144," *Fiction International*; "The Transylvaniess," *Grimoire*; "World's Oldest Living Musician," *The Florida Review*.

For James

CONTENTS

IN THE PINES

Florina

Here's a secret the children know. There's a house at the end of town built in the German style, with gingerbread trim, thick wooden beams, rafters, and windows with Gothic arches. The woods start behind the house, pines and birches spread across the hills. The street dogs gather there, as if they know that's where the wild places begin. Or maybe they're waiting for scraps of the rich food the German man eats. He has a German name so they call him the German but he isn't German, he's American. Maybe he's CIA, probably he's CIA. He teaches courses at the university, but he isn't really a professor. His Romanian accent is uneven but he refuses to ever repeat himself and you must strain to understand him. He doesn't use his hands when he talks, the way Romanians do. He has the soft, small hands of an intellectual, an unruly mustache that he chews at with his bottom lip when he is thinking, and the absent eyes of windows in an abandoned house. You might think the German's house is abandoned, too. The lights are never on in the kitchen; the street dogs gather at the gate. But late at night, the German pulls up in taxis with children, two or three at a time, sometimes four. The children leave in taxis before dawn.

I've been inside the house, been one of the children in the German house at the beginning of the woods. Most of us have gone at least once because we know the German will give you candy, Western candy—Mars Bars and Wrigley's Spearmint if you touch it, and money if you don't get upset when he brings out the camera. He likes boys and girls both, as long as you're not too old or not too young. Just a little hair, he'll tell you once. He won't repeat himself. I'll be too old soon.

There's a real German cuckoo clock in the parlor, so you can count the passing of time and think about how much candy or money you're going to get. He opens up the sofabed. He asks you not to look straight into the camera. Look at each other, look at him, look at his thing. He wants it to be like a real movie. He doesn't like us to wear lipstick. He tells us, what does it matter what clothes you're wearing? You're going to take them off anyway.

In the office, there are calendars of girls in bikinis and signed photographs of the Romanian Women's Gymnastics team. You wait in the office with your candy while he calls you a taxi to take you back down to the Red Bridge, or Tatarasi, or Nicolina, wherever it is that you stay. One of the orphanages, if you're lucky enough to have a bed there and know how to sneak back in at night. I used to, in Children's Home Four by the Red Bridge. I would sew the money into a hole I dug in my mattress.

Or back to your apartment, if you're lucky enough to belong to a family. I never have. Larissa used to visit me, but she never brought me home. Everett would say, I wish you were mine, but I'm too old for his games. Liviu says Everett is looking for me, but I don't care.

I stay under the Red Bridge now. I used to keep the German's money wrapped up in newspaper and stuffed in my underclothes at first. I can't remember what it was I was saving it for. I give it straight to Liviu now. He's the Fish for us. If you give him the money you make, he'll be sure to hurt anyone who hurts you.

You might think we hate the German, but I don't. I like the candy. What I do in the German house at the beginning of the woods is nothing better or worse than what I've done with the older kids at the orphanage. His mustache tickles, but it's all right.

Everett

She left in April. It's October now, and I promised myself I'd find her before winter comes. I keep going over what I could have done to make her stay.

Her name means flower, although I've never seen a child less likely to bloom. Everything about her was faded. Pale skin so that every vitamin shot she got in her arm left a blue-black record, pale clothes hand-washed so many times they weren't red to pink, blue to gray but colors seen through a fog, pale brown hair that didn't hold enough color for her to be considered blonde by the staff at Children's Home Four. If her hair had been blonde, she might have been one of the darlings, the pretty babies that thrive on attention, that learn how to stay alive because someone beside themselves wants them to live.

If Florina had been blonde, it would have been clearer that she wasn't gypsy. You'd think such a pale girl would be beyond suspicion, but the ladies at Children's Home Four have turned suspicion into an art form, and Florina's sulky expressions and the way she faded out until it seemed she wasn't there, how you could almost see through her thin arms as she reached out to us, made it clear to them that she must be a gypsy. Besides, they'd met Florina's mother Larissa, so bossy and with manners so common that if she wasn't gypsy she'd been raised by them. Larissa won't relinquish her rights, so Florina can't be adopted, by me or anyone else.

This year's volunteers from Brigham Young told me Florina had dishwater hair. They wanted to give her highlights, make her cute. They were all blondes themselves, six of them stuck together with their chaperone in their apartment near Cathedral Square. By spring, they were so bored they flirted with me, touching my arm while they asked me to watch the Super Bowl they'd had sent from America. Oh, Everett, they giggled, tossing their ponytails as I walked by.

They know I'm evangelical, that I don't consider Mormons as part of Christ's church, worse than the charismatic churches or the Catholics even, that I would do anything to keep them from converting the babies in their care, but I'm the only American man they know. I'm young enough at twenty-six for them to call me cute behind my back. I play the guitar, I jog, I throw the football around on my breaks. I'm the kind of guy the Brigham Young girls understand, not like the short, skinny Romanians who whistle at them on the street or the teenage orphans who bring them wildflowers, not like the Peace Corps or Soros people who won't talk to the Mormons because they're trying to blend in while the Mormons, in their sweatshirts and jeans or suits if they're going door to door, are staying out of place on purpose. Besides, I'm a missionary, too. These girls understand a mission.

I've been in Romania for four years, since I graduated from Penn in 1996 with a degree in child psychology. My Romanian is so good that the Peace Corps and Soros people use me for translation. They try to pretend that I don't do what I do because the Lord has called me. I've asked Annie, why do they think that being called by Caesar to do what might be the work the Lord wants done is inherently better? This summer, they began inviting me to their parties. Annie's doing, I know. With Florina gone, I've got time on my hands. I play the guitar, I can do Pearl Jam and Nirvana plus endless Beatles covers, I always stay straight-edged but I'm a good guy to have around. They think they might convert me, but they don't get that I went to college with a million of them and they've only met one of me.

If Annie were Christian, and our parents willing, I might be courting her. Her Romanian has a purring village accent from where she spent her Peace Corps days. Sometimes she tries to hold my hand. Once when she was drunk, she kissed me and I let her. Since then, I make sure we're never alone. She's little, dark with pointy features and beady eyes that squeeze tight when she's mad at me. She blends in more than anyone, looking like a Romanian student from the university on the Copou hill, tight black pants, high-heeled boots, cigarettes, and scarves. When she doesn't want her friends to understand us, we talk fast in Romanian, the way I used to with Florina. Annie calls me Mount Everest on the days she likes me.

If I can bring one of Annie's friends over to the Lord, maybe that's what I'm here to do. The economic power, political, the Caesar-power they wield over the world is dazzling. Convert one of them, versus converting one hundred orphans, converting Florina, and I'd stir things up. But the Lord loves each one of my kids as much as any one of those secular missionaries. There's something innately blessed about my orphans. They're the ones who taught me Romanian, taught me because they couldn't believe they couldn't talk to me.

I began learning Romanian with my kindergarten, but I perfected my Romanian with the street children who live under the train station bypasses. That's where I learned all my dirty words, words I haven't let myself use in English ever since I dedicated myself to my mission. Everything those kids say is about f-ing the c—t of their mothers, worst of all, f-ing the c—t of God's mother. If I play my guitar for them, for a little while the cursing, the glue sniffing, the drinking of new wine from plastic liter jugs, the rutting around with each other in the darker corners, stops and they look like children again. Ever since they beat me up and stole my guitar, but I came back to them with black eyes and a cheaper guitar I bought in Bucharest, they treat me with wary respect. Some of them will even come to my classes for the soup and bread I offer. None of them, though, no matter how much I beg, no matter how much I speak in the dirty language, not even if I get them alone, will tell me if they've seen Florina.

There are only so many places where the street kids live in Iasi, and since Florina left Children's Home Four I've haunted them all. She's chosen to be lost to me, deliberately erasing her tracks, perfecting her act of fading out, finishing what she'd been working on since the first day we met. What always scared me the most about Florina's chances was how she was constantly moving from being one of my kids, actu-ally *my* kid if I would admit it to myself, to belonging to the streets and the streets alone.

When I met Florina, she was eight. She didn't even come up to my waist and her wrists were so frail her bones must have been the size of matchsticks. She kept rubbing one wrist against the other, as if the friction kept her warm. I didn't notice her right away. The other children ran to me for hugs and kisses, holding on to my legs as I walked through the cor-ridors. I've read book after book on institutionalized children, but even so, I was troubled by their indiscriminate interest in everyone who walked into their wards. Florina was different. She showed no interest in me.

The month I met her, she came down with double

pneumonia. Her wrists were tied down to the sides of the bed to keep her from scratching. I stopped by to put a cold compress on her forehead at the same time every day, evenings as it was beginning to get dark. My classes for the day were over and the night ones yet to begin, the sky pink over the hills that ring the city. The Romanian poets call Iasi Little Rome. She wouldn't twitch, keeping herself still, her eyes unblinking as the compress came down. I would hold her clammy hand, her fingers clenched up away from me as much as she could with her wrist restrained. After a week, she looked up at me and said, You're always here. And I will be, I told her, and I was.

For the next four years I saved my evenings for her. We'd sing songs together, draw pictures, stroll through Cathedral Square. She'd make me small presents of chestnuts or walnuts, toys and treats that she was given by other foreign volunteers: yo-yos, friendship bracelets, coloring books, Hello Kitty pencils, gum. I learned to accept them all from her, learned that you don't have something if you can't give it away.

I wanted her to belong to me. I realize that people would wonder why a grown man like me would want to adopt a twelve-year-old girl who looks like she's nine or younger. There are some children you fall in love with and some children who fall in love with you, and sometimes you can't tell which is which but you know that child is going to break your heart. The missionary who worked at Children's Home Four before me warned me how hard it is not to have favorites. It's why I adopted three, he said. Remember, it's the multitudes of children who need us, not the one. I tell it to every new group of Brigham Young volunteers. I try to tell it to the secular missionaries who will listen to me, although Annie just laughs at me and reminds me that I'd adopt them all if I could. In spite of our mission, in spite of what the Lord has called us for, it's impossible to love the general without taking delight in the particular.

The last time I saw Florina, she asked if I could teach her the words to songs from Nirvana's *Unplugged* album. She was wearing her ancient Nirvana T-shirt given to her by a summer British volunteer. It went down to her knees, ripped in two places where the fabric had worn through, and the staff ladies wouldn't let Florina wear it unless she sewed it up each morning with her own thread and needle. I tried not to think how much Florina looked like Kurt, his light hair falling across his face as he looked downcast at his guitar. Florina was rubbing her wrists behind her back as she waited for me to say yes.

We sat down on the lone unbroken bench in the orphanage's yard. As I practiced a few warm-up chords, kids gathered around us, squatting and never sitting—Romanian children, orphans or not, know not to spoil their clothes. The Brigham Young girls showed up, sitting cross-legged in the dirt. They have a washer and a dryer in their apartment; they don't know what it's like to wash clothes by hand. They wanted "Love Me Tender" and "Mmmbop" even though they knew I'd take the kids' selections first. Florina asked for "Pennyroyal Tea" and "Jesus Don't Want Me for a Sunbeam."

I said, Florina, Jesus does want you for a sunbeam.

Florina laughed and rubbed her wrists together, but she didn't look at me. She looked out the gate, to the water rivulets flowing down the muddy road. She said, Everett, you want me for a sunbeam. It's not the same thing. I'm not a sunbeam. I'm not a flower, either.

The Brigham Young girls said, in English because they never did learn any Romanian besides please and hello, Oh Florina, we can make you pretty as a flower if you'd let us. It's amazing what happens when you wear your hair a different way. Florina walked with them hand in hand into Children's Home Four. After they combed her hair back, stuck in a barrette with rhinestones in the shape of a daisy (we found the barrette on the ground by the wall) and sent her into the main hall to start her homework, Florina must have gone out the back door, climbed over the iron railing and walked down the road to the end of town, because we never saw her again.

Florina rarely made choices. Ask her if she wanted a cookie or a banana, the blue crayon or the green, English or math lessons, and she'd watch you paralyzed, rubbing her wrists, peering at you through her shaggy pale bangs, waiting for a sign telling her what you wanted her to choose. She chose those songs for me. "I sit and drink pennyroyal tea, still the life that's inside of me. I'm anemic royalty." From "Jesus Don't Want Me for a Sunbeam": "Don't expect me to cry, don't expect me to lie, don't expect me to die for me." I never asked to her to die for Jesus. Over and over, I tried to explain to her that Jesus died for her.

The song I keep thinking about is one she didn't ask for, the Leadbelly song on that album and Annie's favorite. I play it at those parties, but I won't sing it. Annie does instead, in her unwavering alto. "My girl, my girl don't lie to me, tell me where did you sleep last night? In the pines, in the pines, where the sun don't ever shine, I would shiver the whole night through."

I'm no fan of the Orthodox faith, its obedient faithful literally on their knees as they worship a barely literate priest instead of Jesus Christ, Lord, in all his glory, but lately I've been thinking about the legend of Saint Paraschiva. When she died, her body didn't rot. It gave off the perfume of roses. Her chest cavity didn't cave in, as if her lungs were still going about the business of breathing and her heart was still beating on, waiting for that day when body and soul clasp hands and rise to the reward. Her body waits in a gilded casket inside the Metropolitan Cathedral. All over the Moldovan region in the north of Romania, they've built their faith around that wait.

This October, I keep walking through the Cathedral Square as the crowds gathered for Hram, the week-long festival for Saint Paraschiva's hallowing day. I push through the waves of whining orphans tugging on coats and the cripples pulling themselves along in their hand carts or propelling themselves forward by the strength of their arms alone while their stumps drag behind them. Red-eyed street dogs bark on the edges, gypsies hawk their cheap plastic toys at every corner, and in front of the Cathedral, the nuns sell painted wooden icons the size of postcards. The air is thick with newly fried doughnuts and grilled sausages as I move down into the town. I know the new group of Brigham Young girls are looking for me, wishing I'd buy them doughnuts and shoo the beggars and dogs away for them. Everywhere I'm looking for a glimpse of pale Florina. I'm hoping that like Saint Paraschiva, she can keep the rot from setting in, but that unlike Saint Paraschiva, she doesn't die. She isn't dead yet. She can't be. She's got to be somewhere moving on ahead from one state to another, turning into whatever it is she will be when she joins up with the Lord.

Larissa

The researchers only ask me about the babies I didn't have, not the one I did, never about Florina. I must be ruining their statistics, but if they're so lazy to get their subjects from the same clinic it's their fault.

I told the lady that with my first one, I was just a kid. I had to leave school after the eighth form to work as a night janitress at the hospital. He said he would pull out, and it's true he had many times before. He was an intern. It was always clean under his neatly-clipped fingernails. There was always an empty bed somewhere in the hospital.

It would have been easy enough for him to arrange the abortion, but he told me he would say he didn't know me. A neighbor knew what to do. A spindle, a knitting needle, bay leaves. Only it didn't work, and I had to go to the hospital. I bled all over the waiting room chairs. I almost died. The doctor took pity on me and filled the forms out as if I'd had a miscarriage.

After that, I didn't want to have anything to do with men, but that's not how they felt about me. The second time, I tried it myself. The spindle, the oleander. I thought it worked, but I must have been raving because the neighbors broke down the door. They called a nurse who lived across the courtyard. I didn't even know her name, only knew her by the starched uniforms she wore and the silky mustache on her upper lip. She bundled it up in rags and threw it out in the garbage down the block so the dogs couldn't get at it. Someone must have told, because I ended up in court trying to describe my spontaneous miscarriage. I spent two years in prison, as did the nurse who helped me. When I tried to thank her after we both got out, she refused to see me.

I couldn't get a legal job placement because of my prison record. I managed by baking cabbage pies and selling them at the station. That's how I met her father. He was a maintenance man for the tracks. He'd have me do the sewing his wife couldn't because of her crippled hands. He was handsome, a strong chin like a movie star, like that Marcello in *La Dolce Vita*, and silvery hair, too.

I kept her because I was sure he would leave his wife. He paid for a room for a while. He visited Sundays. I'd cook for him frantically, even with my swollen feet, borsch and fried pork the way he liked it. Once she was born, he stopped paying. We stayed on a month before the landlord kicked us out. She was so small, I thought I might break her. I would dream I would lose her in the folds of the quilt or she'd go down the drain in the sink and I couldn't get her back. She cried all the time because she was hungry, but after I breast-fed her she would coo at me as if maybe she could get to be mine. One Sunday, I bundled her up in all of the clothes I had for her plus the two blankets and left her at the orphanage. I was leaking milk, but when I visited, they wouldn't let me feed her. It would be too confusing, the ladies said.

I used to visit her, at Children's Home Four. She clung to me like a monkey. She recognized me right away every time. She'd push the other kids off me to have me for herself. I always told her, don't share your little bird with anyone, not until you're grown and married.

When I was with Nicu, I meant to take her. Then he started hitting his own kids, and me, too, and I couldn't bring Florina into that. I stopped visiting. I didn't want her to see her mother with black eyes. I had two more abortions in those years with Nicu. I didn't need something else to defend.

I got a job here at the clinic because it's funded through Soros, so they don't care about my prison record. They're proud of it, and I'm trotted out to meet foreign visitors. I've got a dormitory room I share with another lady who works at the clinic. There's no room for Florina. Besides, I've heard now that they've fixed up the orphanages with all the foreign money, English lessons, and computers even.

I said to the lady researcher, do you really need to know

anything more? What possible use will this be? What about the one I had? The translators didn't talk in English long enough to match what I said in Romanian. They gave me the money and a pack of Camels and they were gone.

Annie

The Fulbright professor I'm working for this month is named Candy. She's middle-aged but well-preserved, turtlenecks to guard wrinkles, constantly applying hand cream. She's old enough to like it when the Romanian gentlemen kiss her hand. She's spent just enough time in Romania to pick up the paranoia without sensing what to be paranoid about. She keeps asking me, Annie, which person is the one the secret police sent to spy on me?

My answer, the person you least expect, has done nothing to calm her down. I've already picked out my spy. It's my host father's cousin, the one with the harelip who drops in on me unannounced. Candy's asked me to come along to all of her interviews because she doesn't trust her official translator, Hadrian of the oily lips and acne scars and phony Oxford accent. Hadrian would like to sleep with Candy. Candy thinks he only wants a green card, but Hadrian seems interested in Candy's project, excited each morning to interview Iasi's street children, whores, petty thieves, glue sniffers, and ex-cons.

Candy is a sociologist looking at rehabilitation. She wants to blame most of the subjects' problems on being Roma. Maybe she's right, but my Peace Corps time in Truseni gave me village attitudes. I have to be careful to say Roma instead of gypsy in front of her. I'm glad her Romanian is poor because the things Hadrian and I say about the poor fuckers we interview would shock her. Hadrian gets the coffee for us in the morning while I tell Candy what we've got lined up each day. She listens to me leaning out of her balcony, watching the barking street dogs on the Square. Her salmon-colored, nineteenth-century hotel was designed by an architect named Eiffel, but not the Eiffel Tower-Eiffel. Iasi is a town of the almost famous, desperate cousins and second sons.

I haven't told Candy that Hadrian and I have done it before, back when he was a student at the university and I was still living in Truseni. We did it in the woods at the edge of town, pine needles poking us. We did it in his dorm room on his skinny bed while his roommates slept, Hadrian covering my mouth with his hands to keep me quiet. I've promised my Peace Corps friends I would stop dating men with the names of Roman emperors. Since this summer, I've only had eyes for Everett, which my friends think is just as bad. Or worse, they said at our last party. Don't let the fact that he's American fool you. Your cultures are crossed in spite of yourselves.

This morning, Hadrian forgot to bring the Camels, so I had to run out to a kiosk and purchase packs out of pocket. When I came back, Candy gripped my arm and hissed, he's my spy. I'm sure of it.

I have to stay on Candy's good side because I need her recommendation. I want to study anthropology. I told my host mother I'll study her and Truseni. She said, fucking unlikely. Because I spent so much time in Truseni trying to become an insider, it's hard for me to see it now with the eyes of an outsider. When in Truseni, I do as the Truseneancas do—cross myself backwards the Orthodox way, drink all night on holidays, polish my boots when I come back in the house, never bring an even number of flowers unless it's for a funeral.

My adaptations make Everett nervous. Everett's the kind

of Christian that doesn't think anyone else is Christian. He tells me I've picked up all the worst aspects of Orthodoxy at the village church. I think the icons are beautiful, the more unrealistic, the better. The long-nosed Marys, Jesus with his overly attenuated fingers up in blessing, the colors in their faces verging from blood red to a murky green. I like the idea of miracles. I like the idea of submitting to a higher authority that works through a bureaucracy you can't hope to understand. It reminds me of Peace Corps or the Romanian government.

I could talk to Everett about things like that, in ways I couldn't to my host family or my Peace Corps friends. As I walked over this evening to Cathedral Square to meet him, I tried to think about what I might tell him about today's interviews. One of them wouldn't follow Hadrian's questions. She didn't want to talk about her abortions and prison term; she wanted to talk about her daughter. Candy kept nodding and tapping her pencil, even though she hadn't understood anything the subject was saying. If she knew how far afield the interview was going, she would have been furious and Hadrian that much more likely to end up unlucky.

I've been unlucky all summer. I used to think someone should write a short story about Everett and me called "The Missionary Position." He can't date without chaperones. He saw someone in his study group at Penn, but he warned me it wasn't anything I would think of as dating. More like having a very close friend who is a girl that you see for group activ-ities, he said. And I asked her father for permission first. He looked away from me as he said it and held on to his clunky Jesus fish necklace.

Everett hates meeting me at Metro Pizza off Cathedral Square. He wanted us to go to Little Texas, the restaurant run by missionaries at the edge of town by the cemeteries, but I wouldn't go. You have to take a taxi to get there, the waiters smile as if the corners of their mouths have been pinned up by the missionaries in the spirit of customer service, and you'll run into every missionary in Romania.

At Metro Pizza, the waitresses are surly, they never have mushrooms, and the soundtrack is invariably German techno. Everett was waiting for me outside, kicking at the crumbling leaves caught up in the wrought-iron fence by the Cathedral. He's always early. He doesn't want me to wait alone for him. I'll look too much like a streetwalker, I'll invite trouble, there will be implications he can't bear.

He greeted me with a handshake. His hands are long and thin, like the icons. I knew not to hold on for too long. He's growing a Jesus beard. His ruddy cheeks are partially camouflaged by the advance of the beard. His eyes look old in his too-smooth, broad face. He looks like a college boy playing at hippy rather than college boy playing at missionary. He doesn't tuck in his shirts and he wears his Jesus fish necklace, but everything is always clean, too clean. He always polishes the necklace before we go out. He says he has to keep as close to sterile as possible because of the orphanage.

We ordered mushroom pizza but got primavera instead. We asked for the radio to be turned to Romanian pop. The waiter snorted at us and forgot to bring us our drinks. I told Everett about Candy, avoiding talk of Hadrian. He talked about his search for Florina. He'd started to have fantasies that Florina was a modern-day Paraschiva.

Now who sounds Orthodox? I asked.

He blushed under his beard. I wouldn't be able to talk him into going to the Hram Fair now, or walking up on Copou for the fireworks. He asked me to come to a party one of the married missionary couples was having. I couldn't help thinking that having a party on Hram was a good way to keep the flock from being tempted by beer and carnival rides. Everett paid the bill, stalking the waiter and thrusting our crumpled bills into his hand so that he couldn't refuse it. Everett likes to overtip to shame the Metro Pizza staff into customer service.

Yes, let's go play Pictionary with the missionaries, I told him. Forget the fireworks. Forget the Fair. You can draw a triangle, and I'll guess the Trinity. You can draw a cross, and I'll guess the one true faith.

He ignored me. As he hailed a taxi, he said, I'll have an unfair advantage, all those hours I put in drawing with the kids.

In the taxi, I reached for Everett's hand. Mount Everest, I whispered. We're going to defeat them all. He stared at me so I added, At Pictionary. I know you can't be trying to win at too many worldly things at once.

He put my hand in my lap and held it there for a minute. Annie, it's a sin to be with you like that. He took his hand back.

I wanted to tease him, but it came out wrong. Maybe I wanted it to come out wrong. I asked, How do you want to be with Florina? Like that?

Annie. He brought his face closer and closer to mine so I could see the individual hairs that made up his beard. What I want is for you and me and Florina to be a family together. That can't happen until we find her.

And until I change my wicked ways, I said, trying to glide through the conversation. Even while we were having it, I guessed it might be our last.

He reached out for both my hands, holding them the way he would if we were about to begin a Romanian dance, a *sirba*, a *joc*. If my host mother were to see it, she would think we were courting. He said, It would be easier on me. If you changed. Do you know how hard it is to watch someone you care about risk damnation? Don't you know I'm constantly praying for you to find your way?

You mean *your* way, I told him. I turned away from him to look out the back window. We were stopped at a light. The fireworks started up behind us, splintering across the sky. I couldn't believe I wasn't at the Fair, couldn't believe I wasn't back in Truseni for Hram with my host family, couldn't believe I was going to a missionary party. I turned back to Everett. His eyes were glued to a group of street children huddled at the corner around a trashcan fire. A pale girl was haloed in the light of an exploding firecracker. Everett opened the taxi door and jumped out. I watched Everett running after that moon-faced kid. She slipped into the crowd. He never once looked back at me.

I had the taxi take me back home. I sat up in my kitchen drinking gin. There was a confession I hadn't made to Everett. Last week, Candy wanted to interview pimps. Hadrian and I set one up with the *Peste*, the fish, Romanian slang for pimp, down under the Red Bridge. Liviu was an orphan and had spent time in prison. Even under the Bridge, the weather was perfect, the sky the dark blue it has in Iasi sometimes, a metallic blue like an icon. The leaves of the chestnut and linden trees were a brilliant ochre. Liviu was dressed up in a flashy suit and kept winking at Candy. Hadrian found the whole situation distasteful, brushing his hands over and over on the seat of his pants as he checked the interview ques-tions with the mechanical pencil he kept clicking. All I had to do was hold the mini tape recorder steady. As Liviu listed his successes, the number of girls and boys working for him, neighborhoods he wanted to move into as he franchised, my eyes wandered through his kingdom. There, under the dripping Red Bridge, I saw Florina playing tug of war with a mangy puppy. I recognized her from the pictures stuck to Everett's fridge: pale bruised skin, limp light hair, a girl so distinctly absent she'd created a presence.

I didn't call Everett on his mobile phone. I didn't tell him about it later, pretending I didn't realize I was talking to her right away. Instead, I interviewed her, using Candy's standard set of questions. Everett wants Florina's soul and as it turns out, all I'm interested in is her data. Florina kept going on and on about a house at the end of the woods, a house at the end of the woods. She stuttered as she talked, first holding on to the squirming puppy, then rubbing one of her wrists with the other. The usual tics you see in people who've lived through institutionalization. My host mother told me once that everyone in Romania is crazy, that the whole country is a big nuthouse. There was a story Florina wanted to tell that had nothing to do with life on the streets, nothing to do with life under the Red Bridge, something about Germans and a fairy-tale house, but as she began, Liviu came over and had me tell Candy there had been no arrangements for any of his working girls to be interviewed. I gave Florina a pack of Camels anyway.

It's time for me to go home, but where's home? Truseni? Michigan? Where should I be celebrating my real Hram? Sometimes it feels like all of us, all of these bad Americans, are part of some diabolical homecoming leading us straight to Iasi. Tonight at Saint Paraschiva's Cathedral, I'll make my true confession. The priest will mumble something back to me. No matter what he says, I'll hear it as *Dumnezeu sa ierte.* Forgive us, Lord. On my way out, I'll give the nuns a 5,000 lei note and light a candle for Florina, sticking the candle up straight in the sandbox, making sure it doesn't blow out at least until after I've let the cathedral.

Karl

Say what you want, I always fed those kids and no one else was looking after the health of their bodies. No one loved their bodies as much as I did.

If I hadn't gotten greedy, it could have gone on forever, a sad little society chock-full of orphans they weren't keeping track of. I'm not sure whether I chose to be a scholar of Balkan languages or Balkan languages chose me. Slavic, Magyar, Romance, Hellenic—if it was Balkan, I dabbled in it. I received grants to Bulgaria and Romania in the early eighties and never looked back. Bulgaria had better weather and spicier food, but it lacked the orphans. I set up shop with a contract at the university in Iasi teaching American culture. The U.S. State Department used me as a source of information in Ceausescu's weird country. The coeds thought I was sexist, but the truth is I simply had no interest in them whatsoever.

The opening up of Eastern Europe in 1989, the internet, cheap digital technology, all made the business end of my enterprise possible but the more money I made, the more I knew I would lose everything. What a time we had, though, the orphans and me, before it all spiraled out away from us.

The United States Embassy gave me up quick enough once the authorities in Iasi built their case. Too much of what the street children were saying matched the visual evidence of the videos. Too many children were ready to testify, their cute little faces in the paper, on the TV.

The other prisoners would like to kill me. Their shanks are

ready, sharpened and hidden. The guards will let them. The coroner won't be too careful at the autopsy. I'll be stomped to death in a riot, stabbed in the heart by my cellmates. A good way to go in the country of Dracula, as I wrote in one of my scholarly articles. It's a hell to balance the paradise I used to have, those skinny, all-too-knowing virgins in and out of my sofabed. A house to call my own at the end of the woods.

Actually, I can't even remember Florina, and you wouldn't either if the videos with her weren't so popular among guys who like the idea of making it with the saddest orphans.

It isn't a sin to be with you, pretty one. They said during the trial I told her that in one of the videos. The best-selling one. If it's so, if I really said it, I was lying. She wasn't pretty, not like those tiny boys with their coppery skin and black satiny hair, or some of those supple girls that were regular little Nadia Comănecis once you started to film them, back flips in bed and I'd be calling 10, 10, 10 as I came all over them.

If you've seen the videos, shouldn't you be confessing, too? Maybe confession is what you get off on? Some people get off doing, some seeing, some reading. Can you say you haven't ever thought of the possibilities? What would you do with a city of orphans spread-eagled before you? It can become a mechanical problem, a question of architecture, where to arrange the bodies and what you would like them to do with their nimble, cold fingers.

REPORTS FROM THE VILLAGE OF C, NEAR THE GREAT FOREST OF CODRU

One Hansel and Gretel and What They Did There, as Recorded by Grimm, our Comrade on the Scene in the Village of C

Next to the great forest of the Codru lived a poor comrade with his wife and two children. Let's call the boy Hansel and the girl Gretel. It was the time of famine and there was only a crust of bread left in the cottage.

One evening as they tossed and turned upon the soba, the comrade said to his wife, "What is to become of us? How can we feed ourselves?"

The mother said, "We must abandon the children in the Codru so that we won't eat them."

"God forbid," the father said. "It can't be done. I won't do it. Let's die together, rather than let the wolves eat the children."

"Do you want the neighbors to steal the children from our yard? We'll turn against each other in time, when we're hungry enough. Bad if the neighbors eat them. Worse if we do it. At least in the Codru, they could maybe make their way through the forest to the city and be beggars there. The city comrades will have more sympathy for orphans then they would if we came along, too. Man of mine, it is a kindness." She was right. In that time in the village of C or in any of the villages that ring the Forest of Codru, beggars were not given a crust of bread for their troubles. At best, they were ignored. At worst, they were eaten themselves, ending up in the soup pot. Nobody knew what happened to beggars in the city, but how could it be worse? The grain from the village kolkhoz was sent on to the city, once a week in the trucks.

The father sighed. "It's a pity. I do feel sorry for the poor children."

"You sentimental old fool. Feel sorry for us all if you want instead."

Hansel and Gretel were on the soba, too, the whole time, the family in a pile for warmth, and they couldn't sleep because of what they'd heard. But Gretel knew what to do. Once she heard her father's snores and the rhythm of her mother's breathing change, the one time when her parents were the most lovable, she climbed down from the soba and crept outside. The moon was bright, and the white pebbles in the yard glistened like small moons. Gretel filled her pockets with them. She went back into the cottage, climbed up the soba again, and listened to her family until she fell asleep herself. Her father's snores, her mother breathing, Hansel weeping softly beside her.

When they were asleep, when they could sleep, they dreamed of hunger, which was easier than being awake and hungry. Awake, they were nothing but bodies hungering, unable to hold a thought without twitching back to hunger, but asleep, their dreams chased the hunger down. Their dreams were both horrifying and satisfying. In their dreams, they didn't have food, it was out of reach, chickens flying over walls in spite of clipped wings, bread sprouting doughy limbs to run away from them, potatoes that shot out roots to seize the soil forever, soup that would not slide onto the spoon. Sometimes the dreams would eat them, chickens pecking at their eyes, bread growing in their armpits like mold, potatoes digging roots into their veins. They were in the soup boiling by degree. But even when they were the food, it meant there was food, their dreams mimicking the processes of dystrophy, as the body cannibalizes itself as studied in the work of the eminent Dr. V. of Leningrad.

In the morning, their mother woke them, shaking them awake from their dreams and into their hunger. "So lazy. Get dressed and put your coats on, too. Today we're going into the Codru forest." She gave them each a morsel of bread. "Here's your dinner. If you eat it now, you're done, because there'll be nothing left."

Before the time of famine, they would go into the forest for picnics. When they would go to collect firewood, the children still thought of it as a treat, a picnic but without the food, until today. Hansel took both pieces of bread because Gretel's pockets were full of pebbles. Gretel had to trust him not to eat it. It was very hard. She had to tell herself that if he couldn't help himself, she would forgive him.

When they'd walked only so far that they were in the trees but they could still see the houses of the village behind them, the father said, "Gretel, why do you keep stopping and looking back at the village? It isn't going anywhere."

"Oh, Tata, I'm looking at my white cat on the tin roof that is waving goodbye to me."

The mother said, "Foolish girl, that's no cat. That's the morning sun blinking on the tin." All of the cats in the village of C had been eaten at this point in the famine. Gretel had been unusually fond of the family's cat, scrambling up to the eaves to sit with the cat in the sun, listening to the cat purr like the motor on the trucks as they sped the village's food onto the city. The mother had been very cross with their neighbor when he ate the cat because it was a good mouser. Now she was cross because the cat wasn't there for them to eat down to the very whiskers.

Gretel, of course, had not been looking at the tin roof, but had instead been dropping pebbles at intervals to make a path through the trees.

When they arrived at the point where the woods were dense enough to make it dark while day, where they used to hunt for mushrooms when there were still mushrooms to be found other than the poisonous toadstools that the mother worried Hansel might eat in his hunger, the father said, "We'll stop here and collect some firewood. Children, find what you can for kindling. Your mother and I will go a little on. When you're tired, take a nap here, among these leaves. We'll be back soon."

Oh, the whole thing made little sense. Who goes deep into the woods for firewood when there are logs to split closer to home? But Gretel and Hansel kept up the pretense, almost embarrassed on behalf of their parents. The leaves were dry and crumbled beneath them as they stretched out to sleep. As Gretel predicted, Hansel had eaten his piece of bread. She shared half of hers with him now. He was younger than her, and everything was harder for him. As they fell asleep, they could hear their father's axe echoing in the woods around them, but when they woke up startled in the moonlight, they realized it was the wind banging in the dead branches above them instead. Hand in hand, they looked for the moon bouncing on the white pebbles, the little lopsided moons at their feet, and they were home in no time.

They knocked at the gate. Their mother came out to take down the bolt for them, and she said, "You wicked children, why did you stay so long in the forest? We thought you had run away."

But when they crossed the threshold, she kissed Hansel on the forehead and ran her hands along Gretel's braid, and she was happier to see them than they had expected. Her eyes were smiling, victorious, even while her mouth stayed drawn and her face was wan. Their father laughed when they came in the cottage.

"Clever children," he said, but he would not tell them why he said it.

The famine only grew worse. Lent that year was a time not of giving things up, but of having nothing at all, and the harvest was still months away. Everything in the granaries at the kolkhoz in the village of C had been carted away to the cities. One night, when the mother thought the children were sleeping, they heard her shake their father awake up on the soba and tell him, "This time, we'll take them deep into the forest, deeper than they've ever been. Otherwise I don't know what I'll do."

"It would be better to die with the children."

"Fool. Who knows who will die first? Do you want to watch them die? If I could, I'd slit their throats right now rather than watch them die of hunger. I would, if I wasn't too scared of what I'd do to their corpses. No, it's the only way. You and I will make a pact, to eat the other, whoever dies first, but not the children. I worked too hard to bring them into the world to eat them now."

Hansel and Gretel, curled up together on the soba, heard the whole thing. Gretel wondered if they were meant to hear, to know why abandonment in the forest might be cheerier than the fate that awaited them at home. Gretel wanted to get down and gather pebbles, but their mother had locked up the cottage itself, not just the door to the gate, from fear of the neighbor who had eaten their cat and had been looking at Hansel when he walked to the well in a way that made everyone uncomfortable.

The next morning, they all walked out into the forest,

deeper than any of them had ever been before, so deep they were probably more than halfway through to the other side and the roads that would lead on to the city. They could walk the rest of the way, if they weren't so tired, the dystrophy cutting into their muscles. And if they weren't arrested and shot by the regional authorities for being away from their village of residency without official permission papers in a time of famine, they could start over in the city.

Hansel and Gretel did most emphatically not, as some earlier reports suggested, use breadcrumbs to scatter along the path. In a time of famine, who uses his food to find his way home? Food is the home. Food itself is first. If you have food, who needs home?

This time, there was very little pretense. Their father couldn't look them in the eye, looking past them into the density of trees. Their mother said, "Here we are. We're going off into the woods. Sleep now, Mama's darlings. Close your eyes forever." Oh, ominous lullaby. Oh, sleep that is a little bit more than sleep.

When the moon rose, they rose, too, but this time, there were no little oblong moons to lead them home, and Gretel didn't want to go home anymore anyway. She wanted to walk to the city and present herself as a clever orphan who would learn to work the gears of a machine on the factory floor if they gave her something to eat, her and Hansel, too. If they made it without being shot by the regional authorities or eaten by the peasants in the villages they had to pass on the way, it was more likely they'd be pressed to join a gang of thieves and whores, but if they were paid in bread, she'd do it, steal and fuck both, and so would Hansel. She'd make him if he wouldn't, if it meant bread.

They walked further, weakening until they dragged their

legs behind them, and that's when Gretel worried that the wolves would come. When they saw the white bird, they thought it was a hallucination from hunger. There were no white birds in the forest of Codru. It must have been an albino, or some bird that had its color bleached out from blight, from a cryptic bird disease. They followed it to discover what was wrong with it, and possibly eat it, until they came to the house in the clearing, a house that almost blinded them, for far brighter than sunshine on tin is sunshine on pure sugar. The bird wasn't albino, but had dusted her feathers in sugar from crest to claws. They were so startled by the house before them that they didn't notice the house wiggling from its foundations as it came to greet them, teetering on chicken legs and settling in an instant so they could reach out and touch it.

It was a gingerbread house with a roof made of chocolate shingles, and the windows were panes of translucent sugar. The children had never seen anything like it, and I don't mean that it was the first time they'd seen a house made of sweets before. They'd never seen sweets. Sugar was something their mother, before the time of famine, had purchased in tiny quantities in order to make fruit preserves and compote for the winter. They broke off a corner of the gingerbread house and chewed it, their stomachs contracting in agony at the unexpected thrill. Hansel scaled the roof and knocked down chocolate shingles for Gretel. The gingerbread was spicy and the chocolate was bitter, in ways that intrigued them, but mostly, they licked the windowpanes, as if they were deer at a salt lick.

As their tongues were about to push through the sugar glass, a voice called to them, "Who's been nibbling at my house?" The voice resembled their mother's stern but sibilant tone, and they were sure it was a hallucination and kept eating. The door opened and an ancient woman balancing herself on a crooked cane of birch, as white as sugar, as white as her shock of hair, emerged. Women as old as this one had all died off in the village of C months ago. Hansel and Gretel were so frightened they peeled their tongues from the windowpanes and backed away.

But the old woman said, "Darling children, how ever did you get here? Never mind. Come in," she commanded, and they obeyed. They should have been sick from eating sugar on empty bellies, but she gave them milk and pancakes with apples and nuts, which soothed them. She made up beds for them, with white starched sheets. Two twin beds, for these children who'd slept atop a soba their whole lives in a tangle of blankets, and never alone. That was their second mistake, after eating the witch's food. They never should have slept alone, folded into the bedding like letters sealed into an envelope. Their dreams were wrong. Instead of dreaming of food, they dreamt of the house, an impossible luxury rising before them, growing into a solid apartment block of sugar, and then neighborhoods of sugar apartment blocks stacked to the horizon, a city, a sugar Moscow itself. So much luxury, yet all for the collective.

The old woman was, in fact, once one of their neighbors from the village of C, who, instead of expiring so that her family could eat her or at least stop feeding her, walked out into this clearing in the Codru and with the power of her desires, and her memories of desserts from her youth spent not in the Soviet Empire but in the Austro-Hungarian one in the fabled city of Czernowitz, built a gingerbread house as easily as baking it from scratch. What the witch was doing in the village of C in the first place would be a long story involving population exchanges at the start of two wars ago and a case of being at the wrong place at the most horrible time, and suffice it to say that her status as a lover of books, a wearer of glasses, and an eater of dessert, an intellectual and all-around gourmand would have meant, if she'd lived through her ordeal with Hansel and Gretel, years in the gulag at best. It was a miracle she'd made it through the deportation of June 13, 1941, and she'd done it by going out to the woods to hide. She had built her gingerbread house to lure the children of C to her, where she would catch them, kill them, cook them and eat them, according to the finest German recipes of the Great Famine in the years of 1315-17.

In the morning, there she was over their beds, admiring the rosiness that still clung to the hollow of their gaunt cheeks. "Such apples once," she said. "Ah, well, can't be helped. You get what you can, in the time of famine." Pulling Hansel out of bed, she dragged him to the kitchen and locked him in an oversized birdcage, an object from the bourgeois Mitteleuropa childhood of the witch, nothing the children had ever seen before, much more elegant than a chicken coop, which was of course no comfort to Hansel. He screamed and cried for his sister, but it was too late. Gretel sprang up from her bed, kicking out of the covers and racing into the kitchen to help him, but the key was already in the witch's pocket. Gretel thought it would be simple to overpower such an old woman, but she had a wiry, freakish strength, and she'd been surviving on a diet of children, whereas the children had been eating nothing and then sugar. The witch quickly and efficiently pinned Gretel to the kitchen's cold floor, nails from the uneven wooden planks poking into Gretel's protruding spine. Gretel was almost all skeleton and delicate.

For now, Gretel had to do what the witch told her to do, if

she wanted to think of a way to take the key from the witch and get Hansel out. The witch commanded her to cook fattening food for Hansel. This task proved frustrating for everyone involved, as Gretel only knew how to make kasha and borsch, and those, only with the simplest ingredients: buckwheat, beets, cabbage, water, a pinch of salt. Even in the best of times, that was all they had at home. The witch taught Gretel how to cook using the massive mortal and pestle in the kitchen to grind the herbs of the forest, a mortar and pestle as big as Hansel himself. So in the house of the witch, Hansel received the best borsch, and Gretel received the worst kasha, which was still the best food she'd had in years. If Hansel wasn't packed in a cage too small for him, like an animal in the zoo in Kishinev that they'd never been to, the time in the witch's house would have felt like a vacation to Gretel.

Every morning, the witch, who was almost blind, her eyes a rheumy blue with cataracts, shouted at Hansel (she was a little deaf, too, and thought everyone else was) to stick out his finger so she could test his fat.

If the witch had been a well and good efficient cannibal, like their neighbor in the village of C who ate their cat, she would have eaten them up right away. Fattening them up first reveals a tenderness of feeling that the witch could ill afford, not in times of famine. It wasn't as if that many children had the energy to stumble into the forest anymore. Was she eating the birds once their wings were so heavy with sugar that they couldn't fly away? Had she found a way to digest the toadstools? Or was she surreptitiously eating her own house, brick by brick, in corners where Gretel wouldn't notice?

Hansel had found an ominous bone, a sliver of a bone, in his cage, and each day he passed this bone up to the witch instead of his finger. He didn't like to think about who the bone belonged to. One of his classmates, maybe. The little girl who used to swing on her gate when he walked by and would call out, Here comes Hansel!

"Good God, boy, the metabolism on you!" the witch said, squeezing the bone. Hansel took it back and gave it a kiss.

A month passed and they were at the planting season, closer to the hope that there would be food once again in the village of C but further away from last year's grain. The witch could no longer wait. She wanted her feast now. "You there, Gretel," she shouted. "Fetch some water and boil it up."

Gretel cried into the water, her tears providing the salt for the soup that would be made of her little brother. *If only we had been eaten in the woods by the wolves, we would have died together. Or if we had died together at home and never gone into the forest in the first place.*

"Your tears only make my soup the saltier," trilled the witch. "Wicked children, how delicious you'll taste, and I'll have revenge for you eating me out of house and home. I'll bake a boy pie. I need your nimble fingers to knead the dough." They kneaded the dough, Gretel with every push and pull thinking about whether the witch would make Gretel eat Hansel.

"Do climb in, Gretel," said the witch, "to see if it's hot enough."

"How?" replied Gretel in her most obstinate voice, when she was being stupid on purpose, the one her mother hated the most. "What do you mean?"

"You fool," said the witch. "See, even I can do it." She stooped down and stuck her head in the oven. Gretel shoved her, and the witch fell in. Gretel slammed the oven door, bolting it shut. The witch began to howl. "After all my kindnesses. The most ungrateful children." But in time, the words were lost, and all Gretel heard was the howling of wolves. The bolt rattled, but held, and Gretel, although there was a part of her that wanted to let the witch out, didn't.

She had to wait for the ashes to cool until she pulled out the key to Hansel's cage. The ashes clung to her, soot that would stay with her for days. She unlocked Hansel, but he wouldn't come out until the next morning, cowering in the cage, clutching his bone, howling. When he came out, and she tried to kiss him, he shied away like something wild.

They walked from the witch's kitchen into her parlor. Floor to floor were books and papers. There was a clock that told the time. They knew it was mechanical, and they took it. They took the books that were in Cyrillic—they couldn't read the others—thinking they could sell them in the city someday, putting them in a scratched leather satchel that they also hoped would hold value, something they could barter for food. They broke off gingerbread and chocolate for their pockets. They took the dough with them, too—they wouldn't cook it in the oven laced with the witch's ashes.

"I kind of miss her," said Gretel. "She could be funny, when she wasn't trying to eat us."

"I don't miss her," said Hansel. "She wasn't so funny from inside the cage."

"Let's go to the city," said Gretel.

"I want to go home," said Hansel. He still had his bone. He rubbed it in his pocket like a talisman. They didn't know the way, but they started walking. The house chased after them on its chicken legs. It didn't want to be left alone, but they ignored it and it soon gave up, folding into itself like an umbrella, an object the children had never seen, but the witch had known well. After a day of walking, they came to a lake so wide that the other side shimmered like a hallucination.

How had they come to Lake Ghidighici? How would they ever get back to the village of C?

Hansel knelt down at the shore. He didn't say anything. He wasn't much company. They couldn't swim. They could go back into the forest, but there was probably more than one witch in the woods, and they were certainly full of wolves. Hansel and Gretel weren't as weak as they once were, after a month of eating at the witch's house, but that made them all the more a tasty morsel for the wolves or cannibals. While Gretel debated and Hansel meditated on his bone, swans were gliding across the water, a lake so clear and flat it looked like the sugarpane windows they'd left behind, to ferry them across.

The swans were as white as the bird coated in sugar at the witch's house, and Hansel, at first, would not trust them. The cob pecked at him before Hansel climbed on his back. Gretel was drawn to the pen and didn't have to be cajoled. She wanted to recline on that long, slender neck, the plumage her pillow. The satchel with the books trailed behind her, one corner dipped into the water, creating an undertow as they slid across the sugared glass of Ghidighici.

Hansel didn't want the swans to leave. A simple kindness, and he was attached. He pulled at the great expanse of wing, not wanting to let go. The cob unfurled his feathered span and started flapping. Hansel had to release him. He was left with a downy pin feather he hadn't meant to pull out. He hadn't meant to cause the cob pain. He just didn't want to be abandoned. He put the feather in his pocket with the bone.

They walked another day and night, and then the woods were familiar, the toadstools, the bed of dried leaves they'd slept in so many nights ago. They stumbled upon the white pebbles, too, which turned their walk into a race until they could see the houses of the village before them. Some of the gates were open, a good sign that the famine was easing and the villagers trusted their neighbors again, or the most terrible sign of all, that the village was abandoned, everyone gone to cannibals or wolves.

Even though they'd run to the gate of the courtyard of the cottage, they were timid to cross the threshold. They stood transfixed until their father came out to them, running. He picked Hansel up into the air and tossed him. Catching Hansel and squeezing him with one arm, he grabbed Gretel with the other, pulling her close to him so she could smell his sweat. Their father smelled of garlic and onions and the must of new wine. He smelled of food.

Hansel slid out of their father's grasp, but Gretel remained in the nook of his arm, the space where, on the cob, Hansel had plucked out his feather.

"Oh children, it was the saddest moment of my life when we abandoned you in the forest, and it is my happiest to see you have returned. And so fat!"

"Where's Mamica?" Hansel demanded.

Their father shook his head. He never told them anything more. They didn't know whether their father had eaten her, or the neighbor, or whether their mother had herself walked out into the forest to be eaten by the wolves who howled her a lullaby.

They sold the clock to the village's richest kulak, and as for the books, they took them one by one to the city to be sold. Gretel read them first. She'd started the habit of reading in the witch's house. The famine relented. Their father started courting a second wife. Gretel took a look at the boys in the village, seeing who was left. Hansel didn't do much but sit on a stool in the yard's sunny corner, stroking his feather and his bone, but these simple things kept him happy. When he held the feather, he was a cob, soaring with his mate across blue skies with clouds that looked like a village of swans come to greet them, or swimming through a sugar glass lake, diving his elegant neck into the water for all the fish he could swallow down his gullet. Flight, food, flight. When he held the bone, he was a skeleton, stripped of all flesh, stripped of the need to eat, to have muscles to dangle and arrange the aperture of his perfect structure. He was a perfect skeleton, intact, a relic most holy and complete.

They lived happily, the three of them, from the summer of 1947 until the deportation of July 6, 1949. Gretel's reading, her expanded vocabulary, her elementary German, her casual questions put to the village schoolteacher about universities in the city and entrance exams, marked her as an intellectual and if the family didn't have the obvious wealth to be kulaks once they'd unloaded the books and the clock, Gretel's interests marked them with kulak potential, all three of them, even the father who was relatively feckless, even Hansel who was probably insane. The German names of the children didn't help.

Hansel died in the cattle car that transported them to Kazakhstan. The father, with his resilience, started a courtship with a jolly woman in their camp and stayed on. Comrade Gretel came back to the village of C in 1958, to the horror of the family that had been living in the cottage. Gretel's hair had gone white. She wasn't much older than twenty, rail thin with bright white hair. She walked with a birch cane up to the gate. She didn't make claims on the cottage, just asked to sit for awhile on the stool that had been Hansel's, in the courtyard in the sun, holding a feather and a bone that might have been Hansel's, but maybe not. The feather wasn't white, more of a duck's than a swan's, and the bone was translucent, like that of a chicken's. She took up her birch cane, leaned her arm into the crook, raising it up like a wounded wing, and walked out of the village and into the woods. She was never seen again. What kind of house her desires built, we don't know.

IN THE AMBER CHAMBER

The Amber Chamber is missing. How can a room itself go missing? What happened to the Catherine Palace? It's still there—only the Amber Chamber is gone. It is worse than a whole palace vanishing, unmoored from its foundation, the cellars left behind as a gaping maw, worse than a city disappearing into the fog that shrouds it, worse than an island sinking under its own weight into the sea. If the rooms of the Catherine Palace were teeth, now there is a gap, and the other rooms shift and sigh to close it. The Amber Chamber is lost.

If you find it, you will have done the first hard thing. But that is only the beginning.

•

Once there was a man and woman who wanted a baby. But they couldn't have one. They didn't have any money for the medicines that could magically change what was wrong with them. None of their relatives died so that they could take in the children. It would almost happen. Somebody ate bad mushrooms and died. The boys came to stay, too scared to eat anything but cornmeal pancakes and kasha. But then an uncle was found with papers for the City and a chance for the boys to go on to a lyceum, and poof! Somebody's husband was a drunk, and she had to pull night shifts at the hospital. Her little girl came to stay. She would whistle in the house, bringing the worst bad luck down upon them, but she learned the names of all the most poisonous mushrooms and how to talk to swallows. She was very clever, and they loved her. But then her mother was moved to the day shift, and poof! So two times they'd had other people's children for their own, and two times they lost them. The third time, they would have to find something that worked, even if more was asked of them, if everything was asked.

Leave me, the woman told the man. Leave me yourself, he told her. You know, you could have an affair and all our problems would be solved. She lingered by the well in the evenings, and walked on the edges of the fields after the cows came home. The villagers could smell her desperation and left her alone. She was still pretty, but in a hard way. The men were scared of her, and the women scared for them.

She told the man, But you could have an affair, too, as long as you brought home the baby. You could steal him when the mother was sleeping. He was a soft man, gentle hands and a belly like a down-pillow. If she'd had his belly, they'd have thought she was pregnant and it was a miracle. The village women liked to nap upon his belly. They'd have the sweetest dreams. They were children again, but never hungry. They took it as a good omen. They were too happy to do more than sleep on him.

So they didn't have affairs. They took their own chances with mushrooms, and they drank, and they waited for a relative, or even a neighbor, to leave them a child. They spoiled the dog, giving him scraps of meat from the table and letting him inside when it stormed. He often looked at them as if he were just about to speak, his head cocked, his ears pointed, but he never did. He barked and squealed and wheedled, but in spite of their love, he never turned into a boy. Worse, he grew from a puppy into a dog, and then he seemed to want a child as much as they did, staring at them in silent judgment.

So they went to the orphanage in the town. They filled out forms in triplicate that stained their fingers purple. They watched the children who roamed in packs in the yard, their eyes wolfish, howling at each other across the dusty playground. They thought, the dog will like these children, and these children will be clever. They weren't asking for a baby, reserved for the foreigners or the wealthy city people, but a child, even a teenager or two. They were placed on a list, but the harvest never allowed for the bribes that would move them up the list.

They made gingerbread men. The dog ate them when they wouldn't run. The woman planted fields of rapunzel, but no neighbor women were hungry for greens. The log the man found in the woods, which looked as if it were branching into toddler legs, got tossed in the fire once dripping milk into the knot that could have been a mouth got them nowhere. The man carved the charred log into a small wooden puppet. The dog chewed its nose off.

They built a snow girl. They hugged her, their tears melting into the snow. They rubbed her snowy hands until their hands were red and raw and her snow fingers winnowed down to splindy icicles. They kissed her turnip nose. This was the one they were sure would work, a wintery tale for their cold hearts. One of her arms fell off, crashing to powder at their feet. They couldn't think of any other stories to try. Her remaining arm pointed north, and they followed it, out of the village and across the snow, the dog trailing behind them with as much dignity as he could muster.

·

To find the Amber Chamber, you must outsmart the Nazis and the Soviets, something most villagers have at least had a fair amount of practice at trying to do. They worked very hard to hide it, and it won't be in any of the obvious places. It's not sunk at the bottom of the Baltic Sea, packed in crates stashed in an abandoned salt mine, or at the bottom of a dry and poisoned well. It isn't in a Palace of Culture, hidden behind wallpaper patterned with mushrooms and hedgehogs, or in a Politburo office beneath the propaganda posters of fields of wheat and busty peasant woman bouncing along on tractors. The Stasi aren't using it as a torture chamber. It's not in a Museum of Decadence. The Nazis and Soviets didn't sell it piece by piece to the fat cat Americans who look like the guys on the Monopoly board. They were clever for once. They hid it in a story, where it can be found, but never stolen. It's lost and found at once.

When you find the Story of the Amber Chamber, the amber tiles sticking out of the pages like miniature ship masts sailing through a paper ocean, you must rebuild it piece by piece. You have to imagine, how do I want it to look? What shape will the room take? How will I arrange the illustrated pieces? If I turn these carved guns upside down, will they look like flowers? Or if I place them in a row, will I have a cannon? Could these palaces be cathedrals? Cathedrals, palaces? Fat, smiling babies or dead angels in a choir? What kind of Amber Chamber do I want?

•

By the time they saw the amber poking out of the snow, they were exhausted and collapsed before the tiles, the man and woman stretched out like angels, the dog curled up between. The food, the hard-boiled eggs, the brown bread the woman had burned in her hurry to leave, the jars of canned pickled red pepper and cabbage salad, even the turnips, had been eaten to the last morsel. They were thirsty, and they sat up to eat handfuls of snow, blowing on it to ease the chill, pretending it was tea. The dog frolicked, shaking the cakes of snow off his back, rooting his snout around in it, pretending to be puppyish again. It was all practice for the imagination it would take to build the Amber Chamber.

At first, the dog was making too many choices, and the room was scaled to his size. The woman thought the baby might like that, so she was willing to humor the dog, but the man wanted his son born in a big room, at least as big as their house in the village which although only one room, was a roomy room. So they started again, tile upon tile, clinking against each other like fingernails upon a typewriter.

•

Once you build the Amber Chamber, it will give you what you want, but only within the walls of the room. It is its own world. It is its own sun. It glows from within, a yellowing flame that never flickers. The Greek word for amber is electron, because of its ability to hold a charge. The Germans called it Burnstone because you can set it on fire. The Russians call it sea-resin, and that's what's special about amber, that it can hold the properties of fire but be found in water, as if it's frozen fire.

Czars played cards in the Amber Chamber before it was lost, their luck improved by the light of the room. In the one that you build, anyone can play cards, anyone you want, Nazis, Soviets, villagers, good fairies and bad, Baba Yaga and her jeweled toads, and czars, if you want them, can do whatever you want them to do. Want a Cinderella czar, dusting and dusting? Washing the amber floor on his knees with the rags and buckets of dingy water? Done. Want Catherine to go at it with her horse? Done. Want to add Peter the Great and Ivan the Terrible? And all of their horses? In every combination? And afterwards, they all play cards? Done and done.

If you give birth in the Amber Chamber, and try to take that child out of the room, the Amber Child can never be yours outside in the world. The child belongs to the Chamber. You can give her away to somebody else, starting off another story, but you can't keep her, not unless you stay within the walls of the Chamber itself. If you try to keep her, she will disintegrate in your arms until you're left hugging shards of amber wrapped up in a blanket. Even if you try to take those shards back to the Amber Chamber, the Chamber won't give you back that exact child again, only an amber copy.

If your ultimate objective is a child at all costs, and you're not picky, you could use the Amber Child as a changeling in the world outside, sneaking her into a crib and taking the crib's original occupant for yourself. In the short term, the Amber Child will adapt her features to match the baby she's meant to mimic, although there are no promises beyond the first couple of days or so. If the family doesn't take to the changeling, the Amber Child will turn brittle and break into dust, as amber does when it isn't cared for. But the Amber Child is charming, and it usually works out. No promises that the baby you've exchanged with your changeling will amount to much, either, but that's always true unless your baby is an Amber Child and you've imagined every bit of her in advance.

·

The woman didn't believe at first that she was giving birth to a changeling. She thought this was the child they could keep, their third chance, the one where they risked everything. Surely that risk deserved rewards? She was certain. Her labor started the moment they used up the last tile. She crouched up against the walls, the electric-charged warmth of the tiles against her spine. The man patted his belly and wondered if in the Amber Chamber, he could have a baby, too, but he couldn't pull off the leap of imagination he needed. The dog decided absolutely he did not need puppies. He sat down next to the woman and nobly let her pull his fur when the contractions came. The man got stinking drunk on amber vodka and sang her favorite songs off-key. It was better than she had hoped for.

It was a horrible birth. It lasted for a day or a week or a year, they could never be sure in the Amber Chamber where it never went dark, and the blood she bled was yellow. Buckets and buckets, with the slimy baby sliding out into the room across the streams of blood. The man wrapped the baby up in his coat. She wailed and stared at him, the tiny features as sharp as if they were carved into amber. Tiny eyelashes, miniscule flaring of the nostrils. He carried her over to his wife proudly, as if it had been his labor after all. She was still leaking yellow blood. He handed her the baby, and she clasped it to her breast. The little yellow head rooted around for the nipple. The woman stroked the baby's patchy down. She turned paler and paler, as if nursing the baby ebbed her last bit of strength. As if the baby was eating her up.

If they had been able to have a baby back in the village, without the help of the Chamber, back in the beginning of their story, if the doctor from the town didn't come in time, she would have died. She was beyond what midwives can do. Maybe the baby would have made it, if a wet nurse could be found. Maybe not. In that moment, the man thought that maybe they should have let things stand the way they were. Maybe they weren't meant to mess around with the Amber Chamber. Stay in the village, hope for a better harvest, hope for someone to have a child that needs fostering for whatever reason, hope to die and their story to end off that way. But they were in the Amber Chamber, and so he could imagine a different end. He could have all the skills of a surgeon in his clumsy hands. The man had to stitch her up, which he didn't know how to do, but when she hissed, Pretend you know how, he found himself threading the amber needle and imagining that his wife's dangling bits of yellowed flesh like rotten meat gone through the grinder was golden cloth, bolts and bolts of it before him, and the dress he was sewing was for his daughter's wedding day.

They had a girl, which is to say, this story has all been prelude to another story. Snow White isn't about the queen who wishes for a daughter white as snow. The child born within her mother's tear, the teardrop her womb, and who springs to life before our eyes, is the heroine of her story, not the weeping woman. Anne Boleyn isn't the story of Elizabethan England. Those children are haunted by their lost parents, but they go about having their own adventures, including the adventure of not having any children themselves. Once you decide to wish for children, your story ends and theirs starts.

They can't tell if she is jaundiced. She isn't a rosy baby, but they like to think of her as sunny rather than sallow. She throws her toy turnip and the dog catches it. She claps her hands in glee. They are entranced. They know it's time to leave the Amber Chamber, they know time is passing, but it's as if they're trapped, trapped like flies in honey, trapped in frozen fire, trapped in amber. If it's a trap, it has been set by their own desires.

They understand now about the changeling bargain. The Chamber has whispered it to them, sung it to them in their sleep, illustrated the story along one of the walls, a part of the Chamber the woman tries to avoid, although when the Amber Child sleeps, the man finds the woman pacing along the wall, looking for a trick, a loophole in the story. There isn't one. They can only keep her if they stay. If they plan to use her as a changeling, they will need to leave as soon as possible.

The longer they stay, the harder it is to imagine that she won't be theirs. When she learns to walk, toddling across the length of the room, holding on to their hands with each of her own, the dog right behind just in case she needs to fall back onto something soft, the woman starts to wail. Why can't we be the ones to bring her up? I don't want the real baby. I want my changeling. When the Amber Child begins to babble mama and papa and doggy, the man wishes the words would catch in her throat, so she'd be stuck as a little baby. But he doesn't wish it hard enough for the Chamber to make it happen, and besides, now the girl has wishes, too.

•

Amber isn't hard. It's worn like jewelry, but it's no stone. It's easy to break and it will burn. Remember, the Germans called it Burnstone, and you should think of the word as a command. So when you are ready to leave the Amber Chamber, all you need to do is crack a hole in the corner, ripping a hole in the seam, like breaking an egg from the inside. Then light a fire, and as the room burns to a crisp so that its contents can't be used against you by future inhabitants of the Amber Chamber, slip through your hole into the stinging light of the world outside. You can come back, if you're willing to take on all of the tasks you took on once before, but most don't have the energy to return, and those that do return never leave at all.

•

I can't give her up, she said. Let's just stay here, he said. The dog grayed first. He couldn't control it. The man and woman aged themselves piece by piece to match their daughter's growth, adding wrinkles, losing a tooth, stiffening their joints, but when they weren't thinking, they fell back into the age and health they had when they entered the Chamber.

The Amber Girl grew faster and faster. Once she could talk, she wouldn't stop, and once she could write her own name, all she wanted to do was read in the library of the Amber Chamber. At first, they liked playing school with her, splitting the subjects between them, but when she worked past the ninth form, further than they'd been in school, and wanted to tutor them instead, they didn't like it anymore. The cooking lessons went better, the woman coming up with soups with twenty-seven ingredients and sauces that were reduced down to the very elements themselves in order to keep the Amber Girl interested. The man specialized in walks though the woods he'd raise up in the center of the room, little amber trees like bonsai, and they'd go mushroom hunting. It was especially hard to spot the poisonous ones when everything was yellow, but the Amber Girl never made even one mistake. So when she ate a poisonous mushroom on purpose, they knew it was over.

We'll make an Amber Boy for you to play with, promised the woman. It's going to be better, soothed the man. When you're older, and settled down here in the Amber Chamber.

I can't settle down with my brother! cried the Amber Girl, and the look of resentment she shot them, her delicate features frozen into a sullen mask, told them it was time to leave the Amber Chamber.

It's too late for her to be a changeling, said the woman.

Don't you think she kind of already is one? asked the man. Where has our charming baby gone?

The Amber Girl balanced on the dog's back to punch a hole in the wall up by the carved choir of amber babies. The air of the real world outside rushed into the room, dulling everything within and making them itch. They said to the Amber Girl, You go first and we'll light the fire, but she said,

Not a chance. I'm not leaving you behind. I'll feel guilty and it will be like I never left. The woman lit the fire while the man went first, creeping into the world. The woman followed, holding the dog, and finally the Amber Girl came, her braid almost catching in the last smoldering gasps of the fire behind them. She brushed the ashes off the tips and kept walking.

So this is what it's like to feel old, said the man as their knuckles swelled and their hair thinned. Their backs curled in and their shoulders bent as if they were folding up wings, and they held on to each other to steady themselves. They wouldn't accept any help from the Amber Girl.

Once they came to the fork in the road, the village one way, the city the other, the man said, If we were to keep you, you'll turn to dust.

What if I kept you? said the Amber Girl. Somebody else has probably moved into your house in the village anyway. Why don't we start over in the city together?

Why don't you send for us when you want us? said the woman, thinking, *if* you want us, and you probably won't. She said, The village will be like a holiday after so much time in the Amber Chamber. They each gave the Amber Girl a papery kiss on her forehead. The woman pressed the last of the food, a hard yellow cheese and yellow grapes, into the Girl's hand. The man tucked the woman's arm into his, but they didn't start down their road until the Amber Girl began down hers.

Every time she looked back, they were still waving, her father almost foolishly, her mother sharply as if she were saluting. The Amber Girl wasn't going to take the dog, but he wouldn't turn back even when she threw stones at him. He walked with her once she relented, his paws crunching in the dry road of summer. They shared her cheese together as she planned herself a future in a field of sunflowers. In the Amber Chamber, they would have been arrayed as a court, bending to her whim. In the field, they turned their heads away from her and toward the sun.

When she got to the edge of the city and saw the tiny stars sparking off the trolleys racing along their wires, she was drawn to the electricity, and as they walked beside the tracks, the sky grew brighter and brighter until she almost thought she was back in the Amber Chamber once again. An impossible city, glowing as if made of frozen fire, rose up before her. As she stepped into the electric, humming world, even the dog lost sight of her in the press of the crowd.

CHILDREN IN THE TIME OF FAMINE: REPORTS FROM THE VILLAGE OF C.

*Collected by Comrade Grimm, as requested
by the Truths of the Famine Committee*

Once in the village of C, region of T, Soviet Republic of M, there was a woman who was so poor that she didn't have even a crust of bread, not for her or her two daughters neither. They were starving, showing the signs of dystrophy as documented by Dr. V. so ably in the siege of Leningrad: what the body will do after the requisite period without food. The body will eat itself, shredding muscle from the inside out. Dystrophic and desperate, she said to the oldest girl, "I'll have to kill you so there will be something to eat, for me and your little sister both."

But the girl begged, "Please don't kill me, Mama. I'll go out and find something for us to eat without having to beg for it."

Beggars in the town of C in the time of famine were not tolerated. No one opened their gates to them, and in fact, the beggars risked being pulled into the house and eaten themselves if they banged at the door too loudly. It was a time of not announcing one's presence, slipping cleanly through life as a cat. Not that there were any cats left in the village of C.

We'll call the girls Tanya and Natasha, as that was probably their names anyway. Most of the girls in the village of C are Tanyas and Natashas. Tanya was the oldest, Natasha the youngest. When Tanya said she had a way to find something to eat without having to beg for it, she must have meant prostitution, and at that time in the village of C, it was before the purge of the richest peasants, so there were potential clients, houses where there was a little more to spare. Famine first, then purging. Comrade T had two cows. Comrade P had a herd of goats.

She either prostituted herself to one of them, or maybe one of Comrade P's two sons. She probably tried the sons out first. They had been good-looking boys before the famine started, which had wasted them away a bit, but since they started out plumper than most of the villagers, they could afford to lose more. The older one was two classes ahead of Tanya in school, the younger one in her class. Perhaps Tanya liked them. Perhaps they liked her. Perhaps they had always thought of her as a bit of a whore, the kind of girl that will sell herself for a crust of bread to feed her mother and her little sister. Maybe it was quick, done and done, the crust of bread slapped into her skeletal palm before the second brother pulled out. Maybe it lasted all night. There weren't many distractions in the village of C during the time of famine. Maybe they wanted to do something with their bodies while they still had them. Certainly Tanya had nothing left to lose, considering her mother had already announced her intention to eat them all.

In the morning, Tanya came back to the little house and put the crust of bread on the table. The mother, regaining some of her composure, took the good knife and cut the crust into three even parts. She boiled water so they could pretend they were drinking tea, but still the bread stuck in their throats. It did so little to ease the pangs of their hunger, their dystrophy, that the mother said to Natasha, "Now, little one, Mama's darling, it's your turn."

Natasha said, "Oh no, Mamica, spare me, too. I'll go out and get something to eat with no one the wiser." She meant, steal it. At that point in the famine, the vigilance of the villagers was beyond reproach. Nobody's gates were open, and if a cat burglar like Natasha climbed the walls, they would find everything within the gates locked up, too. The surly guard dogs had been eaten weeks ago, but any grain that was left in the village was guarded by a surly human with a knife, and that surly human was just looking for an excuse to cut someone, make a corpse, and have a dinner.

The only food that could be stolen that early spring of 1947 in the village of C was from the kolkhoz's granary, and the only way to do it was to wait for the trucks to pull out for the long road to the cities and then pick up the grains that had fallen to the ground in the moment of transport, from the wheelbarrows out of the granaries and up on to the trucks. Kernels of wheat. Bits of kasha. Something always spilled, no matter how careful the comrade. Barely enough for a bird, stuck in the mud rivulets of the road, but in that spring, enough to die for. Natasha would have to fight bigger children, fight women, even men, and risk being shot if she tried when the trucks first pulled out. But she was clever. She waited, perched in the oak tree outside the granary gates. She sat for hours. When it was dark, and not just dark but velvet, velvet being something Comrade Natasha would have only read about, so let's say fur, not that there were any animals left in the village of C other than wild ones, she dropped down and quiet as a cat in the shadows, made her way to the muddy rivulets, stuck both hands in the mud, squeezed, and ran.

At home, there was enough bulgur wheat in her fists once they unclenched them to make a tiny porridge, enough for everyone to have a bite. The mother insisted that Natasha take an extra bite for good luck. Tanya flinched when her mother said it. How could Tanya still feel jealous when all she should feel was hunger? What was the point of Natasha having an extra bite as a treat if the mother was going to eat them anyway? Natasha's extra bite would become the mother's extra bite once she ate her. The mother might have wanted Natasha to know she was beloved, especially more than Tanya, but everyone knew that already. That information didn't take a famine.

After a few hours spent huddling together on their soba, the fire in the stove grown cold, nobody with any energy left to step down to light the kindling let alone collect firewood in the forest, the mother smoothing Natasha's hair but Tanya sliding out of her grasp, Tanya knowing what's coming and hating her mother for it, Natasha knowing what's coming, too, but unable to even imagine another end—her whole life had been lived in bad times, want and famine, her best skills stealing grain dropped by others, scavenging garbage, scavenging happiness by climbing trees to leave this earth for awhile—they knew that the pangs of their hunger have not been eased. The mother told them again, "You'll have to die, otherwise we'll all die." She didn't say, I'm going to eat Tanya first. She didn't say, I'll save Natasha for last. When she said, You, it's you, plural, you, sisters, you, daughters. She was saving herself.

Natasha said, "Darling Mamica, we'll just lie down and go to sleep, and we won't rise again." She nudged Tanya, but Tanya didn't want to agree. What, just die? Make it easier for their mother, so she wouldn't have to kill them as they squirmed against the good knife at their throats? But Tanya was tired after her night of fucking. She didn't have the energy to climb off the soba and out of the door and offer herself again to P's sons, tell them they could eat her if they fed her first. Natasha had already curled up in their mother's lap, the lap she'd stolen from Tanya since the day she was born. Without even noticing it, Tanya's head fell back on her mother's bony shoulder, the way it did the one time they rode the bus to the town of Cahul together to see the church of Saint Vasile and kiss the bones in the reliquary, before Natasha was born, before the war, before their father died, before the time of famine. The mother, in spite of her intentions to wake up and eat her children, fell asleep, too, her head tilted back on the soba's tiles first, but later, coming to rest on Tanya's head still pressed upon the mother's own shoulder.

She must have woken up, and left, because her bones weren't found in the little house like the girls' were. Whether she woke up and ate Tanya and Natasha, or whether she couldn't bear to do it in the end and walked out of the village to avoid the temptation to eat her own children who died for her on command in order that she might eat them, no one in the village of C knows. Someone ate the girls. All that was left was bones in a pot on the soba, cooked for soup. But there was no sign of a struggle anywhere in the little house. They seem to have died peacefully. The crime of cannibalism was committed in this house, but not murder. Let's not investigate this one too closely, shall we? As for the mother, not a soul in C knows where she is to this day.

Nobody is descended from this Tanya or this Natasha. Their bones were buried in the corner of the graveyard set aside for the victims of soup. What's left was as clean and as picked over, down to the marrow, as the ancient bones of Saint Vasile in the reliquary of Cahul.

I've redacted C's name in this report, as requested, but the villagers know who they are.

REPORTS ON THE CAPRA FAMILY IN THE VILLAGE OF C

Another chronicle of our intrepid Comrade Grimm in his investigation into the rumors of the famine years, and just how many cannibals live amongst us in C to this day, and how we should be kind to them because it's in their nature. And the potential uses of this instructive tale for relationships between the classes of goat and wolf within our new glorious society, as the wolf now truly lies down with the goat. (See the reading primers for second and fourth forms and their three-toned illustrations of slightly edited but still gleefully murderous versions of the tale.)

Once there was a widowed nanny goat. She had three kids, which is to say, two were a pain in the neck and the youngest, a nanny girl goat worth gold, worth the others put together.

It was the time of famine, and the nanny goat had to go further and further to find food for her kids. Their garden was gone and there was nothing in the village of C, not even a crust of bread. She had to walk off to villages that still had food, far off, and beg. Because she was still a little, pretty nanny goat, with lovely, shapely teats that some comrades greatly enjoyed to fondle, she could, at least for now, bring something back for the kids, although she knew there would be a time when the villagers of C or the villagers far off who enjoyed, for now, to only sample her milk, would remember how much they liked the taste of roast goat.

She gathered her kids together and sang them her song,

softly and sweetly. They were not to open the latch on the door unless they heard this song, and in her voice:

> Three little kids with tiny horns,
> For your dear mama, open the door!
> Mama's brought you leaves in her lips,
> Salt upon her back, milky teats, and more!
> Corn within her cloven hooves, flowers
> Tucked inside her legpits, all four!

Unfortunately, her song was overheard by the eavesdropping wolf, her neighbor, the witness to the wedding with her dead billy goat and the godfather to her kids. Although he'd been generous to the Capra family in the past in his role as godfather, his lupine nature in the time of the famine was becoming harder to ignore, and Comrade Lupul had nothing but malevolent intentions on his mind.

The kids busied themselves in the house. The eldest did the dishes, the boy started on his schoolwork (there wasn't school anymore due to the famine, but he greatly enjoyed solving equations), and the little girl played with her dolls, a little goat family formed from sticks and felt, in the corner by the soba. The toy nanny goat sang her song, leaves, milk, flowers, and the toy kids let her in. They fell on top of each other in a shaggy goat heap, bleating at each other in greeting. No sooner had the little girl goat fallen silent did they hear at their door their mother's song. Her big sister and brother rushed to the door, but the baby sister called, "Wait!"

"What?" asks her brother, his hoof already on the latch.

"Didn't you listen? It was her words, but not her voice."

The older sister nodded. "She's right. It was gruff, like someone with something caught in his throat. Something he needs to hack out." [Editorial note from Comrade Grimm: Probably one of Comrade Lupul's earlier victims. Unfortunately, due to his wealth and personal charms, the wolf was godfather to many children in the Village of C.]

Comrade Lupul, thwarted from his feast by the cleverness of his goddaughter, threw back his noble shaggy head and let out a howl. He remembered her baptism, how she peed through the christening gown when he held her squirming at the altar. She'd always been a disagreeable kid. He ambled down the road and into the market until he found the blacksmith.

"I need you," he told the smith, to "file my teeth and tongue until I can sing soprano."

"You're crazy," said the blacksmith. "Do you think it will soothe your hunger?"

"Yes," said the wolf. "And I will pay you."

"Save your kopecks," said the smith. "Unless you can give me bread?"

"Who has bread?" asked the wolf, all the while thinking about the delicious goat he planned to eat. When the smith split his tongue and whittled at his fangs until they could cut through steel, they were so sharp, the wolf didn't complain, just squeezed his paws against the anvil.

He walked back up to the house of the goats. The nanny wasn't back yet; the latch was still in the door, the curtains still drawn. He sang the song again, as softly and sweetly as he could, pretending he was a crooner on the radio beaming over to them all the way from the city broadcasts.

"Don't open that door!" cried the little one, trying to wedge herself between her brother and the door. But she was so little, and skinny enough in the time of famine, that he was able to slide her aside and throw the door open. In the instant before the wolf was fully revealed to them, standing at the threshold, a dandy in his city suit, ecru kid gloves stretched over his paws, a velvet waistcoat with a little pocket for a handkerchief where he'd casually tucked a paw away while he surveyed the kitchen, a blood-red silk cravat at his throat where the singing that sounded so much like their mother came from, the little one scrambled up the soba and into the chimney, her white hide blossoming with soot. The oldest managed to crawl under a barrel and watched the wolf from the hole made from the knot in the wood.

But the brother stood still, mesmerized by the sight of the glamorous dandy. As soon as the wolf crossed into the kitchen, he swiped at their brother and ripped out his throat. He decapitated his head and swallowed the rest of him whole, with an almost painful gulp.

Over in the barrel, the oldest kid couldn't help herself. She was very polite and imprudent. Or maybe she was so horrified at her brother's brutal murder and devouring before her eyes that what she wanted was her own death, as quickly and painlessly as possible. She whispered, "May it serve you well," the phrase her nanny goat mother had taught her to wish her elders after they ate or drank something. It was the post-eating (or in this case post-mortem) equivalent of wishing a comrade a good appetite before they ate in the first place.

No sooner had she whispered the words than had the wolf pulled up the barrel and rolled her out of it. "Why, who do we have here? Come a little closer and let me kiss you!" he said. He ate her, too, again leaving the head behind, as he had with his decapitated first victim. Perhaps Comrade Lupul did not enjoy the eating of heads, which was unusual because it was a rare cannibal in the time of famine who left a head behind. At the time of our investigations, many heads were found in many soup pots. Perhaps Comrade Lupul bore an unusual hatred toward Comrade Capra and in fact, the entire Capra family, because he stained the whitewashed walls of the kitchen and the porcelain tiles of the soba red with the blood of the kids. After that dishonor, he took their heads and placed them on the windowsill, where before the time of famine, the nanny goat used to leave her dried apples and quinces in the winter so that the house would smell of summer, and poked his claws into their mouths to twist their lips into grins.

Having eaten his full, he longed to take his revenge on his last goddaughter. But the littlest kid didn't make a peep, a bleat, a whisper, and if puffs of her breathing exited the chimney, the wolf wasn't outside to see them. He climbed up on the soba to take a nap, planning to eat the littlest kid and maybe her mother, too, once she came home. He'd always had an eye for the nanny. When he woke, he remembered the radio back in his own kitchen. The Capras didn't even have a radio. Maybe they'd owned one once but had pawned it long ago for bread, or maybe, even when Comrade Gentleman Billy Capra was alive, finances hadn't permitted such a luxury, something that couldn't be eaten or worn or used to make food or sew clothes. He wanted to hear the broadcast from the city. They never reported on the famine. In fact, in the Empire as a whole, everything was in abundance. He liked to imagine himself a city dandy, a city wolf. He leaped from the soba, out the door, and soared over the fence into his own yard.

The littlest kid didn't come down from the soba's chimney until she heard her mother crying for her lost kids. She slid down the chute of soot, bounced off the blankets on the ledge, and bounded to nuzzle at her mother's chin. Her mother sat on the kitchen floor, a place she never sat, for to sit on the cold floor was said to bring bad luck and render you infertile. The littlest kid knew her mother didn't care anymore. The nanny had pulled down the heads from the sill and had them arrayed in her lap, kissing them in between her crying. The littlest kid would have liked to kiss her sister and brother good-bye, too, but their hideous death grins terrified her and she couldn't bring herself to do it.

When they both calmed down, when the mother fed her last kid some bread and milk, when they'd placed the heads under a blanket on the kitchen table, as if they had a whole corpse and were getting ready for a funeral, after they washed the heads in holy basil and water and scrubbed the blood off the walls, the kid told her mother what had happened and how the wolf had tricked them and eaten them.

Comrade Capra began to plot her revenge. She'd never liked the wolf. He was the godfather, but he took too many liberties, squeezing her teats when she had to brush past him on her way to the well. She didn't like the way he had looked at her older daughter, measuring her, sniffing in the air when she walked by, trying to figure out when she was ready to become a little mother herself. She didn't like how he'd cuff her boy when he was caught listening to the wolf's radio, or how he would pull the littlest into his lap and tickle her until she screamed for mercy. The nanny would have never stood for Comrade Lupul being godfather if her husband hadn't been so insistent and Comrade Lupul hadn't been so rich, but also never would she have dreamed that he would murder and eat his godchildren, her kids. Were these unspeakable lusts always within him? Did famine drive him, or bring what was always within him out? How can goats and wolves share one village?

She sent her kid to the well for water, and brought out the leaves, the milk, the salt, the cornmeal, the flowers. With what she had from her own body, she'd make a soup so rich it would drive the old wolf crazy. She dug a pit in a corner of the yard and filled it with still-burning embers and logs. Next, she covered it with her carpet, then scattered the carpet with leaves and dirt to disguise it. Last, she took the candles and shaped a stool out of wax, so thick it could hold a wolf in comfort.

Locking the last kid in the house, she walked into the forest, singing her song, salty tears staining her shaggy whiskers that ran down her chin. It didn't take her long to find the wolf, strolling in his ridiculous suit, blood still smeared on his ecru kid gloves. He seemed to be hunting for mushrooms, squinting at the toadstools at his feet. He was too vain for glasses. The fur on his long, aristocratic nose wrinkled up as he thought.

"Comrade Lupul," she greeted him. "Dear Godfather. A most horrible thing has happened in my home today. While I was out, somebody came in and ate two of my kids. Whoever did so also kindly left me their heads so I could kiss them one last time, and bury them. Will you do me the honor of being my guest at their funeral feast? I know my dear dead husband Comrade Billy Capra would have wished it that way. In this time of famine, it is important for customs to be kept up, and you and I, wolf and goat, could serve as examples to the rest of the villagers of how to set things right."

The wolf was flattered and couldn't resist a pinch of a teat, which she stoically endured, although one more unbidden tear leaked out along with the jet of milk. He didn't notice the tear, gobbling at the milk with his treacherous maw.

"Comrade Capra," he said, sated, wiping the dew of milk

off his muzzle with the cuff of his jacket, "I'm delighted to attend, but I must confess I was far happier to attend your wedding than be there on this solemn day. I remain the god-father to your final kid, and I would be honored to honor the memory of the kids that have gone on."

Gone to your belly, you old lecher, she thought, but all she did was smile, a smile as ghastly as the grins on her kids' decapitated heads as they rolled against each other to settle on the windowsill, like the quinces did once before the time of famine.

The rest of the villagers turned up for her feast, partially out of respect but mainly because of the promised soup. How had she managed to make something taste so good in a time of famine? There was a bit of the witch about the nanny goat. Nobody sat in the waxen stool, because the littlest kid announced to everyone who tried that the stool was reserved for her godfather and no other comrade.

When he arrived, preening the fur on his front paws, digging at the claws one last time, the littlest kid shivered in fear, her shaggy coat rippling prettily, but she solemnly walked up to him and took his hairy paw with her hoof, leading him to the stool of wax. He'd left his bloody kid gloves at home, out of respect. His suit was buttoned up over the waistcoat, and he'd changed his cravat to a sky-blue one, as if to emphasize that his godchildren had been sped on to heaven, and he'd been a help along the way and not a hindrance.

The villagers ate bowl after bowl of the soup, Comrade Lupul included. Soon, the nanny goat and her little kid added so much water to the soup pot that what the comrades were eating was largely liquid, but the original scent hovered in the air and soothed their hunger. Or maybe it was the smell of the blood on the walls. The nanny had scoured and scrubbed, but a coppery echo of the blood remained. After Comrade Lupul's fourth bowl of soup, at last, the stool of wax melted, first his fur catching in the melting, as painful as when he was caught in the zipper of his trousers, then his wolfish weight collapsing the wax and burrowing through the dirty carpet until he crashed into the pit below and was entirely engulfed by the flames. He burned slowly, tenderly, like barbecue, with ample time to beg Comrade Capra for help and forgiveness. "Dear Comrade Capra, mother of my godchildren, dear nanny, forgive! I'm just a wolf, an old wolf, and I know I've wronged you, but I beg you, think of all of our ties and pull me out of this pit of fire. Think of dear Billy Capra, who was like a brother to me, and be a sister to me, dear nanny. I'm burning!"

She bleated back at him, "I've only followed the holy words. A death for a death, a burn for a burn." As he howled, the other villagers backed from the pit themselves. There wasn't one of them that would make a move to help him, either because they hated and feared him, too, or because he smelled so delicious. His fur was singed entirely across his pelt, and now the fat was beginning to sizzle.

The littlest kid threw the first stone. Then the nanny goat dropped down a rock as big as the heads of her dead kids. They stoned Comrade Lupul to death, the two of them, as many stones as there are villagers in C. Then all of the villagers gathered to dance and celebrate and feast upon what remained of the wolf. Some of the comrades, and certainly the goats themselves, had qualms that by eating the wolf who had eaten the kids, they themselves were eating the kids. But it was a time of famine, and what was done is done.

This tale, comrades, as we all know, became a useful instructive legend. The bourgeois wolf, the peasant hero mother with the many teats and many children. We all know the story from our school primers. You think the story predates the revolution. You think it belongs to Creanga, the storyteller. You might have seen the animated short on TVMoldova. You might have heard the long-playing record of the opera on the headphones in the library of your own village. You think Creanga was the first to tell this story? Do you think it happened only once? It happens over and over, whenever there are wolves and goats and famine.

There is a documented history here that can be traced back to the town of C in the time of famine. The wolves are all gone, eaten like Comrade Lupul or deported, as surely he would have been if he'd lived long enough, the old greedy kulak himself. But it's the littlest kid who's the most terrifying, up in the chimney, leading her godfather to the chair of wax, throwing the first stone. And she's the one we're descended from. The wolf ate her brother, and the wolf ate her sister, but littlest kid ate her godfather, and it isn't in a goat's nature to eat a wolf.

CHILDREN LEFT TO BE RAISED BY WOLVES

The children in the photographs in the old woman's album had no style. Or maybe, it would be more accurate to say they had a style, but one that was alien to me, both ancient and inappropriate. Scraggly, wild hair. You couldn't tell the boys and girls apart, like they were all one kind of creature, and wild, furtive eyes, ready to bolt, the way they had when the police came calling. The jeans were clean, but bulging at the cuffs, as if the jeans wanted to grow out, too. They had sandals barely covering their slender feet. They had flowers in their hair. I thought the taller one was the man. There was so much hair flopping in their faces that I couldn't tell whether there were beards, sideburns, something that would guide me other than height, but the old woman corrected me, pointing to the tall one, saying, that's your mother, that's my daughter. See, she's pregnant in this picture, see how her blouse catches a curve? She traced it with her bony, spotted finger. Here. See?

I didn't see it.

She grabbed my hand, pulled my finger to the curling snapshot, and made me trace it with her. That's you, she said. Until now, it was my only picture of you. It's my last picture of her. She was taken before you were born. She was at seven months when they took her. He'd just finished building the crib. We kept it right there by the bookshelf. I kept it until you turned four. I figured, if I found you then, you'd climb out anyway. And look at you now.

She was crazy, crazy as her daughter in her own way. My

knuckles hurt where she had squeezed. She stared at me, hard, as if I would look like either the baby in the belly or the tall girl in the peasant blouse with the hair in her face. Any of my friends would have left then, but me, I'm polite. I have the courtesy of my mother, the one in pearls, the one smelling of gardenias, the one who I know is a woman because she has every feminine grace. And maybe I have the curiosity of these other people, these wild animals. Maybe I was already marked one of them since before I was born, and my parents as well as this woman have always been waiting for wildness to out.

How could I come from them? The wild children in the photographs, playing guitars and sticking flowers in their hair? How was that a way to run a revolution? They must have never gotten anything done, unless they only took pictures of their most innocuous activities. If you listen to my parents, the children of the left were dangerous radicals with bombs, who got what they deserved. If I listened to this woman in this room, the only bombs that went off blew up the radicals themselves.

How could I come from my own parents? My father in his pressed uniform, my mother in her pearls, coming in to kiss me goodnight before they went to one of their parties, promising to kiss me again when they came back home. I'd wait for them for hours, building my blankets into a tent with the bedposts, until I finally fell asleep, blankets tangled around me, and who knew if they kept their promise. I would pretend that when they would come home, it wouldn't be them, but wolves wearing their faces as masks. When I told my mother one morning at breakfast, she took away *Little Red Riding Hood*. She must have known, then, that it was her face that was the mask. If they are wolves, the children of this woman here in this room where I couldn't breathe were sheep, and I was a lamb that shouldn't be. I should have been killed in my mother's womb along with my mother when they killed my father. They waited to kill her until I was born, and then they pushed her out of an airplane into the sea. That's what the old woman is waiting to tell me, the old woman, my grandmother.

We all should have died together, the three of us. Everything would have been simpler, cleaner. My grandmother would have had no hope, but she could have spent the last thirty years taking up a hobby instead of standing around the square holding pictures, waiting for a baby, a girl, a woman who never came. But if they killed my mother before I was born, my own children wouldn't be, my boys, wrestling each other on the kitchen floor, picking me wildflowers when we walked in the park, tugging at my hand with their sticky fingers, demanding it was their turn now.

How could I come from this crazy old woman, who let her daughter dabble in revolution when she should have been studying? This woman was not the grandmother I would have chosen. I wouldn't have wanted to spend my childhood visiting this stuffy, small apartment in this outskirt neighborhood, one I've never had reason to venture to before in my entire life. There wasn't a garden, just a balcony facing traffic, draped with laundry. I couldn't bring my own children here. There would be no place for them to play among the piles of books and papers.

She didn't offer me pastries, just hard candies melted down into the chipped porcelain bowl. The tea she brewed for me was so weak I couldn't tell whether she didn't have money for more, or that was how she liked it. The cup was thin with a pearly sheen, nothing but a checkered, black and gold Art Deco design on the rims. Her family must have had money, once, either before they came to this country or before they joined the left and didn't believe in pretty things anymore.

She must not have believed I would come this time or she would have surely supplied pastries. I'd turned down the other invitations, and I'd only accepted this one because my mother took me aside to whisper, it might go better with your father's case if you made a visit. Just one, just once. Until the DNA results are established, darling.

The old woman wanted to keep looking at the photo album. It was the old kind, cream corners glued to black thick paper to hold the snapshots in place. Some popped out as the pages turned, and she wouldn't move on until everything was back in place. Most of the photos were black and white, and in the ones in color, the colors were off, garish like a Technicolor movie, as if that decade never happened except in documentaries.

She paused at a picture of radicals seated around a campsite. The green of the forest made me see spots after I stared too long. She said, He would play the guitar for you and she would sing. Before you were born. From the day she found out about you to the day they took her. Do you sing? She was an alto. What are you?

Soprano.

And you're so short. But you could have gotten that from him. He was short, but feisty. Real tough, like he had something to prove. But he was the kindest of all of them, his group of friends. He took care of everyone. They didn't have enough money for their own place because so much of his paycheck went to making sure his students had enough to eat. I knew him since he was a boy. Oh, if only your other grandmother had lived to see this day. She came to the demonstrations until she got sick, and when she couldn't come anymore, I would hold up his picture, too. This one.

He was in an old man's suit for first communion. It was too big for him. Maybe it belonged to a cousin first, but if so, why hadn't somebody altered it for him? Maybe there were more cousins coming down the line. He clutched his Book of Saints to his chest. His hair was cut short and it stood up in spikes. You could see his big, luminous eyes. It was easier for me to think of this boy as my father than the hairy short man in the first picture she showed me, even though it was impossible for this boy to be a father. It seemed like a strange choice of the other grandmother to bring this picture to the demonstration. They hadn't killed this boy on the day of his first communion. They killed a radical, a wild, shaggy man, a dangerous man. The other grandmother must have been hoping they would see the boy within the man. The fact that this very boy became the man, for somebody like my father in the uniform and my mother in the pearls, was all the more reason to kill him. In their eyes, he turned out to be a wolf in sheep's clothing.

It was the photo of my mother on the first day of school when I knew without doubts. I knew, but I didn't say anything to her yet, this little old woman, my grandmother who wanted so much more from me than I would ever be capable of giving. Not just because of what had happened to me, but because of what was in me. Maybe I changed in those last two months in my mother's womb, when she was being tortured in detention. Or maybe I was the kind of baby who couldn't protect their parents, who couldn't make them choose safer, easier ways. My boys were that kind of baby. I wouldn't risk anything for myself, but everything for them.

I knew because the nervous grin of my mother holding her mother's hand at the school door was the one my youngest son flashed at me when he wanted to tell me he was worried, but would be all right. That I could go, as long as I came back. Now when I would watch him, it would be like seeing a ghost, exactly the ghost this old woman was so hungry for. I didn't say anything, though, until we'd worked backwards through the album, to baby pictures that looked like me except the surroundings were wrong, the decade twenty years earlier than mine, as if I'd been photoshopped into somebody else's movie set.

Now you see, she said to me, closing the cover gingerly. Now you know what the DNA results will show you. I didn't want science to show us why we are family. I wanted history, the history that was stolen from you the way that you were stolen from us. But she couldn't help herself, and the phrases she'd been practicing since the first grandmothers found their grandchildren through DNA were not enough for her. She had to add, The history that was stolen from you when those people murdered your parents.

You are telling me, I asked her, my voice starting out cordial but wavering as I went, that my parents murdered my real parents? Which am I meant to be most distraught over? That my parents aren't my real parents? Or that they are murderers? One alone might be enough for today. I was polite and my mother's daughter. Only the teacup trembling in my hand gave me away.

She wasn't polite, this crazy woman, her dark eyes feverish, bony hands waving wildly as she talked. Your parents are murderers and you are not who you think you are. I've spent the last thirty years looking for you. Every child who came to look in the library where I worked at the circulation desk, I'd stare into their eyes. When you were at the university, I'd walk through the halls on all my lunch breaks. I thought, maybe you'd like music, too. She grabbed a folder and spilled out the ticket stubs of decades' worth of musical events. Why did you deny what you love? she said. Why weren't you where I looked for you? Why did I have to look so hard?

I wasn't allowed to go to the library when I was small. My father, with his deep and abiding love of private ownership, always said, any book worth reading is a book worth owning. I didn't finish the university. I started with my class and attended the lectures, but I was too nervous to sit for the exams. I didn't go to concerts often, because they made me cry. I sat at home and played records. My ex-husband called me agoraphobic, first as a joke when we started dating and I wanted to stay at my home or his but not go out, and then for real when he said my problems were scaring the boys and pretty soon nobody would go outside anywhere.

I have a lovely apartment with a garden. I don't get out much now, except to the market and to take the boys to the park. The alimony is good, and even if it wasn't, my parents would help. The wolves, I mean, the uniform and pearls, not the parents dropped from the plane into the sea. My ex-husband is a successful dentist putting braces on the city's upper-middle-class children. The kind of child I was, once. Dentists aren't often found on the left. They rip out people's teeth. What they do would be considered torture if you didn't have to pay them so much. My ex-husband has asked me, no matter what I find out, yes or no, not to share it with the boys. Or with him, either. He says he doesn't care. He already knows me, and he's already found me wanting.

I don't have grandmothers anymore, I told her. They both died years ago, when I was little. So you can be my grandmother if you'd like. I thought I was making a grand gesture, more polite than my mother in the pearls, as kind as my brand new father clutching his children's Book of Saints.

I *am* your grandmother, she wailed. I don't need your permission to be what I am.

But I've been waiting my whole life for permission to be who I am. Lambs have to ask the wolves. Wolves don't ask to be lambs. They just put on the masks.

•

I didn't take a taxi to the house on the hill. I rode the metro, packed with people, packed with DNA and history. I imagined swabbing the insides of people's cheeks, pulling at stray hair on the collars of coats. So many ways to find out you weren't who you thought you were. You could go around asking about political parties now and those of thirty years ago, but most of the older people on the metro car would lie and the young wouldn't care. DNA doesn't lie. I've watched enough soap operas, though, in my years as a housewife, to know that results can be contaminated by human error, or human desire if there's enough money involved. I didn't care anymore what the results would be. I knew from my child's nervous grin on the face of my mother as a girl. I'd known my whole life that something was wrong with me, and now I knew there was something wrong with everybody else.

My mother held her pearls at her throat and said, What a lovely surprise. She had the kettle on and there were éclairs that the maid had picked up that morning, so they weren't fresh, she could send the maid out again, but I told her I didn't care. My mother was worried to see me out of the house and wanted to know first where the boys were. When I said, with the neighbors, she didn't like the answer. She never liked the neighbors. She wanted me to bring them up the hill, where she could watch them, which meant the maid would watch them. There had been many maids since the one I'd loved when I was a girl, the one who'd read me *Little Red*

Riding Hood, who sang the songs that my mother must have sung to me. Not this one in pearls, the androgynous one in sandals, the tall one who towers over her man. I can't figure out how to say "real." They both are unreal, the wolf, the wild one. Maybe mothers are always unreal.

She fingered her pearls with her blood-red fingernails and waited for me to speak.

You knew what the DNA results would be all along, didn't you?

You have the results?

I don't need the results now.

So now you think you know something. You know nothing. You don't know what it's like to want a child. Yours came so easily. I held my breath for you, and you didn't even know how lucky you were, both times.

She was jealous of me and my fertility, jealous of my hairy flower mother and hers. Which was worse, the murder or the kidnapping? The kidnapping. Because if you hate people so much you want them to die, you shouldn't want their children. She must have been so confident that she could turn me into her. A book worth reading is a book worth owning. A child worth raising is a child worth owning. I didn't say anything. The cream oozed out of the éclair as I pressed it with my thumb.

There were five miscarriages before you, darling. Five. You didn't have one. You can't know. So many dead babies, so much blood. I couldn't try again. The doctors said it would kill me. But your father needed a son. And I needed something to love.

But I wasn't a boy.

Your father saw you and he fell in love. He didn't care whether or not you were a boy once he saw you, so little you fit in his two hands, like a puppy or a kitten, so tiny! How nervous we were as we waited for you to grow. And I, of course, never cared as long as you were ours.

The words binding me to her again. Ours. If you wish it, it must be so. If you wish it, your adopted daughter will dutifully forge a relationship with the crazy old grandmother so that when your husband stands trial, the court will see that his attitude toward radicals and their families has relaxed. He's a kind man, a gentle man, a father, not a murderer and kidnapper anymore.

Why didn't you try what you said you did, when you told me I was adopted? Go and see the nuns?

You fell into our lives, don't you see? We didn't have to try anything. You were there. You needed so much care. You were so little. We gave you everything. It wasn't something I thought about. It happened. Wasn't it a good life, darling? You remember when the boys were little, how much there is to be done, how you never sleep, but you don't care because there is a baby in your arms?

The idea of my mother, sleepless, a baby in her arms. It must have been maids who were sleepless, the maids she ran through as if the job description stated it was only to be temporary. I don't mean that she didn't love me, didn't take care of me. But her vision of herself never matched the reality. She couldn't see her mask, although she could see that I couldn't manage keeping mine from slipping.

They'd admitted I was adopted when I was first contacted by the old woman, when her letter stayed in my pocketbook for days before I could bring myself to finish it. Yes, I was adopted, she was right about that, but not the rest, that was crazy. I was adopted, but they hadn't wanted to tell me to make me feel I was anything less than theirs because I was, I was their everything. I was from an orphanage, nuns handled the paperwork, but from what they understood, my parents died in a bus crash that I survived, and the distant relatives still in the countryside, although heartbroken, were too poor to take me in. No loose ends. Everything virtuous. Poor but noble. The perfect orphan story, straight from a soap opera. Rags to riches because I was such an adorable baby. I earned my fate through my cooing.

They had to tell me I was adopted because they knew the first court-ordered DNA tests would reveal that the DNA was an impossible match for us, and the next step would be to match my DNA with one of the grandmothers, the whole group of them who stood in the square, and although they weren't sure there would be a match, they knew I would know I was adopted. My parents were doling out truth and building new lies for scaffolding. When the DNA showed my grandmother was my grandmother, were they planning to claim the nuns had tricked them into taking a baby without knowing the origins? Without knowing that the baby's parents had been killed by my father? Bad origins twice: the murdered and the murderers. Bad by nature, worse by nurture.

What child doesn't think, maybe I'm adopted? Waiting for the wolves who wear the masks of parent faces to fool the careless child. My father, on the stairs of the house on the hill, sneering down at me, when he'd found out that I hadn't failed my university exams, but hadn't taken them in the first place: you're no child of mine. He was right.

I put the teacup down. The pattern that had once seemed so delicate resolved into a military crest. The pearls themselves were a uniform.

Your father will be home soon. Can't you wait to talk to

him? You can help him. You're the only one who can. I'm losing you, maybe my grandchildren, too.

I didn't respond.

Don't let me lose him. He's all I'll have left.

I can't keep him from prison.

But you can decide how long he goes. Darling, he isn't young. All I ask is that you remember how much he loves you. She folded her hands around her teacup and crossed her ankles together. The interview was over. She wouldn't say another word because she wanted to end on this sentimental note. All I ask is everything of you, darling.

•

I stood in the garden waiting for my father. The cushions were out for the chaise lounge, and I could have walked to the gazebo, but to sit in comfort would reveal me as part of the world of the pearls. I'd wait to sit in my own home, on chairs paid for by skillful dentistry. The rosebushes were pruned so tightly they looked skeletal, and the lawn as regular as Astroturf and as lush as a painting. A green so bright I thought of the Technicolor photographs at my grandmother's.

I knew my father wouldn't approach me in the garden. He didn't meet people, not even halfway. People came in to talk to him, either once he was ensconced beyond the massive oak desk in the study or propped up in his club chair in the den, cigar in hand. He didn't enter rooms or exit them. He was already there, the space already claimed and shaped by him. I tiptoed around him when I was little. I only came to him when I was called. Which is not to say I didn't love him, or that I feared him. When I was little, he would pull me up into his lap and listen patiently while I narrated inventions. He would hide candy and small treats he thought I would like in his pockets: change from other countries, stamps with birds and flowers, pencils with cartoon characters. He wanted to see me every day, no matter how late he returned from his office. He called it the viewing, and sometimes I would turn it into a performance, ballet steps, warbling I called opera, poems about rabbits in the garden. As I grew older, sitting in his lap seemed ridiculous, and I became self-conscious about the viewing. I didn't want to perform, and what teenager wants to be looked at? I stopped seeking him out, and he didn't meet people halfway.

He was done with me when I dropped out of the university. I wasn't a boy, which would have meant an army career. What my mother had hoped for me was at least a few years at the university and marriage. When it was a few months at the university instead, she found me my dentist, the son of a childhood friend of hers. I'd known him all my life. When he came to my house or I went to his, he expected a viewing. He liked to examine my teeth. He found mouths erotic, and it was an efficient step to kissing and things that can be done with mouths that would horrify my mother. When I married my dentist, my father warmed up to me again, although I never remember speaking to him alone, always my mother and my husband in the room instead, as if we were trapped in some play on a country estate where all principals must be on stage at once. When I had the boys, he was transformed, bringing out tin soldiers to scatter on the rugs, the patterns terrain. When I was divorced, it didn't matter to him because I'd produced the boys. His heirs were here, an heir and a spare. They could run two branches of the armed forces between them. I could be dumped from the plane now.

My mother called me back inside. Darling, he's in the study. You can take his tea in to him, she said, handing me the tray. As if I needed a reason to talk to him, when he was the one desperate to talk to me.

I didn't take the tray. She had to put it back on the sideboard. Behind the desk in the study, he looked shrunken, not that much younger than the old lady who was my grandmother, and his uniform didn't fit so well anymore, as if he was shrinking too fast for adjustments. The medals gleamed; epaulets framed his shoulders. He waited for me to say something, as if I were the supplicant. But I waited for him to speak first.

Your mother says the situation has changed, he said.

Yes, I said.

What do you want me to do? he asked. I was the supplicant. He couldn't ask me to save him. It wasn't in him, wasn't within the uniform.

Can you kill her, Daddy? I don't want to go back there. You should have seen her apartment. And it's so sad, her story.

He scowled. It isn't funny, he said. We didn't raise you to be flippant.

What do you want me to do, Daddy?

His eyes flickered. He knew what my mother wanted him to ask, but he couldn't do it. Either he didn't want to debase himself and ask a favor of me, or there was something in him, maybe the part that put those old knees down on the rug for my boys, that wanted to be punished.

Nothing, he said. There is nothing for you to do. What do you want from me?

I do want to know if you were the one who killed them. I know you must have killed radicals. Killed their friends. But did you kill them. Did you kill my mother and father?

Your mother is in the garden. I'm your father, sitting here before you.

But we both know that's not true. At least, not wholly true. I have many parents.

What would you believe? That I killed them? That I didn't kill them? If you know the truth before the DNA results have come, you must know this truth, too.

I did. I knew. He was a man who liked to delegate, but wouldn't shirk from something hard. He prided himself on being a hard man. There would have been bargains between brothers. He would have tortured and killed other mothers for fellow officers who needed babies, too. He'd be complicit in the crime, but able to look at his child and not see a copy of his victims' eyes. If the wolf had killed my parents, I would have felt most bound to him, I think. He would have been the parent who mattered most. But he lacked the courage of his convictions. He was a murderer, just not my murderer.

You didn't kill them, Daddy.

Thank you. Tell your mother I'd like my tea now, darling, will you? He didn't look up from his newspaper as I left. I didn't stop to talk to my mother. I walked all the way home, down the hill, the whole city spread out before me.

•

I didn't testify for leniency for my father, the murderer, and my mother, the kidnapper. I didn't testify for my grandmother, either. I stayed here, insulated by the money of my dentist, bringing up my own wolfpack. We're alone, set adrift in the island of childhood, those years before school when a parent is everything to a child, but we're surrounded by family. My father snug in the prison, my mother high in the mansion on the hill, my grandmother out in her tiny apartment, my parents falling from the plane into the sea, if you drew a circle, there I would be in the center, with my boys, neither left nor right. Nothing will be the same. Everything will be the same. I'm the one who's right. I'm what's left.

THE INN OF THE FORMER RURAL FARM WORKERS

In the City, you can find anything you want, all the things we wanted on Yorn, so why is it that week after week we file into the Inn of the Former Rural Farm Workers? To eat the inky noodles, the "pig-squirrels climbing a tree," moonflower mash stewed in its own pollen, and most dangerously, the peppery spider food?

Beyond the rain-streaked windowpanes of the Inn, the City glows purple and orange. Pod launches break the color up into pulses, but we're too far away from the port to feel the vibrations. The elevated ribbon slides by, spitting out passengers who kick through the debris caught at the metro steps and on the city floor. Old newspapers in the slanting Yornese script cling to the glass of the Inn and slide slowly down. The Inn is in what the real estate agents charmingly call the Yornese Ghetto. The warehouses ship around the clock, and so the crowds in the Yornese Ghetto and the Inn are constant. It's never crowded and never empty.

The Inn never closes, and sometimes it's hard coming in knowing that there will be no reason to leave. We receive our first round of moonflower moonshine without having to ask. We order off the secret Yornese menu we've learned by heart.

All of the food that made us so sick those first six months, whether we took our pills or not. The food my host mother force-fed me when I was sick in bed, too weak to walk over to the capsule dinners stashed in the valise, too feverishly incoherent to ask her to do it for me. I'd stare down the end of the spoon at the peppery broth, the inky noodles curling in tendrils at the base, the ink leaking onto the spoon staining it black, but when I shook my head, she'd say I was asking for more, and when I wouldn't open my mouth, my host father would pinch my nostrils closed. The villages were competing to see which Rural Farm Worker could be fattened up the fastest. But I vomited up everything and was a disappointment.

Fattened up for slaughter, we joke now at the Inn, as if we were nothing more than roly-poly pig-squirrels at Festival time. As if the Yornese had requested Rural Farm Workers from the City in order to eat them. As if we were the solution to Yornese agriculture not because of our knowledge of Irrigation, our knowledge of Flood and Drought and Flood-Drought Conditions, but because the Yornese needed us to add a few more strings of protein into the peppery spider food to take the Yornese cuisine up a notch.

K says, once he's had his first drink, I would have rather been someone's dinner than have eaten food out of the mouths of Yornese babies, day after day after day. When the Yornese didn't have enough to feed themselves first. Why didn't they send us enough capsule dinners to share with our hosts? Or at least enough to last us through our stint? We were such an imposition! The Yornese should have eaten us the moment we exited our Pods.

But that's K. There's Former Rural Farm Workers who never really leave Yorn, even when they're in the City. There's Former Rural Farm Workers who didn't leave Yorn, who died and whom we mourn. And then there's Former Rural Farm Workers who only go back to Yorn on the nights when we drink moonflower moonshine and eat peppery spider food at the Inn of the Former Rural Farm Workers. K's the first kind, Z's the one we lost, and M and I are the kind who can keep our nostalgia to the Inn. M, I think, isn't even all that nostalgic. She just really likes inky noodles.

The Innkeeper asks us if we want another round. We order and ask him to sit down with us. He's Yornese himself, always sweating in the warmth of the City, and he drinks moonflower as if it were water. He didn't know us on Yorn, but his village is in Z's region. He pats my arm, marveling at my thin City sweater. But it's not cold out yet, he says, laughing. Such a hot rain. He grabs my hand and slaps it to his clammy brow. If he had done that in my village, my host father would have taken him out to the barn and beaten him bloody, then demanded a pig-squirrel, and I always wait for K to do something, but K has never been very invested in my honor. M doesn't even notice, her eyes on her noodles.

The Innkeeper's wife shouts, Hands off! and the Innkeeper gracefully takes my hand and places it on K's. We like the Innkeeper, in spite of his flirtations, maybe because of his flirtations which remind us he's a boy only recently off Yorn. We don't like his wife, who like us is a Former Rural Farm Worker. We know the Inn has been designed to manipulate our nostalgia too precisely, and even though the Innkeeper is the genius behind the operation and is manipulating her nostalgia, too, we blame her. We don't like the fact that she is the one in the kitchen, because the peppery spider food should be prepared not only by a Yornese but by an Initiate, and she is neither, in spite of all the time she put in spying in the kitchens of Yorn. She waves, scowling, from behind the stove. She doesn't like that we know she isn't Yornese, can see past the scarf embroidered in moonflowers and wrapped around her forehead with wings on the sides and the tail in the back, can tell that she only glows Yornese blue because of a steady diet of inky noodles. We were bluish once, too.

We brought back valises of those scarves for gifts. I've got one in the pocket of my sweater right now. We know she's not Yornese because she's just B from our very own group of Former Rural Farm Workers.

B would like us to start going to Blue Earth, Yornese Kitchen, Moonflower Village or any one of the other Yornese eateries in the City, instead of coming to her Inn. When we began meeting, we used to rotate, but Blue Earth is expensive, Yornese Kitchen infested with insects, Moonflower Village a blatantly obvious Yornese gangster hangout. As we dropped eateries, we kept dropping Former Rural Farm Workers from our list, too, until it was only K, M and me who were coming regularly anymore. M always asks if we could count B, too, but I don't think we can since she wouldn't be here if it wasn't her Inn.

We keep going to the Inn of Former Rural Farm Workers because M lives only one elevated stop away, K goes to other eateries on other nights in his perpetual nostalgia, and I like watching B and her Innkeeper. I don't think they're going to last. It's hard for a City girl to stay on Yorn, but the Yornese boy you bring to the City seems awfully Yornese once you get him there. My host parents found me suitor after suitor from our village, and I turned each one of them down.

The slogan for the Inn, up on their site and painted above the door in letters slanted to look like Yornese script, is "The ideal spot for the nostalgia and dreams of those who once worked in rural production teams." K's dreams are nightmares of being eaten, M dreams of all the noodles she wants, mine are of Z with us again. We can't figure out why B doesn't want our business when we are so clearly the clientele she and the Innkeeper planned for. Is it that her dream is to be Yornese, and an Initiate? And that she can't pretend when we're there to blow her cover?

Tonight, there's a group of Yornese teenagers furiously typing on their Devices in a corner, and two groups of Former Rural Farm Workers holding far more jovial reunions than ours. They drink round after round. They are older than us; those years were happier on Yorn. Years of snows and the crops that came from them. There is cake: not a Yornese dessert, but all the sugar the City can pour in. They beckon us over to their tables, but K waves them off. He'll only talk to people who like their nostalgia bitter, or people he knew then, like M and me, so he doesn't have to explain himself. Although he does. He turns to M, saying, I like my nostalgia bitter.

And you drink your moonflower tinged with tears, she says. It's a traditional toast from her village and K's favorite. The Innkeeper laughs and downs his drink. He pours us one more before he moves on, yelling at the Yornese teenagers to go home in Yornese. I'd almost forgotten the way the consonants blur in Z's dialect, and the teenagers in their sullenness reduce it to an impossible mumble. When I visited Z in his village, it was almost easier to pretend I didn't know Yornese rather than try to understand his host family, although his host mother was very sweet, plying me with moonflower tea, saying in a million years she'd never be able to warm me up.

When Z wrote me to tell me he was going to marry his host sister, I was surprised and not surprised. Even when on my visits they cuddled together under a single blanket by the family fires, two pig-squirrels up a love tree, as his host father said, even though I'd started dating K during training (although since we'd arrived on Yorn he preferred to stay in his village) and Z and I were just friends, I'd thought Z and I were going to end up together. When they assigned us our letters in training, since the Yornese would never be able to pronounce our real names, there we were at opposite ends. I'd loved Z since he'd whispered, What a hot little pig-squirrel you are, in Yornese, when we danced the scarf dance our very first night on Yorn at the welcome party. When I threw up in my hair, he used the scarf to clean me up and said, You're still a beautiful pig-squirrel.

I thought that after our years on Yorn, once we were back in the City, we'd decorate our apartments with Yornese scarves and cook the peppery spider food together, whether we were Initiated or not. Breaking those rules would turn us on in precisely the way that only City-dwellers who did a stint on Yorn could understand. Yorn would pepper our lives. We would continue to study Irrigation, I would paint City landscapes but with pig-squirrels going up the tree, Z would play his Yornese melodies on his guitar, maybe we'd give our children Yornese nicknames. Maybe we'd go there on holiday, our host families laughing and crying when we exited our Pods, returning against all odds. But we'd never live there again.

Z's wedding was held during Festival time. K and I took our Pods down together. Most of the group came, some we hadn't seen since the welcome party. Everybody was eating Yornese food now, the capsule dinners long gone or frozen solid in freezer-burn blocks. The Yornese were proud of us, but proudest of M, who won the competition of the fattest Rural Farm Worker. Which is not to say that M was very big at all, just that she hadn't lost weight and had managed to put a little on over the winter and her love of inky noodles. They took a picture of her between the bride and groom. She was a good sport about it. Z kissed M on the cheek, kissed me, kissed his host mother, but mainly kissed his host sister, who was now his wife.

She was a classic Yornese beauty, pale, elegant blue, the color of a Yornese sky when the moon is out, her hair as wild as inky noodles, her features delicate and sculpted the way Yornese girls are before they blossom. They bloom, they're beautiful, and then it falls apart and they've got the blunt faces of pig-squirrels, my host mother told me.

Every time the villagers chanted, Life is bitter, bitter, bitter, and Z and his wife had to answer it with a kiss, Z kissed her like it was their first and they were alone under a blanket. I'd seen grooms in my village look annoyed after the first couple of hours, but not Z. Not even the three days of a Yornese wedding got him down. When I listened to him tease his wife, pull at her scarf's tail, he sounded not just proficient at Yornese, not just fluent, but Yornese himself. The Trainers told us that Yornese humor wasn't something that could be taught, but had to be lived. K had mocked them instantly. What's so funny about drinking yourself to death with moonflower? All your babies dying of ice pox? That's so hysterically funny, we've got to get them up on a City site, performing their Yorneseness. Z had laughed then. But he wasn't just understanding Yornese humor, or performing for the Yornese, or performing for the other Rural Farm Workers. He was changing inside. The blue cast to Z's skin started to shine like the heart of a flame. If I'd never met him before, I would have thought he was Yornese.

When we left on the last day of the wedding, K looked cross. I teased him that he'd been in love with Z, like the rest of us. He said, abruptly, bitterly, clearly not pausing to consider whether or not I was the one in love with Z, no, that wasn't it at all. That he wanted what Z had, to be so completely a part of Yorn. They don't like me in my village, he said. They come to make fun of me, to mock me slurp at my inky noodles. They want to fatten me up while their own children waste away. It doesn't make any sense. But they like K? Who steals away their daughter? Who will either take her away to the City like a prize, or eat their food and live off them for the rest of his life like he's their prize? Why do they like him? It isn't fair.

K wasted away in his village, skeletal, less and less blue as he tried to survive on the mash alone. He was sent home early, something he's always considered a dishonorable discharge. He wouldn't let me snap a photograph before he stepped into his Pod. I don't want to remember this, he said. I don't want to remember any of it. He swept his arms back and forth, slicing through the Yornese air around him. A storm was coming, and his Pod had a brief window to launch. I didn't bother to ask him if we were breaking up or not. I didn't think I would ever see him again. When he found me off the site and kept typing amusing Former Rural Farm Worker acronyms at me until I responded, I typed M and together we started gathering our group of letters to move through the Yornese eateries on the list.

But Z wasted away, too. The Yornese got him, ate him, in a way, not the people but the ice pox, the one you breathe in during the icy season when it hurts to take a breath and you wish there was a way you could stop without dying. The ice pox that the peppery spider food is designed to fight off, to build up immunity. Z must have stopped taking his pills, thought he could rely on the peppery spider food alone, but he hadn't had a lifetime of eating it, only part of a stint as a Rural Farm Worker. Or maybe he never stopped taking his pills, and was just unlucky. They told us in training that if we kept taking our pills, we'd be fine, but we knew not to believe them. The City has all sorts of diseases all its own, ultimately the ideal incubator for exotic strains from everywhere else. Yorn mainly has the ice pox. It was all Yorn needed.

Z got sicker and sicker. He stopped typing altogether. My Pod wouldn't work in the weather, but my host parents drove me down in their sleigh. As soon as I saw him, I typed Headquarters in the City to come get him, but it was too late. The Device kept breaking up. I couldn't follow their instructions, whether they wanted me to keep him cold or keep him hot, give him ice water or tea.

His wife kept saying to me, I want to die, too, but I can't get sick from this. Not anymore. Let me take care of him, not you. She pushed me away from the sickbed.

She fed him inky broth and put her scarf over his fevered brow. Z's host mother burned moonflowers, and the cloying smell made me claustrophobic, so much so it was all I could do to keep myself in the room and not to run out through the snow. I knew him longer, but his wife knew him better. She wasn't going to let me take him away in a Pod. She knew I wouldn't bring him back, that I would keep him. I'd say it was because of the ice pox, but it would be because of me.

But she had to sleep some time, and once she nodded off at the foot of the bed, I knelt down and took Z's icy hand into mine. A, you've got it all wrong, he whispered. You and K. You don't understand. They're us. They're not different from us. You can't learn it in parts. It has to be swallowed whole.

You stopped taking your pills, I said. Was it some sort of experiment?

What are you talking about? It's never been an experiment. It's not just who I am now. It was who I always was.

It took both Z's wife and my host mother to pull me away. They locked me in the kitchen until Z died an hour later. It was cold in the kitchen, and it smelled like pepper. My host father tried to get me to play cards, but I wouldn't. The Initiate wouldn't let me prepare anything for the spider food, but she let me stir up the dough for the inky noodles. I saw her throw it away in the corner when they came to tell me Z was dead. They wouldn't let me in the room. I could hear Z's host mother lead the ululation. When they brought in the moonflower, through the open door I saw a flash of Z's host sister/wife stretched across his body as if she would be his blanket. Nothing would ever warm him again. His host father took out the ax to break the ice for the grave. I slouched to the floor clutching moonflowers in my fist. My host father picked me up and carried me out to the sleigh.

He wasn't for you, my host mother said. See how weak he was? You're going to beat the ice pox. She was right. I thought about going home after K left and Z died, but once it was clear the ice pox wouldn't kill me, just leave me marked with these lacy scars like snowflakes along my cheekbones, I wanted to finish up my stint. I went around with some Yornese boys, but never from my village. I didn't want my host family to get their hopes up. I wasn't going to stay on Yorn and I wasn't bringing anybody back to the City. I liked being pig-squirrels under the blanket in the winter, the flash of a blue ankle, the turn of a blue wrist, a blue ear poking out of a scarf and walking through the moonflowers in the summer, but none of it was that different from being with K or boys in the City when I was studying Irrigation. It might have been different for Z.

I kept thinking about how K and Z used to talk in training about whether we were on Yorn to help the Yornese grow food for the Yornese themselves, or whether we were there to help them build a surplus that could be sent on to the City. About whether it mattered if in the end the Yornese could eat more than their subsistence diet. If in the end more of their children could make it out of infancy. At first, K said the means justified the end, and Z cared about the means and was skeptical of the City's agenda. Once we were on Yorn, K flipped positions and Z didn't want to talk about it anymore. I have had more than enough time to hear from K and his thoughts on food production, but I wish I could have asked Z what he thought before he died. But it might have been that he didn't think about his part of the means, as if his trip to Yorn had no purpose behind it other than to deliver him to his waiting village, to the blanket with his host sister, to his ice pox sickbed and his Yornese shallow grave.

B calls out, no desert tonight, but then she sends over some moonflowers in aspic anyway. The Innkeeper eats most of it, sticking a moonflower on M's fork, then mine.

Tonight, I'm going to take the Innkeeper home with me, and when I start to think of Z, I'll have something to distract me. It will mean I can't go back to the Inn. The Innkeeper will tell B, a knot for him to tie on to his scarf, the proof of his prowess. B won't let me back. I'll have to pick one of the other eateries for my nostalgia. At least I've finally got enough money to eat at Blue Earth, enough to treat M and K if they'll join me. They keep bumping me up at Headquarters. Pretty soon, I'll be leading a group of Pods to Yorn myself, and after that, Theria, Livert, who knows? There are so many places with Flood/Drought Conditions, so many chances to travel.

In the end, the City eats us all.

THE POETESS WRITES UNANSWERED LETTERS

Varatec, Romania, June 10, 1889

Dear Emin,

When I arrived here at the convent at Varatec, I knew I was done. I'm thirty-nine, and I won't marry again. I won't move to the woods, write poetry, and live on cornmeal like the forest nymphs you talk about. I'm done, Emin, and it's you who've done me in. I'm ready to give myself over to God's work and to sing his praises, hosanna in the highest with the nuns.

I wasn't going to move from spare room to spare room in my daughters' houses anymore, or move from one shabby flat to another in Iasi. You've seen those little rooms of mine—chambers, you always insisted on calling them, and you never once visited without three flowers for me to stick in the water jug on whatever battered dresser I was using next. You weren't kind to me when I complained that those chambers were small. Cozy, you said. Cozy. It was easy for you to be above matters of money with your drinking partners footing your bills.

Even easier for you now in the asylum: Mihai Eminescu, the maddest man in Romania. They say you think the stones in the yard look like diamonds, the leaves, money. Of course in your madness you've found a way to think that money does grow on trees.

My dear Emin, you weren't ever kind when I complained about matters of money, either before or after you went crazy with syphilis. There, I've written it, what the doctors would never let me hear, what your sisters would never tell me. As if I wouldn't know what the mercury cure was for. Or why you were raving. You said it was Albanian. But you don't know Albanian, Emin. All across Europe, the poets are raving mad. How in vogue you've become.

The first time you said you couldn't marry me, you told me I was raving mad, a lunatic, and in a way unbecoming to a muse or a poetess. Remember? After Stefan died? Nine years ago, when I briefly thought I had the chance to become a wife to the poet, perhaps a better poetess in my own right because I'd be freed from the worry of rumor and want, but above all from the steady pain of missing you, mourning you when you weren't the one who was dead. You were alive and I was alive and how could it be mad to marry? An unbecoming lunatic, you said. As if I'd ever, with my responsibilities, my girls, my reputation, had the luxury to wallow in lunacy?

So I'm a lunatic, but you, sir, are a coward, I told you. I said it again in French to make sure you'd understand me. You with your effete French habits, the cane with the scarab-design at the tip, the pince-nez, the moustache that wriggled above your lip like a mouse trying to slide into his hole. Because a real Romanian would have married me first and thought about consequences second, I told you. It was the most cutting thing I could think of to tell you. You were trying so hard to become French you became as cautious as them, you who had built your career in and for the Romanian language, you, the national poet, Emin the eminent who would get our little local language noticed in Paris, in Vienna, in Berlin, in the real Europe just a train ride away from our Turkish backwater.

No one will let you keep this letter. No one will read it out loud to you, smooth the poet's brow, and unfold the perfumed letter to Mihai Eminescu locked up in the asylum from his notorious mistress locked up in the convent. Where would I get perfume anyway, at Varatec? I've said goodbye to the charms of women and am trying to welcome the nonchalance of crones. I've rubbed acacia blooms across this page for that smell of sex you found so intoxicating when we stumbled upon it in the gardens at Copou, when I was an adulteress and not yet a widow, when you were a poet and not yet a syphilitic.

I've unpacked my trunk for the last time. My poor books, photos of the girls in silvered frames, my plainest dresses pressed and wrapped in paper. The ivory mirror, comb, and brush set Stefan gave me as a wedding present. The cottage in the convent still smells like newly cut pine. The fretted eaves are painted pale blue and there's a veranda where I'll pray for us all, for the girls and their families, but for you and me, Emin, too.

I arrived at Varatec in my fur-trimmed hat. Ermine. The one I refused to pawn. Remember when you told me you always thought of me as "Veronica Micle ensconced in fur and velvet?" When we were still formal with each other, never a *tu* between us, never an Emin or Nicutza, but when the flirting had already started? You had just started your job as the university librarian in Iasi. I was wearing my hair the way you liked it best then, most of it piled up in a chignon but with strands loose over my shoulders. You said I looked like a little girl.

When I was a little girl in Neamt, and we would go by sleigh, my mother would tuck a bear fur blanket around our legs. In winter at its coldest, we'd get the warmed brick at our feet. You used to tease me about how cold I could get, that it made me more appealing because I needed a gentleman to warm me up. But when we took the Iasi-Bucharest train together last April, when your crippled sister Harieta begged me to take you back to Dr. Sutu because you were getting worse again, I was the one who wrapped my arms around you. We hadn't sat so close since you finally ended it with me and ended up in the asylum. For the last six years, we've always kept a respectable distance, my skirts swishing over the floor as I paced while you told me about your days in Bucharest from across the room. In April, you were in one of your rare lucid moments. You patted my hand and whispered, my old girl. Nicutza. Nicutza. But once, you called me Harieta, and your eyes then had the faraway look of a little boy who needs to nap.

My girls wanted Varatec for me because of the stoves and six chimneys in the convent church. They know I need to be warm. It's pleasant as I write this letter on the veranda. The convent's garden is shaded by cedars. The walls are white-washed and dappled in the afternoon sun. The nuns run back and forth from the cottages looking for gossip.

The nuns eye me warily. I've never liked starting over with new people—maybe one of the reasons I was determined to wait for you so long? I didn't have to introduce myself to you. Stefan did. You met Stefan first in that Viennese hotel lobby, two countrymen speaking their own language in the imperial city. I was Doamna Micle to you instead of Veronica, and certainly not Nicutza, when the three of us went into the coffeehouse together. You and I ate a Sacher torte and talked about French literature, Baudelaire mainly but a little Flaubert, while Stefan read the papers. You let me have most of the torte. I thought you were a plump, overgrown schoolboy who liked to list the books he read but couldn't explain why he read them.

The first time you came to our house in Iasi for one of my literary evenings, you didn't want to hand over your cane and hat to the servant, and you wriggled so awkwardly out of your greatcoat. I saw you down the corridor as I conferred with cook about the wine-soaked pears. You looked different than you did in Vienna. In Romania, you seemed wild, disheveled, and clumsy, a poet, not a student. When you sat down in the parlor, you didn't balance your teacup on your lap. You drank it down to the leaves and left your cup on the rug. You leaned back in your chair and crossed your arms as you listened to the monotone poetry Titu Maiorescu offered that night. You audibly sighed before Titu was done. Stefan snored in the corner, but he woke up for yours. You didn't read yours so much as proclaim it. Even Stefan said he liked your poem. Afterwards, when you took your leave of me, you didn't kiss my hand like everyone else. You asked me, tell me, Veronica, what do you think of my poem? You asked me to write out a copy of one of mine. You said it was pretty. You didn't say I was.

I know you always wondered if you were my first love affair. First other than Stefan, that is. You weren't my first because I do count Stefan. You never did. You saw him as an old man, tried to think of him as a fatherly gentleman, never my husband. You'd rather imagine me with other young men, create phantoms to be jealous of rather than think about Stefan. When I met Stefan and we married, when I was fourteen and he was forty-four, he was a glamorous figure to me. I adored him. I was still in braids. He wasn't yet the rector at the university, but he was an established professor in physics and chemistry, and the equations he wrote out for me seemed a different kind of poetry. I was already trying to be a poet, writing whenever my father let me have some paper. I liked his leonine head, his peppered hair, his shoulders that were broader than my father's. Stefan's suits were purchased in Vienna and Berlin. I did love him.

Everyone always asks me what I thought the first time I read your "Luceafarul." They want to watch me squirm as I think about what it's like to be called too beautiful by your lover. Or your husband to be called old and cold. But what I always thought, once Stefan died and you still wouldn't marry me, is that yes, I'm the too beautiful girl, and yes, "Luceafarul" is our love triangle, but you're not the youth and Stefan wasn't the distant Evening Star whose bride is stolen beneath his stellar gaze. You're the Evening Star, Emin, you're Luceafarul, removed from the rest of us in the glittery, cold world of your own imagination. There's no way it could have ended well.

All of Iasi still recites "Luceafarul" and your poems about the poplars. Your favorite linden tree in the Copou gardens is already a tourist destination. They've put up a wrought-iron fence around it, and a sign that reads "Eminescu's linden." I wouldn't walk by it, though, not even when I was staying in Copou. If I'm there on a Sunday evening promenade, everyone starts whispering, there goes Veronica Micle in her fur-trimmed hat, the woman Eminescu loves, the woman Eminescu jilted, paying her respects to Eminescu's linden, poor thing.

You let Titu Maiorescu, that sloppy poet, that colossal bore, talk you out of marriage. Titu! Really, I should have known you were crazy then. I know he's arranged your finances since your illness, I know that when you were healthy Titu championed your poetry, got you the librarianship and editorial position and all the jobs you've ever had, but why did you have to listen to a man who can't keep a woman himself? You were a prompter for the theater troupe when you first came back from Vienna—was Titu prompting you? Feeding you the words that would get rid of me? Titu didn't want you to "stop crying so beautifully." He said happiness would destroy your writing and that you must make this sacrifice for art's sake. You kept telling me you would marry me if you had more money. Who should I believe, you or Titu?

Am I supposed to believe that I drove you crazy? After you broke it off with me, when you were living down in Bucharest, you told Maiorescu you wanted to become a monk. (How strange that I'm the one who ended up a nun.) You went to Capsa Coffeehouse, brandishing a revolver and shouting that the king must be shot because you were a liberal now. Everyone laughed. They thought you were trying on political humor. Then you locked yourself in a public bath for eight hours and let the water flow out, streaming down the corridor, and Titu started talking to Dr. Sutu.

If we had been married, I would have bathed you, I would have taken care of you, better care than Dr. Sutu, better care than Harieta, as tenderly as I cared for Stefan. We would have had to live simply, but our two small incomes joined would have meant we could have lived better together than apart. In the end of the day, Emin, why did you save me from marriage with you when you didn't spare me the knowledge of your body? Who else would marry me? I've no desire to sit here holy in the convent. It calls for a kind of patience I sorely lack.

The younger nuns have such simple wishes and prayers for the families they left behind. The older ones have stories much more complicated than mine. Most of their days are taken up with prayer. They don't write letters anymore. They've told me they've outlived everyone.

       Love, your old girl,
       Nicutza

Varatec, August 4, 1889
Dear Emin,

You've been dead for two months. I've been praying since you died. Do ghosts get mail? Remember when you first moved to Bucharest and we would argue through letters about reasons to choose life or death? You thought I was bringing up thoughts of suicide to goad you into marrying me? I don't think you realized how desperate I was then, with two small girls and no clear sign about what would happen to Stefan's pension. Like most powerful men, he forgot to think about what would happen when he was gone. When he died, I was so intensely happy I had to cross myself constantly to make up for it. Every afternoon, I went to the Cathedral to pray for Stefan. I felt like I'd killed Stefan by wishing for you. Yes, Stefan was sick, yes, Stefan was old, finally it was a kindness for him to die, but I was thinking about you while I fed him his chicken soup and gave him his sponge bath. When you wouldn't marry me, I wanted to die. If I could have found a way to die without orphaning the girls, some kind of poet's trick to have things two ways, I would have done it.

There were many days when I would play a game. A letter from you meant I would have to let myself live. No letter, and I'd begin to plan my death again. It's funny, but on the days I planned for death I felt the most alive. I counted the hairs on the girls' heads as I did their braids with the ivory comb and brush Stefan gave me. I made polenta and sausages for supper and let the chambers get smoky with the smell of burnt meat. I burnt my tongue on too-hot tea. Evenings, I'd look for the evening star and wish on it for you.

I'm done with life now but there's no way to tell you. Not that I could tell you much these last few years, anyway. That's what I've missed the most, talking to you. There's no one left alive I'd like to stay up all night talking to. I don't want to wait here, ensconced in the convent, if my brain is going to turn to sponge the way yours did.

When I'm done writing this letter in this in-between time, after lunch and before vespers, I'll sit on my veranda with a glass of tea. I'll pour in the arsenic I've gathered in Iasi. I traveled to every pharmacist, from Copou to Nicolina, asking for a bit of arsenic to use as rat poison. When I said I was moving to the convent, they gave me a little more. No one wants to think of a lady fighting off the rats alone in her cottage. Or maybe they understood that a lady might be going to Varatec due to a great disappointment and a little extra arsenic could be a great kindness?

There's an embroidery school at the convent. Girls from the village come to sew. I wanted to be a weaver when I was a girl in Neamt. I cried when my mother told me that was for peasants alone. Embroidery is delicate, silly. It's what Titu called my poetry. He's right. My poems were little nothings. My real talent was in recognizing talent, in finding you, in promoting the poets of my literary salon, getting haughty Bucharest to notice provincial Iasi, in pushing my daughters to be artists, too. Before I drink my tea, I'll watch the embroidery class walk home together, the little girls darting in and out of the group, trying to catch up with their sisters. They'll hold hands the way my daughters used to do.

They'll bury me here, by the embroidery school near the convent gardens. I'll be a tourist attraction, like your linden tree. The embroidery schoolgirls will walk back and forth along the path next to my grave. They'll want to do embroidery like an art, embroidery like painting, like what my students at the Art School did.

You must remember the time you took me to the Balta Rece cellar tavern? You took me late at night, almost midnight, when the girls were visiting my mother in Neamt. I didn't wear my fur-trimmed hat, but a boy's cap that shielded my eyes and held my hair up and back. I wore pantaloons. We sat in a booth in the corner. At the tavern, drinking new wine and making up poetic parodies, I had a hint of what it might be like to be a man, to be yourself in a place neither at home nor out on the street but somewhere in between, a place where it was possible to relax your stance and loosen your tongue. At first, unencumbered by petticoats, crinolines, bustles, I sat with my legs together, tucked in at my ankles, but as I watched you and the others, I let them loose to fall as they wished. Uncaged from a corset, I leaned forward to make my points. I interrupted you and your friends whenever I thought of a bon mot, even if it wasn't the cleverest phrase at the perfect moment. I blurted out my real opinions of people and their poetry. I wasn't just tipsy, but drunk. It was our best night, but also the first time I should have realized that there was a chance you wouldn't marry me. You nodded at Titu when we came in, but we didn't go to his table and he didn't come to ours. I didn't know it yet, but Titu was winning the argument. You wouldn't marry me, for art's sake, for money's sake.

You told me I had the laugh of a drunken Gypsy girl, tinkly and high-pitched. You said the cap was the kind of fashion a Gypsy girl might choose. I told you that your eyes were like those of an old Jew's, wrinkled at the edges like the skin was squeezing to hold the eye in the socket, irises nothing but darkness.

You took my hand and pulled me up the cellar stairs. You kissed me out on the street, pushing me up against a building, as if I were a whore. We walked out to the cemetery at the end of town, then back again. We hid behind poplars to avoid the town watch. We watched the sunrise in Copou gardens at your linden tree, your head resting in my lap. When we went back to my chambers, our hair still smelled like linden. We had that whole day together in my bed before your night train back to Bucharest. It was the only time we were together and completely alone for so long.

Do you remember it? Were you thinking about poems you wanted to write the whole time? Poems that weren't about me? At the train station, you were looking past me even as you kissed my forehead. A beggar tugged at the hem of your coat as you turned for the Bucharest tracks, but you brushed by her. I waited for you to wave goodbye. When you did, it was a regal wave, an arc encompassing the arm from the socket to the tips of your bony poet fingers, meant for crowds, meant for someone standing at a greater distance than I was, somebody in Bucharest, Vienna, Paris, and Berlin. I balanced on my toes to watch you bound up the steps. You didn't turn again. I tossed all the coins in my purse, money I needed if we were to eat meat that week, into the beggar's shaking palms.

So when Harieta sent us together to Bucharest to Dr. Sutu, when you clutched my hands and sighed and drooled on my shoulder as you slept, I thought of what might have happened if I hadn't let you board that earlier train alone, if I'd run after you. All I would have done, though, would have caused a scandal, the Micle widow loose in Bucharest instead of safe in Iasi where you could mourn her. You'd already decided not to marry me, before the night in the Copou gardens and the Balta Rece tavern. Maybe you decided even before Stefan died? Maybe you decided the first time you saw me, in the hotel lobby of the Viennese hotel as I blushed, lowered my eyes with my eyelashes fluttering as fast as I could make them go, and waited for Stefan to introduce us. Maybe you decided when you met Stefan that morning and learned he had a young wife? Maybe you decided that you would never marry at home drinking tea with honey in the kitchen with Harieta when you were just a boy, that you would never marry because she couldn't, trapped in her twisted body as much as you ended up trapped in your twisting mind?

What dirty, dirty things you must have done as a student in Vienna! Which whore with open sores gave you syphilis? Did you see something of her in me? Did you sleep with her before or after we met in that Viennese hotel? What was the size of your chancre? What shape did it take? Now there's a subject for poetry. Was it still blooming when you slept with me? In the end, which one of us mattered most? We're the real triangle: Poet, Poetess, Whore. You might have loved me more, but she's the one who shaped your life. In the end, she's the Luceafarul, the distant star guiding us through all of our furtive, intimate embraces. It's the whore I can't stop thinking about. Oh, Emin, I pray for her, too.

Were you raving at the end? They won't tell me. The nuns twitter around me and I know they want to know what the chances are that I'll follow you to your crazy grave. Down, down, down, drown me at the well, drape me in Ophelia's flowers, mark me as Emin's mistress. I'll speak Albanian at last.

> Love,
> Nicutza

Calcutta, September 16, 1930

Let the moon be out. There should be a moon their last night. They deserve it, considering what's coming. They are at the lakes again. Just the two girls, the driver, and the Romanian: one Mircea Eliade, who studies Bengali and lives in their house like a brother. Ma has asked him to call her Ma. Mircea won a scholarship from the Romanian government, the first student ever from his country to research his dissertation in India. He is proud of his position; his chest puffs out whether he wears his Western suit or a dhoti.

They practice saying his outlandish name, Murcha, Murcha? Maitreyi is sixteen, the little one, Chabu, is ten. Mircea is twenty-three and has never been outside of Romania until now. He says, It's the same moon in both countries. Look how big it is, round as a bindi mark, and they giggle.

Papa and Ma feel poorly that evening and say no to the walk around the artificial lakes at the stylish end of town, away from their boring bourgeois Bhowanipore. Too hot, too tired, Ma has a headache, maybe even a temperature, but you go, Mircea, with the girls. Go. The driver is a distant village cousin. They trust him.

The girls are always fighting, Chabu wanting whatever Maitreyi has. She makes sure to sit between Mircea and Maitreyi as they climb into the Chevrolet. Chabu jabs Maitreyi in the ribs. Maitreyi won't turn around, her eyes stuck on the low black ceiling. The problem is, Maitreyi has things now that Chabu can't understand, not toys or sweets anymore, but a poetry career and Mircea's adoration.

The crowds drop off as they approach the wilderness of the Southern Road and the artificial lakes. The town is not just a town but a massive Indian city, not just any city but Calcutta itself. Out at the Southern Avenue it is jungle still, plants greener than Mircea has ever seen, greener than the Carpathians in the height of spring. Maitreyi will see the Southern Avenue turn suburban, then urban as Calcutta spreads and the world of their childhood is swallowed up. Mircea will leave Calcutta at the end of this year, 1930, never to return, but he will carry the map of the streets in his head for the rest of his life. He will ask strangers at academic conferences and dinner parties, Do you know Bhowanipore, the Tollygunge Circular Road, the Southern Avenue? Have you been to the artificial lakes?

Maitreyi tries out lines in her head, not on Chabu, not on Mircea, not, good God, on the driver. She is preparing her first book of poems for publication. Tagore will read each poem and comment; he has promised. Before Mircea came, Tagore was the one she loved, even if he is sixty. He's not just a poet, he's the Poet. Mircea isn't a poet, he writes supernatural novels and philosophy, he's hairy, he's European, and when they talk they both clutch dictionaries just in case they'll need to look up each other's words.

Mircea has been studying Bengali and teaching the girls French. They catalogued Papa's books together in the afternoons while the rest of the house napped. They were almost alone then, but never quite, someone always outside the door, servants' footsteps down the hall, Papa's snores two rooms away, Chabu racing in and out to see if they can come and play, Ma asking if they want tea, more tea, samosas.

But Papa and Ma aren't at the lakes this night. It's just the lovers, the deliberately obtuse driver, the suspicious little sister. The lakes are almost deserted tonight when they arrived, straggling families turning their last late circles. Ma's indecision cost them time, the driver said, but all Maitreyi and Mircea can think of is what a gift it is to be almost alone out of the house.

At the lake, the driver stands over by the car, talking to the other drivers and kicking up dust together as they complain about their households.

Go away, Chabu, Maitreyi says.

Mircea says, Go away and I'll give you a sweet.

Mircea stands behind Maitreyi, trying to find the outline of her legs beneath the green sari catching against her in the wind. She's beautiful, even if she is dark, beautiful because she is dark; she is India to him. He hasn't learned yet that one person can't be a country, if he ever learns it. It is a mistake he will make again and again in his fiction. This man is Romania, this woman the essence of all gypsies. This man is Man, this woman Woman. He likes concepts.

Why won't she come talk to him? The driver won't care. Why does Mircea want her? He catalogues his desire. Her eyes are wistful. The lids droop as if the weight of her earrings pull her whole face down. Even when she's laughing, her eyes make her look older than sixteen, almost as old as Tagore. Her mouth is larger than European girls, designed for pouting. Her hair is thick. She's a head shorter than him, and when they embrace he rests his chin in her hair like a bird settling into a nest. It smells like jasmine at night.

She says it should smell like ink, for all the times she accidentally brushes the tips in the inkpot as she writes. Ink's the same color as my hair, so how would you know?

Maybe my blood itself is ink, and I wrote myself up, she tells him.

He wants to write about her. Make her a temptress in his next novel? She'd be less maddening, in his version. She says she knows she's pretty, everyone says so—Tagore, her family. She doesn't care what Mircea says, she tells him, if he says she's too dark or her eyes too sad. She's so smart, and funny, quicker than the cleverest girls at the University of Bucharest. At sixteen, he was working on his first novel and finishing up at the lycée. She is the first person he has ever met who matches his own ambition.

Chabu pulls at his hand. Come here, she commands. But Mircea won't. Chabu sulks, her lips vanishing into her mouth. He's waiting for Maitreyi, Maitreyi over by the tree chanting poetry in a language he can't truly understand. Even Chabu says his Bengali is like that of a small child's. Maitreyi loves Tagore the Poet more than she loves him. She leans on a eucalyptus tree, stretching her back against it. The image, girl and tree, is held in the still water of the lake. In her green sari, she seems to belong more to the world of trees than she does to the bustle of Calcutta.

Once she told him her first love was a tree. Can you be jealous, even of that? she asked when he wanted her to stop talking about it.

Jackals call at the end of the road. Chabu copies their screams. She yanks both of his hands and drags him over to the edge of the glassy lake. He catches fireflies for Chabu, cupping them in his hands and letting them fly off. Their lights blink like the electric lamps that line the paths along the lakes, another sign of Calcutta's modernity.

We're not primitives, Papa warns him regularly. Don't romanticize us.

Chabu flaps her skinny arms, chasing after the trails of light. Once Maitreyi must have looked like her, and played her games. Chabu is dark, darker than Maitreyi. In his journal, he has written that she reminds him of the gypsies of his own country.

Why can't people fly too? Like fireflies? Chabu asks.

He shrugs.

Can they fly in your country?

He says, Only the gypsy witches.

The smell of lotus petals lifts up off the lake. Chabu sneezes and the fireflies are gone. Ask the driver to walk you once around the lake, he begs her.

I don't want to; you'll be with Maitreyi while I'm gone.

Oh, please do go, Chabu.

Will you love me best?

Yes, Chabu, hurry. You'll find more fireflies if you start off now.

Chabu skips off with the driver, looking back over her shoulder three times, each time more wistful than the last. Mircea takes Maitreyi's hand. It's soft, except for the callus where she holds her pen. Almost everyone has left the lake and the driver will make them leave soon. Chabu will be back in minutes, she sighs. I'm almost done with my poem. He slides in between the tree and her, his back to the tree. The green sari twists and settles as he spins her around to face him. He kisses her roughly, biting her lower lip, his hands moving down her spine to the small of her back. She chews at his mouth, pulling at his unruly hair, brown and stiff at his neck like a dog's. Don't leave marks, she reminds him. Ma will see.

It's why he leaves marks. He wants them to be found out, to have it all done, their love public, decisions made, Maitreyi to come home with him to Bucharest in triumph. Even better, settling down in Calcutta. Hinduism, curry all his days, Maitreyi in his arms, his kitchen, his bed. What could make him happier?

Maitreyi murmurs, You're reckless, Mircea. Mircea? He runs his hands up and down her legs, but always with the cotton of her sari between them. He knows if he reaches underneath the sari, she will move away and he will have to chase her. He's wearing a dhoti tonight. She has said it becomes him, that he looks truly Indian.

But she thinks he looks like he belongs nowhere, his European doughy face and skinny student body stuck inside Indian clothes, lost in the folds of fabric in which Tagore looks so dignified. The heat makes his whiskers grow faster than in Romania, and he hasn't learned to shave more frequently to keep up. His spiky chin rubs against hers when they kiss. They can't marry. Even if he were Indian, what were the odds he would be Bengali, Hindu, Brahmin, the right kind of Brahmin? Not that she believes in castes, and Papa and Ma say they don't, but when they discuss her future husband he is always all the exact things required. And a poet, too, for Maitreyi, Ma adds. Maitreyi and Mircea can't be together, she needs to focus on her poetry career, he can't understand the best part of her.

She slips out of his grasp and as always he lets her go too easily. Kneeling by the shore, she casts a lotus petal into the water. Will it sink? she asks Mircea.

No, he says, so she drowns it with her hands, pushing it underneath the water with the slightest press of her fingertips.

There. It's fragile, she tells him. The image alone would have been enough for Tagore to follow her meaning. She has to tell Mircea, Our love. Our love is that fragile. She doesn't always have the right words in French and Mircea won't understand her Bengali. Their last conversation will be awkward and too simple. But they must have it soon. The cataloguing project is done. Ma will feel better and won't miss future trips to the lakes. They are becoming careless, and drivers can be bribed by parents as well as daughters.

Chabu races up to them. I caught you! she says.

Caught us at what?

You were kissing! I saw! The driver shakes his head and starts the car.

Chabu, listen, you didn't see anything at all. We were standing close like this because Maitreyi was telling me about a poem. That's all. Mircea shakes Chabu's bony shoulders. She wriggles out of his reach.

Kiss Maitreyi, Mircea, do, Chabu says. Please kiss didi. Mircea is all too happy to oblige. He swoops in for a Rudolf Valentino kiss, dipping Maitreyi back to make Chabu giggle. When his lips press Maitreyi's lips, Chabu freezes. Mircea doesn't see Chabu from his angle, but Maitreyi does. Mircea doesn't get that a kiss on the lips is always serious, never for play, that Indian movies won't show kissing. Maitreyi likes the film version of the Bengali novel *Devdas;* she doubts that Mircea would understand that it's more romantic when the couple doesn't kiss, let alone get together in the end. What's romantic: Devdas and Parvati longing for each other for the rest of their lives. For a moment, Maitreyi freezes too, trying to play, trying on the pose of a Hollywood movie poster. Her lips graze against Mircea's. She twists away, hopping on her left foot and righting herself. Mircea is ready to play the Sheik again, this time with Chabu. She squeals as he moves closer. The driver honks the horn.

Mircea, stop your joking. Maitreyi grabs Chabu and holds

her close. Her brow is hot, her cheeks are flushed. Chabu, you don't feel at all well. Like Ma. You made her walk around the lake. She suffers, so we're happy? Help me get her in the car. They place her in the center, between them, like always.

Chabu falls asleep, her head resting on Mircea's left arm and her legs draped across Maitreyi's lap. Mircea's arm goes numb, but he won't move Chabu. She's so little, and sweet, really, and none of this has been her fault.

At home in the comfortable house in Bhowanipore, Chabu in her fever tells Papa and Ma, Mircea kissed Maitreyi. When she's out of her delirium, Chabu regrets her betrayal. Didi, didi, I'm so sorry. What have I done?

Maitreyi says Ma, Ma, only on the forehead. But Ma knows about Europeans. She has read her Maupassant. No one will believe Maitreyi, least of all the driver. Two days later, after both daughters have been thoroughly interrogated and the worst of Chabu's fever has passed, Mircea is asked to leave their home. He is in disgrace.

His bags are tossed into the car after him. Papa won't even speak to him. He hands the letter to the driver for Mircea. No contact with the family from this day forth. You don't know us, we don't know you. Mircea can't bring himself to dial South 1144, to address letters to Bhowanipore. Now that he's exiled, he obeys Papa implicitly.

•

Chicago, April 13, 1973

Did they do it or didn't they? Not the kissing, let's not be coy, of course they were kissing. They're in agreement about that. Everyone is. Chabu, Maitreyi, Ma, Mircea: The driver. They kissed. Did they do *it*? She says they didn't, he says they did.

Back in Bucharest still smarting from his disaster in Calcutta, he wrote a novel about her, *Maitreyi.* In the book, Mircea didn't change her name, her address or phone number. It's all there, Maitreyi, phone number South 1144, Bhowanipore. He wrote in his journals, It was inconceivable to me that the novel would be read in Calcutta.

In Mircea's novel, Maitreyi visits him at night, to the joy of shy, neurotic Romanian schoolboys everywhere. Then the novel is translated into French, and Maitreyi starts to notice that Europeans giggle when she is introduced to them. Was this novel an act of revenge? Yet he was the one who left the house in Bhowanipore, left India, left her. Shouldn't she be the one to seek revenge?

She's here in Chicago waiting in his office to get it straight with him. His desk is solid oak, the kind of desk she thinks dictators might have. Eliade was involved with the fascist Legionnaires in Romania; it's why he had to go to America after the communists took over. Now, he's Mircea Eliade, the University of Chicago scholar, the expert on world religions.

She's glad to be physically awkward, perched on the edge of an American chair too large for her. She sits in the chair in front of the desk and waits for Mircea. He tells her, I'm waiting for a tax officer, and shifts his papers. He has his back to her. He's stuck in the corner with the filing cabinets. Tagore was never at his desk. She remembers Tagore writing underneath a tree, herself at his feet. There are different ways to work, different kinds of work. Mircea's filing cabinets make a fortress of the office, his attempts to catalogue the world, catalogue the East, catalogue the mystical as if it could be catalogued. Not that she isn't a writer herself, not that back home in India there isn't a room topsy turvy with books, but she's always resisted this kind of regimented order.

His office is drafty. The red, tailored coat she bought in Paris is more stylish than warm. She tucks it more tightly around her middle, surprised at her vanity after all this time. Why did she want to look good for this cranky old man? When the student guide escorted her up to Mircea's office, the girl took Maitreyi's arm as if she'd been told the visiting Bengali poet was infirm. Maitreyi wanted to shake off her grasp.

Okay, maybe it is not how things are done, to look up his office number in a campus directory and show up unannounced. She has sent him letters, but he hasn't answered them. In the novel, he asked for Maitreyi the character's forgiveness, but he doesn't seem interested in the real-life equivalent. Her friends in India think his wife Christanel must open all his letters. She's said to be quite controlling. She's said to have made his career.

Maitreyi is here to lecture on Tagore in Chicago. She's got on a red sari interwoven with silver threads, a style she helped to pioneer back in the thirties; she has to look the part of the Bengali grand dame. Her theme is "The Man Behind the Poetry." If people think of her in Bengal, the man they instantly think about is Tagore, her guru. It's only the giggling Europeans who think of her linked to Mircea, think of her as the woman behind the pornographic novel.

When she told her husband she was going to see Mircea on this trip to Chicago whether Mircea liked it or not, he was amused. Ha! said her husband, not looking up from his newspaper. Her husband is an engineer, not a poet. An arranged marriage, but one she agreed to. Tagore always thought her husband was saintly.

Mircea rolls his chair back around to face her, but he still won't look up. His knuckles bulge as he holds on to the edge of his desk, his pen scratches across his calendar book, his bald head is shining in front of her. She imagines she can feel the smooth, hairless skin stretching across his skull.

Hey, it's Maitreyi. Don't you want to see what I've become, after all this time? she asks him.

After so many years of listening to Americans, her Indian accent sings to him, with a hint of Bengali poetry behind it. There really is an accountant coming. Christanel doesn't trust him to file his own taxes, and also of course she likes to check up on him.

Maitreyi in Chicago. He can see her in his mind, the sad wise eyes, large lips pursed, the marvelous legs for such a short girl. He'd rather squint than have to look at the dumpy old woman before him now. To have her in his office in Chicago, before his desk where the anxious students stand, it's like being visited by a character from a book. What next? The evil ghost Miss Christina from *Miss Christina*? The murderous men from *Hooligans*? The man who would not die from *Youth without Youth*? Dante shouldn't have to look at his Beatrice, he scolds. He smiles weakly at her.

Beatrice? she asks. Dante had to die to meet Beatrice. Me? I came to Chicago. I made it easier for the both of us. Mircea, so tell me, why did you mix up fact and fiction the way you did?

She leans into his desk from the edge of her chair. He rolls back a little in his. He blinks behind his glasses. Why is she so anxious? Why does she need to cling to the good reputation of a Bengali housewife? Wouldn't it have been more interesting if they *had* done it? Which is why he made sure it happened, set out on the seduction of his guru's daughter. He wasn't going to leave India inexperienced.

He explains, I wanted to make you a goddess, a Kali.

Kali, she says. Kali? Dark and ugly? In the book, you asked

for my forgiveness. You wrote you would look me in the eyes if you saw me again.

He finally looks up from his desk. Straightening in his chair, peering through his thick spectacles, he looks at the wrinkles around her eyes intently. He avoids the irises, as if they might punish him. It's always dangerous to look at Kali head on. He mutters in Sanskrit, *Na hanyate hanyamane sarire.* It does not die when the body dies.

He's not entirely sure whether he means to comfort Maitreyi, that they'll die but their spirits will live on, the best parts of them, the parts that talked about literature and philosophy for hours, the parts of their characters that had such affinity for each other that their eyes kept meeting across the room when something amusing happened; well before they were in love, this affinity started. Or whether he means to point out that they'll die but the cycle of revenge that started when Chabu said Mircea kissed didi will continue, that over and over Papa will kick Mircea out of the house in Bhowanipore, over and over the novel *Maitreyi* will dial South 1144 and whisper, Maitreyi came to Mircea's room. Take that, Papa! I didn't seduce her, she seduced me. What did you expect when you let her play those dirty games with Tagore? What were you training her for?

Or that he's haunted by those days in Bhowanipore and what might have happened if he hadn't left. Or found a way to take her with him. Or guilt over what happened to Chabu? She was such a little girl, and she ended up so desperately ill.

Maitreyi nods. She relaxes. Her dangling feet, in sandals in spite of the cold, kick slowly around her chair like a schoolgirl. Like a child. Like Chabu. He knows she must be thinking that their souls will live on. She's still too easy to flatter. Do tell me where you are staying? asks Mircea, pushing his glasses up his nose as he reaches for a piece of paper. Please do be so kind as to write down your phone number. Christanel and I will have you over for dinner. She hands him the paper, and he clasps his hands around hers. So unbelievable to see you, Maitreyi, he says, shaking his head.

He watches her walk away from his office window. He presses his nose up against the glass. Her strides are purposeful, magnificent, the sari's edges whipping in the wind, the silver threads flashing in the sun. She doesn't look down at the ground as she goes. He loses her in the gray Chicago afternoon. Christanel calls him to ask what he wants for dinner. Stuffed cabbage? A piece of fish? Both. He keeps his eyes on the window.

In his journal, Mircea writes about this encounter: "April 13, 1973. Meeting with M. After almost 43 years! It all seems unbelievable, unreal, false—and in a sense, in bad taste." Always, as if his life were a novel. He is at once hero, writer, critic. Christanel watches him writing with her pinched, faded eyes, rubbing her arthritic fingers as she sits patiently on the sofa.

Maitreyi walks from her hotel room in the Loop down to Lake Michigan in between her lecture obligations. The park along the lake is lined with trees, but they're not the palms and eucalyptus of home. There are no smells; it's too cold. How do the Americans remember anything with their noses plugged up with frost? Because of the bikes whizzing by, and the children on roller skates, she watches the path for disaster before each step.

The lake stretches before her like the Indian Ocean, nothing at all like the artificial lakes in Calcutta but a sea she can't see across. Waves bounce across its surface, the wind stirring up the water. The water is too rough for her to possibly catch any reflection of herself. She hadn't known it would feel so overwhelming, the lake filling the horizon, the Sears Tower poking at the sky, everything overdone. She could never feel at home here.

She wishes she had asked him if he remembered Chabu, how clever she was as a little girl, how she never left them alone. She wanted to ask him about why he had to kill Chabu off in his novel. He made her die of grief and guilt. It seems worse than what he wrote about Maitreyi in the end, that in desperation she slept with the fruit seller so that her family couldn't marry her off to someone of her own background. He was unwilling to imagine a life for the girls without him. Chabu had to die, Maitreyi had to be degraded. An adult Chabu, glossy and plump as she bosses her family around, couldn't be. Maitreyi married, Maitreyi a successful poet, Maitreyi old, couldn't be.

He didn't change Chabu's name, either. When she was reading his book, Maitreyi couldn't escape the sensation of her own irritation at Chabu, at the forcefulness of Chabu's nagging jealousy. Mircea captured Chabu accurately. Why capture her, only to kill her? It's like pulling wings off insects once they're already pinned in the collection.

Maitreyi plans her novel about Mircea, the one she will write once she's home in Calcutta. They kissed, nothing more, not just on the forehead, on the lips, okay, yes, on the lips, but no sex. In her parents' house, when had they ever been alone? In India, in Calcutta in 1930, when could they be alone? Young married couples sanctioned by the family can't get enough privacy, let alone illicit lovers. Her novel will be about her coming of age as an artist and as a woman, about how her encounter with a foreign student changed the way she viewed her family, her city, her country, her poetry, even if in the end she continued on much as she might have without having met him: the arranged marriage, her writings on Tagore as well as her own work. She'll give herself a fictional name, Chabu, too, but she'll call Mircea by his real name just as he did to her. She won't kill Chabu off as Mircea did, simply let her fade away as sisters do when they grow up and live apart from each other. She'll get in one last dig: when Chabu begs her to run away so she won't have to marry the man her parents pick for her, Maitreyi will write, and in italics, *but you drove away the one I wanted.* That's Chabu's final scene, nothing on Chabu's own marriage, nothing on Chabu's life that isn't part of Maitreyi's romance. Maitreyi doesn't kill her, but she doesn't set her free, either.

She'll end the novel with her awkward encounter with Mircea in Chicago. She'll turn it into poetry instead. A phoenix plucks her out of Mircea's office and carries her home. No need for Air India. No need to listen to him talk about tax officers or vague invitations for dinner. She'll let the phoenix blast his office into bits as the massive wings struggle to take off.

She calls her novel *Na Hanyate.* It does not die. What hasn't died? Chabu? Not this time. The gossip about them? The sexual love between them? The sting of his revenge, the purity of her reputation? What's left to matter after forty-three years?

If you dial South 1144, will Chabu pick up the line? Will she know the answer to whether they did it or not? How much does it matter? It certainly will matter to Chabu. Her jealousy's not going to die. Chabu's the one missing from their reunion in Chicago. She's part of the triangle, essential for them to keep their balance. Mircea, Maitreyi, those performers, jokers, egoists, they need an audience, demand an audience, want to expose their secrets, demand that their secrets be paid attention to. If Chabu had been there, she would have been able to sort out the clues, play detective, be a careful reader of the most grandiose lies they tell themselves. Chabu knows. It's why Mircea had to kill her off, why Maitreyi reduced her to a bit part in the second half of *her* novel, why neither one of them let themselves get too angry with her when she tells, Mircea kissed didi, in the first place.

In Chabu's novel, the one she didn't write but arranged through her artistry for all of them to live through, the little sister is the heroine. The big sister is the monster, the foreign student the innocent patsy. The patsy is banished, the monster punished, the family's reputation secured by Chabu's bravery. Chabu knows and she's only telling part of her story, only the part about the kissing. Chabu likes to keep secrets cupped in her hands. If Chabu keeps a secret, she has something Maitreyi doesn't have.

HOW THE ROMANIANS RUINED CHRISTMAS

In Romania, what holidays do you celebrate?

You're sloppy interrogators, hardly like the Securitate back home. Sometimes we don't even give you our names when asked, pretend we don't understand. For the times when the three of us have to talk, we practice what to say together, particularly what to say for Gabitza. She's too little so we have to speak for her. We tell her what she needs to remember, what to tell, and when to keep quiet.

Taticul promises us that this year in America, we'll celebrate a real Christmas, with Old Man Christmas coming instead of the communist Old Man Winter. In Romania no one has a real Christmas anymore, no fir trees with candles, no boys in goat masks banging drums, no braided sweetbread full of raisins. There aren't any raisins even if your bunica queues for days on end. They do decorate the trees in Cimisgiu Gardens, and if you have enough money you can get a picture taken standing in the snow with Old Man Winter. We had one taken when Gabitza learned to walk. We're lined up in a row oldest to youngest. See Silvica's braids lifting in the wind, see me, Cornel, balancing a snowball on each mitten for each sister, Gabitza crying as Old Man Winter squeezes her hand! We have the picture with us in America.

Besides, we're Jews. We're not supposed to celebrate Christmas but we can have New Year's, Women's Day, or National Day like everyone else. Bunica said before the war we used to have Shabbat every Friday, plus interesting holidays like Yom Kippur and Rosh Hashanah.

Mamica said to Bunica as they smoked in the kitchen, draga, are you crazy? Shabbat—a day without electricity *on purpose*? Yom Kippur—entirely too much fasting. They're skinny enough already. Please don't talk about such things in front of the children. The neighbors are so nosy, Ma, like you wouldn't believe.

We like that Bunica talks to us. Bunica is Mamica's mother, but you'd never guess. She's skinny and smokes, not like anybody else's bunica. When Mamica was at work, Bunica answered our questions, including the ones she's not supposed to. Bunica said, But don't tell people that we're Jewish. It's not supposed to matter, but it does matter for the university and jobs. We weren't supposed to talk about the parties Mamica and Taticul went to at their classmates' apartments to drink brandy, play bridge, and make up rhymes about how stupid the Ceausescus are. Or that Bunicul had a wireless locked up in his bookcase that can pick up the BBC World Service, or the letters Bunica received six months late and ripped open from her cousins in Israel.

When we applied for our visas in 1987 until we got them in 1989, the Domnul from the Securitate in his trenchcoat and his Warsaw-bought double-breasted suit came to talk to Taticul once a week. Sometimes the Domnul took him away over night and Mamica waited up in the kitchen in the dark. We said, *Buna ziua*, good day, to the Domnul and nothing else, ever, like Mamica asked. We took Gabitza out of the parlor and into the kitchen when we heard the street dogs bark and saw the Domnul striding through the courtyard with his long and careful steps, the trenchcoat billowing behind him.

Once we're in America a month after the visa came

through and Taticul promises us a Christmas in December 1989, Mamica instantly realizes what the problem will be. Mamica says, God, what have you said, Octavian, you know we can't have a Christmas with the Jews coming over here almost every day. How are they going to feel after what they've done for us? What will they say when they see a tree?

Draga, we'll hide it, Taticul says. Aren't we good at hiding things? He blinks at her twice. He is highly myopic, but rarely wears his glasses.

We come from a long of line of myopics. Sometimes it's not good to let people know you have glasses. They'll know you have enough money to get them. They'll know you need them because you read too much. If you need glasses and you don't wear them, the world looks different. It blurs and you can see your way through to the end that you might want. Sometimes if you can't see someone, they can't see you, and you're safe.

In America, the teachers say we need glasses because we can't see the blackboard. They also wonder if Silvica's gotten the right things to eat in Romania. She's too short for ten. I'm all right though, at eight, stocky even, and Gabitza at five is too little so they can't tell yet.

At the synagogue the American Jews are impressed with how quiet we can be, even Gabitza, how carefully we pay attention. They don't know that in Romania, the teacher hits you if you fidget. At the synagogue door, Mamica says, draga, darlings, Silvica, Cornel, Gabitza, straighten your postures. Chin up, always. Since Nadia Comaneci, the Americans expect it of us. Particularly these American Jews. Don't forget how much they did for us, to get us here. None of your snot-nosed ways from home. Let's just say I'd like your naughtiness to stay in Bucharest where it belongs.

Do you have any pets?

We think we belong in Bucharest with Bogdan, our favorite street dog who kept the other street dogs away from us when we play in the courtyard. Bogdan isn't the biggest, but he's crazy when he fights, so the other dogs stay away from him. All the dogs in our neighborhood had stiff, tawny fur and yellow eyes.

Bunica used to joke, I don't know how you children can tell which is the dog you think is yours. They're all vagabonds. We knew Bogdan right away because he only has one eye. He let Gabitza pet him, but nobody else. Gabitza sat in the courtyard on the steps with her arms draped around his thick neck and he didn't mind. His stubby tail wagged, and he looked almost for a minute like a pet instead of a stray, none of his wildness in his yellow, unblinking eye. But if somebody else tried to pet him, he'd snap at you, even if you gave him a piece of bread dipped in soup first. If someone tried to get too close to Gabitza, he growled low in his throat and his eye rolled back into his head.

We couldn't take Bogdan. Taticul told us, you can't take a dog on an airplane. And we'll have an apartment in America, not a villa in the country. Really, do you think we'll be in Chicago and—poof! — then we're rich? Besides, he isn't even our dog. Someone else in the building will look after him.

Where do you live?

But we don't get to go to Chicago. The Jews from the synagogue who sponsored our visas live just outside of Chicago in the Village of Skokie, Illinois. Skokie is the worst place we've ever seen. It's not the city, but it's not the country either, and it's like no village we've ever been to. It's nothing like the village where Bunicul grew up. No one has chickens or cows and there are no meadows or forests to play in. There is a small yard with weeds in one corner and dog shit in another, and some anemic evergreen bushes growing next to the house. There is only one other family in our Skokie building, the Goldsteins, who walk us over to the synagogue on Shabbat.

In Bucharest, our courtyard ran the length of a city block. The courtyard was covered in layers of dust that blow in the wind, but where the cement cracked along the edges, people grow flowers. We never had to play with each other because there were so many kids, plus Bogdan. Gabitza has got a matted clump of his fur in her pocket that she hides from Mamica.

The Goldsteins say the building is called a two-flat. The two-flats are little, squat and pink, built in a brick that is almost the same pink as the Skokie sky is at night. Taticul tells us the electric lights make the sky pink. We think, what a waste to try and light up the sky itself. How very American. Gabitza worries the pink sky will catch on fire and Mamica has to pull Gabitza onto her lap to quiet her. Gabitza sticks her hands deep into her pocket.

Mamica isn't being as careful about housekeeping in Skokie, otherwise she would have found the fur in Gabitza's pocket and fast, too. She says America makes her bone-weary, even though in Bucharest she taught algebra at the high school and in Skokie she doesn't do anything but wait for us to come home from school and then for Taticul to come home from the hospital where he works as an orderly.

Taticul says in America, maybe his children will be doctors. In Romania, Taticul was a scientist before we were born but lost his job because of his myopic-style politics and became an electrician instead. He wants to become an electrician in Chicago. The perfect job for the myopic man, he says.

Mamica can't teach here because she doesn't know English. She knows French, German, and Russian. She props an English textbook open next to the sink when she does the dishes. Most of the time, she waits in the kitchen smoking and looking out the window, even though Taticul asks her to sit in the living room in front of the picture window when he comes home from the hospital. She wears a checkered house-coat all day, taking slow drags of her cigarettes, scratching at her hennaed hair as she thinks. We think Mamica is beautiful, with her black hair dyed dark red and her aquiline nose, high nostrils flaring at everything Taticul says these days.

The living room. That's where the living is supposed to happen, draga, he tells her. The picture window is for looking out, pretty as a picture onto this wide street. The Goldsteins wonder why you don't sit on the loveseat with the floral print that they went to such trouble to arrange for us.

Maybe they shouldn't have troubled, she says. Maybe you shouldn't trouble me, either.

Gabitza barks to stop them from fighting. Taticul gathers her up and places her on his shoulders. What's this? He says. A beautiful little girl, or a beautiful little puppy? They run around the apartment, crashing into the rest of us, barking. We, all three of us, collapse onto the floral loveseat and tickle Taticul. Mamica smokes another cigarette in the kitchen and flips through the pages of her English book. She leaves ashy thumbprints.

What's your name, little girl?

More and more, Gabitza is barking instead of talking. At the school, they think the barking is Romanian. Ham ham

ham, says Gabitza. The teacher says American dogs say bow-wow, but when we listen to the American dogs as we walk home from school we still hear ham, ham. We hear the dogs, but we can't find them. They live locked up in people's yards and don't go out on the street to play with children. Gabitza sticks her fingers through fences to pet the dogs even though Mamica told her not to. Her hand is so little that if she balls it into a fist, she can stick it through the chain links. The dogs sniff her fingers and lick them. She rubs the spot where their floppy ears meet their heads. These dogs are Labradors, terriers, retrievers, the fancy dogs we can't have until we're rich like the Americans.

No one can spell our names. Gabitza's name in Romania didn't have a zed, it's Gabita with a *t* with a tail, Gabitza's favorite letter because you can draw it to look like a puppy, but the teachers say we have to add the zed so people can pronounce it properly. Silvica and I learn the new alphabet quickly, but Gabitza hasn't learned the Romanian alphabet perfectly yet so the new alphabet is hard for her. They want Silvica to spell her name, Sylvia, and to drop the diminutive. I have a girl's name. You start calling me Cornelia and then Nelly instead of Cornel. Apparently Nelly is the name for a mean girl with fat yellow ringlets in the book *Little House on the Prairie*. At my recess, I have to hit you when you call me Nelly. The teacher makes me take times out to cool down. It's cold outside and I can see my breath growing in front of me as I wait.

Silvica is in trouble, too. She can draw so that things look real, but she can't draw from her imagination, only from her memory. She can't draw a monster from *Where the Wild Things Are* or Lincoln's log cabin, even when the teacher puts the picture on the board to copy. The teacher makes her skip recess until she can draw a Wild Thing dancing with Honest Abe.

Gabitza bites into another kindergartner's parka at the kindergarten recess. They call us out of our classes to calm her down. The parka lies on the chair in the principal's office. It's blood red with a pattern of lacy snowflakes scattered across the quilting. A piece of the lining fluff is stuck in Gabitza's teeth. I'm Bogdan, she says, in Romanian so only we can understand. She says, You must address me as Bogdan now and not Gabitza. There is no little girl here.

Draga, we call Gabitza. Draga, darling, dear, it's going to be okay. But the other kids think we're calling Gabitza a dragon. You think she's a dragon, she thinks she's a dog, the teachers think she's very bad indeed.

We get a letter from Bunica and Bunicul. Draga Gabitza, Bogdan is living in our courtyard. We feed him and he sits by our entryway door. Gabitza doesn't believe it. She tells Mamica that Bogdan climbed to the top of our building and jumped off the roof in grief, calling ham ham as he fell.

When Taticul comes home, Mamica tells him about Gabitza biting the parka, about the letter, about Gabitza ham hamming. They talk softly in the kitchen. They come sit on the loveseat and talk loudly about the Christmas tree. Taticul says, We'll have little electric lights everywhere, like the Americans do.

How will we pay for it? asks Mamica.

Draga, this is America. Power is cheap as air. Besides, it's Christmas.

What games did you play at home? What games do you play now?

In Bucharest, I played football in the courtyard. In Skokie, what you call football is a game so dangerous that players wear armor. It's forbidden at recess so you play something called kickball with rules between baseball and football, and something called dodgeball, which has no rules. I spend recess when no one calls me Nelly running around the field, kicking my real football from home, a gift from Bunica and Bunicul because we were leaving. Here, such balls are called soccer and only rich boys play. During the lunch recess, we all play this soccer together, just the three of us, even after it snows. Gabitza is goalie.

In Bucharest, I shared a football with the other boys as we ran up and down the courtyard. The girls played Going to Warsaw and My Baby's Sick What Can You Give Me? Gabitza tried to teach Bogdan to write. She traced the alphabet into the courtyard dust with his paw. When it's winter and dark inside, Silvica used a candle to read Bunica's forbidden art book on Chagall. While Silvica drew pictures by candlelight, I worked on my football teams, made up of pictures cut out from the newspaper of players from Dinamo and Steaua. Gabitza sat at the window and watched Bogdan. She begged Mamica to let Bogdan in the apartment.

Never, Gabitza draga, said Mamica. Do you think we're rich, to have a dog in the house?

When it was dark in the winter, when the house was cold and we had to put on both our best and second best sweater and maybe our mittens when we sat in the kitchen, we helped Mamica cook. You haven't asked yet about wh,.at we eat. In Bucharest and in Skokie, we eat borsch and stuffed cabbage and fried potatoes and pork cutlets and *w,,,,ll./*. Pork cutlets are something we must keep from the Skokie Jews, especially when we have it for supper on Shabbat.

In Bucharest, when the queues were long and we had to stand outside with Bunica for hours on the icy sidewalks, when the rationing levels got bad and we were always a little bit hungry, we played Maybe There's Something Besides a

Potato on My Plate, Guess What I Found in My Borsch?, and Something Funny Happened in the Toilet Paper Queue.

Sometimes, when Bunica sent us home and queued alone because it was too cold, and we waited in the apartment for Bunica, Bunicul, Mamica and Taticul, we played a game called Mamica's Never Coming Back. Gabitza would ask, When is Mamica coming back? And we chanted, Mamica is never coming back. It's just us, forever and ever. We laughed when she cried. She would run outside to sit with Bogdan until Mamica came home. We watched her from the window and tried to lure her back in with a cup of tea with extra sugar, a picture of a dog that Silvica will draw for her, permission to play with my paper teams, but Gabitza stayed with Bogdan. Bogdan would growl at us when we tried to pry her off him and drag her in.

Whenever she came back, Mamica would be cross that we let Gabitza outside but would make tea for all of us. Silvica would make a picture for Gabitza, and I wouldn't mind when Gabitza ripped Dinamo's midfielder the slightest bit. After the Domnul took away Taticul for the first time, we never played that game again, because now we know it's true that someone can never come back.

When will the revolution start in your country?

As the changes begin in Europe in 1989, the teachers ask us and the Jews at the synagogue ask Mamica and Taticul this question. You don't ask us; kids don't care. The closer we get to Christmas, it becomes clearer that the Romanians might do something that will ruin Christmas.

When school lets out for the winter holidays, we start a new game. We stand outside in the small yard, yelling, Down with the Goldsteins! Instead of Down with the Ceausescus! The Goldsteins are at work so they don't mind, but Mamica minds.

She says, Do you want to suggest that this nice family who has done nothing but help us are dictators? What's the matter with you?

As soon as she goes back inside, we start again. She doesn't call us inside to play because she has a headache and wants to be alone in the bedroom with the shades drawn and a washcloth over her eyes. She tells us we need the fresh December air. We pretend that the yard is the central square in Timisoara. We take turns being the jailed Hungarian priest. The chain-links are our prison bars. We wrap our mittens around the links.

When Taticul is home, he listens to National Public Radio. He translates for Mamica. When the Ceausescus flee from the Central Committee Building in a helicopter on December 22, the Goldsteins tell us it's going to be on television on the evening news. Mr. Goldstein says, Isn't it exciting to watch the changes in your country?

The television feed from Romania is grainy but we can see the gray buildings in the snow and the people huddled together on the streets in fur hats. The Central Committee Building isn't so far from Cimisgiu Gardens. Gabitza asks if we will see Bunica, Bunicul and Bogdan. Romania is shown for seven minutes. We sit together on the loveseat, no one wanting to be the one to turn off the television.

When Taticul calls Bunica and Bunicul, he can't get through, but there's a click on the line which means the Securitate is listening. We ask if it's the Domnul. Taticul says, We're in Skokie now. Don't think about these things. Don't think about the Domnul. Just think about Bunica and Bunicul, walking in Cimisgiu Gardens hand in hand.

We figure out how to use the fire escapes to climb to the roof of the two-flat when Mamica goes to the store. We use a ladder from the Goldsteins' toolshed to pull the fire escapes down with our own weight. There isn't much of a view up on the two-flat but Gabitza counts the dogs she can see in the yards. We make sure she doesn't stand too close to the gutters. We draw matches to see who gets to be Ceausescu. Gabitza wins. She wants someone to be Elena Ceausescu with her, but we say then there won't be enough people to shout down below. We use the matches to melt the ice off the edges of the fire escape steps. We climb down and stomp in the snow while Gabitza waves at us and squints at the sun. She's to wave her arms above her like a helicopter and disappear from view down the fire escape. Then she'll join us and we'll all cheer together, take a walk to a pretend Cimisgiu Gardens in the back of the yard, eat pretend cakes made of real sugar poured into snow. We'll be done before Mamica gets home.

But Gabitza won't come down, and she kicks at the ladder until it falls in the snow in front of us. When we try to put it back up, she throws snowballs at us and threatens to drop icicles on our heads. All along, she's barking and saying, Down with Silvica and Cornel! Down with Skokie! Ham ham ham.

As the sky across Skokie turns pink and the little white lights on the houses for Christmas and the blue lights for Hanukah in the homes of the Jews go on, as the neighborhood dogs bark and race along their fences responding to Gabitza's call, as Mamica is approaching the front door and Mrs. Goldstein's car is entering the garage, down Gabitza goes, like a dive, like she's performing a trick.

She lands in the snowy, scraggly evergreen bushes. Mamica screams and runs. We run, too, to see our sister splayed out across the bushes as Mamica squats down to touch her forehead. Gabitza's eyes flutter open. Her corduroy pants have ripped through and some of the blood on her scraped knee leaks on to the snow to make it sickly pink. Her right ankle is bent back beneath her and she howls as Mamica pokes it. It's sprained, Mamica whispers as she gathers Gabitza up. Not broken. Gabitza yawns and settles back into Mamica's arms.

We were playing Ceausescu, we tell Mamica breathlessly.

Good god, what's with you? It's bad enough what Ceausescu does to your Bunica and your Bunicul but you decide to do it to your little sister?

No, no, Mamica, you don't understand. Gabitza *was* Ceausescu. She flew down by helicopter.

Mamica looks at us like we are crazy. Do you know, she says, what's real anymore and what isn't?

Mrs. Goldstein has come in through the garage. Is everything all right? she asks.

Okay, okay, all okay, Mrs. Goldstein, Mamica tells her in English. Her pronunciation is terrible. If she went to the school, the kids would laugh.

Mrs. Goldstein smiles, that toothy American smile everyone at the synagogue and at the school uses. She says, That little one's simply got too much energy. Let's see about getting her into classes at the J.

When we're back in the apartment, Mamica yells, I knew it was just a matter of time before the Americans tried to turn you into gymnasts. Too much energy! How could anyone have too much energy! Get me the iodine. The iodine turns Gabitza's knee a crusty dark green. She sits on the loveseat and gets to watch what she wants, ice on her ankle wrapped in a dishtowel. She flips through the channels looking for dogfood commercials.

Taticul brings home a tree, smuggling it in his overcoat so

the Goldsteins won't see. It's a small tree, what they call an apartment tree, Gabitza's size. The branches are much fuller than the ones in Bucharest and it doesn't smell much. It can't be fir. Mamica puts it in a bucket of water next to the television. Taticul arranges the cord with little lights he purchased at the pharmacy. When he plugs the lights in, Gabitza claps.

We turn off all the lights but the tree lights. We sit on the loveseat and look at the tree while we drink our tea. No one wants to sing. The songs O Brad Frumos and O Christmas Tree are the same song, we learned in school. Of course they are, Mamica says, it's a German song, O Tannenbaum. She wants to sing it in German but nobody else does. We don't know the Romanian carols, the *colinde*. We couldn't learn them in Bucharest. The poems we know about Old Man Winter seem babyish now. At school in Skokie, we learned O Hanukah O Hanukah Come Light the Menorah, but Mamica and Taticul don't know it.

Taticul turns on the television. We watch a program about poorly-drawn orphans with a beagle who buy a scraggly Christmas tree. They love it so much it grows. Gabitza asks if it will happen to our tree, and Mamica tells her to hush. Look, Gabitza, we have a nice tree, the tree your father got for us, truly a Brad Frumos here in our new country.

Mamica takes us to pick up our new glasses. She makes us talk to the optometrist. We have to translate for her. We complain that because she won't talk, our frames are hideous, bulky and plastic. We will never wear them. You will never like us now that you can call us Four Eyes. Besides, we don't want to be marked myopic like this. Mamica walks us home all along Dempster Road, the cars speeding past us, without saying anything to us at all. Gabitza's nose is running, but no one stops to wipe it. We want a car like the Americans, a new one, a BMW, a Ferrari, a Ford, Chevrolet. We're tired of waiting for the bus in the snow and the cold.

When Taticul comes home, he says, Why, what has happened to you, my little owlets? Now you look like your parents and grandparents. We tell him we have decided to wear the glasses inside the apartment. We like being able to see each individual needle on the Christmas tree for the first time without standing so close it pokes us. We didn't know that other people could see so much. But Silvica says she plans to take off her glasses when she draws, me, when I play soccer, and Gabitza when she talks to dogs.

Christmas morning Gabitza wakes everyone up in turn by kissing us on both cheeks. Silvica pours the tea while Mamica fries up the pork cutlets for breakfast. I turn on the tree. Gabitza waltzes through the rooms of the apartment while Taticul brings out the presents. An American football for me. Aquarelles for Silvica. A stuffed dog for Gabitza. Gabitza says it doesn't smell real but is softer than Bogdan. New clothes for everyone, because now we are so plump. Mamica gives Taticul a tie and Taticul gives Mamica a scarf. We laugh because they are almost the same pattern, white polka dots on a field of blue. Like the night sky, Mamica says.

We are still admiring our presents when Mr. Goldstein knocks on the door. The cutlets are still frying, the Christmas tree is still on in the living room. Mamica hisses at Taticul, What happens when the Goldsteins come up, see the tree, smell the pork cutlets? I run to turn off the tree and Silvica turns off the burner and sticks the frying pan in the refrigerator. We are still good at hiding things.

Mr. Goldstein knocks again. News, he calls out. Turn on the television! Mamica lets him in and offers him a cup of tea. He sits down on the loveseat as Taticul turns on the television.

There's been an execution. Elena and Nicolae Ceausescu have been executed by firing squad in Tirgoviste. The newsman announces that the images will be graphic. Mamica and Taticul make no move to take us out of the room, to tell us not to watch, to remind us that we are children, to tell us to take off our glasses once again and resume our myopia. The image is quick, flickering, grainy, but we know it must be bloody. We know how to resolve those grains. Now that it is in Silvica's memory, she's got something new to draw.

The monsters are dead, says Taticul.

Who will be the new monsters? Because it will be just a matter of time, says Mamica.

Mr. Goldstein says, You must be so happy. Now everything will change there, too. Maybe you can bring more of your family over, or go back if you want.

Taticul says, Yes, it's wonderful. Thank you, Goldstein, for sharing news with us. Please stay for breakfast. Bring Mrs. Goldstein.

Mr. Goldstein looks at the tree. He isn't smiling. No, I don't want to interrupt. He waves to Gabitza as he backs out the door.

Taticul says to Mamica, We really can't be so sure that everything will change. It's too quick. Too okay. It can't be okay. They whisper about a coup instead of a revolution. The helicopter escape was too convenient, this trial and execution a kangaroo court run by the army. Mamica says we're going to have some explaining to do about our tree at the synagogue. I turn on the tree again and Silvica gets the cutlets back on the stove. Taticul pours brandy for everyone, even a sip for Gabitza, and we toast the health of Bunica and Bunicul.

Viva Romania! I say.

Maybe, says Mamica. Gabitza ham hams. She asks, When

are we going home? Like Mr. Goldstein said? Mamica straightens Silvica's braids and watches me put my new American football away and take out my real one so I can practice my footwork outside in the morning sun. Silvica starts to draw the execution. Her new red aquarelle is left a bloody stump when she is done.

Draga, Mamica says, pulling Taticul's arm. Draga, Octavian, it would be such a simple thing to get the children a puppy.

CHILDREN IN THE TIME OF FAMINE

*An inverted, perverted tale from the original, in which a
mother plans to eat her children in order to survive, as collected by
our Comrade Grimm, our man on the scene in the Village of C*

Once there was a mother who gathered her children around
her and said to them, "Children, I will die soon, and when I
do, you must eat me."

They began to cry, tugging at her skirts.

"Stop wailing and listen," she said. "You'll have to be fast.
You must eat my corpse before the neighbors come to take
it."

They cried harder, the youngest climbing under her skirts
and holding on to her bony leg.

"Stop that," she said. "Pay attention. What must you do?"

"Eat you," said the baby Natasha. She wasn't a baby anymore, but sometimes she acted like one. She was the age for
school now, if the school still ran, which it didn't.

"Yes, Mama's darling."

Tanya, the oldest, didn't want to eat her mother. She was
a the age where her mother disgusted her, the heavy, sagging
breasts like udders, the sweet and stinky smell of milk, the
black hairs sprouting on her chin. None of these defects were
rendered more beautiful by the effects of famine. The breasts
drooped further. The smell of her mother was sour now. The
stray hairs here and there produced silky fur.

"Let's not eat you, Mama. I'll go out and find something
to eat without having to beg for it." In this time in the village
of C, beggars didn't come back from their rounds, dying on

the road, ending up in a soup pot, or shot if they showed too much interest in the granary at the kolkhoz.

When she said, "without having to beg for it," Tanya meant prostitution, but as she walked around the village, strolling through the empty square, where once before the famine, the market was held on Saturday mornings and the dance on Sunday night, nobody watched her with longing the way they had in her prime. Any bit of roundness, any dumpling of fat on her thighs and breast, was gone now. She'd only started to bloom when the drought began, and it was all over. Girls in the village of C had a brief flowering between being little girls and plump cows, baby in the belly and another at the breast, to die as hags, as dried up as prunes. To be called big girl and not little anymore was an honor and a privilege, and the famine was wasting Tanya's big girl year. She'd never know a man now. To curl up with bony Tanya, to be stabbed by her pelvic bones while you tried to stab into her with what was left of your meat, wasn't worth a crust of bread. Wasn't worth even a crumb.

Tanya came back to the house with nothing.

"We'll eat nothing, then," said her mother, and they played a game of cooking water on the range, trying to trick the steam as it rose above the water as it boiled into taking a substantial form, an essence of meals they'd once eaten. She put the boiled water in bowls and made them drink it with spoons. Their mother was crazy. The slurping of water at the table three times a day gave them a structure to their slow dying.

After the bowls were washed in the same hot water they'd been eating, their mother said again, "You must eat me. And here is how you'll do it. Slit my throat and let the blood run out into the pot. Catch it for the soup. Cut off what you can to fry. There's still oil in the pantry. Use it. There's almost no fat on me left, so you'll have to use more oil than we used to do. The bones and the head are for the soup."

Natasha started to cry. "Mamica, I won't eat you, I won't! I'll go out and find something to eat with no one the wiser." She meant she would steal it. She was little and cute and at first during the drought, villagers pitied her and would give her something. Once the drought turned to famine, their mother wouldn't let her out of doors for fears the neighbors would see something little and cute and think, easy to catch, easy to eat. But Natasha would escape sometimes and wait at the kolkhoz granary. She wouldn't fight with the big children for the grains that rolled off the truck taking the village's stores to the cities, but wait until the scuffle was over, until the guards left with their rifles, until all she had to fight with were the birds that came to peck at what was left, and if Natasha caught a bird, she could bring it home for the pot and be the hero.

This time, though, there was nothing, not a kernel of buckwheat or bulgur to bring back to her mother. The guard swept the yard with a broom before the trucks left, swept it onto a newspaper from the city, and slid the residue from the newspaper into his own pocket, then hopped on the truck. There was not a crumb, nothing but husks and hulls. Natasha picked those up so that their water might have the taste of food, the smell of food, food's echo, and slowly walked home. She did not want to eat her mother. She'd eat Tanya in a minute, but not her Mamica who hummed as she washed the spoons which only touched water and then went into their empty, cavernous mouths, saliva sticky stalactites in anticipation of the imagined meal before them, their mouths the gateway to their churning bodies, and the spoons back to the water again.

As soon as Natasha came into the house, her mother fetched the bowls and began boiling the water. Natasha dumped in the husks. Tanya sulked, refusing to eat the pretend soup.

"More for us, then, silly," her mother said, humming. Natasha's spoon clinked against the empty bowl. Otherwise, silence.

Their mother washed the dishes. Natasha dried. Tanya went to get water from the well. There was no one up and down the road, everyone holed up in their courtyards, gates barred. For the first time during the famine, Tanya didn't have the strength to turn the crank. She stared down in the well at the bucket. Once, if she went to the well for water, boys her age and older would be lined up to assist her, making time with the big girl. Now, it wasn't worth it to wait. Nobody would come. There wasn't even the sound of birds. Every chicken in C had been eaten, and the other birds knew better than to alight in the land of famine.

Tanya walked with the empty bucket back to the house. Her mother and sister were already up on the soba under the blankets.

"Come sit, my Skin-and-Bones," her mother said, shifting closer to the wall and making room for Tanya. Tanya hated it when she called her Skin-and-Bones. They all were. It wasn't a useful or endearing nickname. What was the reason that Natasha still was Mama's darling? Look at her, sitting up so close to her mother that she might start rooting around for a nipple at any minute, as if she was a real baby instead of an infantile child.

Tanya climbed up onto the soba. Her mother put out a hand to help her, but Tanya wouldn't take it.

"You'll have to eat me, or else you'll die," her mother said again. Neither girl said anything.

She tried to sleep without touching either her mother or sister, but once she fell asleep, she couldn't help sliding into a triangulation of limbs with the rest of them. With their bony frames, they fit together like architecture, masonry, bone on bone, Tanya's skull on Natasha's knee, Natasha's skull upon her mother's pelvic bone, her mother's claw hand hooked through Tanya's elbow.

It would be so pretty to leave them there in the story, like remembrance bones in a reliquary.

But the girls' bones weren't found in the house.

Just the hero mother. Her head in the soup pot.

What happened to the girls, not a soul in the village of C knew. Whether they woke up and did eat their mother as she wished, or they woke up and fled the house in the morning at the horror of eating their mother and some neighbors stopped by to finish the feast instead, nobody knows until this day.

The girls might have made it to the city to join a band of orphans begging at the train stations. They might have grown again, plumper, taller, breasts to aid them in their prostitution. Maybe they got along, Tanya looking out for Natasha, Natasha using her skills at soothing people to ingratiate herself and Tanya into larger groups of successful orphans. But this investigator doesn't know what happened after the head got into the pot, or what happened before, either.

Nobody in the village of C is descended from either Tanya or Natasha. The house stayed empty for a time, but after 1956, somebody whose house had been taken over by somebody else after the deportation came back, and the village soviet assigned the house of the hero mother to somebody who needed a house. Calling it the Hero Mother House started as a joke, in homage to the statues of heroic mothers built after the war in the town squares across the Soviet Union. Like a statue by Vera Mukhina, with the woman as muscular as any man, but with sadder eyes. Names of Mukhina statues: Fertility. Bread. The Worker and the Kolkhoznita. We Demand Peace, with a mother holding a dead child in her arms. Who was a bigger hero mother than the mother who asked her children to eat her? Most of the villagers in C don't know why it's called the Hero Mother House, but those who saw the head in the pot can't forget. There's no statue of that.

THE GENERAL AND HIS WIFE ATTEND THE GRADUATION OF THEIR GRANDSON

Getting Dressed

What my daughter wants me to say is that I don't deserve it, the invitation. She hopes I have the decency not to come at all. I am lucky that she deigned to send me an invitation in the mail asking me to attend my grandson's graduation. My daughter doesn't call, not because there is a chance she might have to talk to me. I never pick up the phone. That's what secretaries and wives are for. I don't remember the last time I made a call. But our Beatriz doesn't want to talk to her mother, either. Since the results were revealed, we only see her on set visits she arranges with Graciela by e-mail.

The visits are with the boys. Beatriz is there, because she wouldn't let us have them alone, but she reads a magazine and barely looks up from the pages. When Graciela tries to engage her in small talk, Beatriz cuts her off.

I want to ask her what she allows that woman. If that woman gets to see the boys alone or if Beatriz stays during the visits there, too. If Beatriz chats with her. When that woman dies, will we get Beatriz back? That woman must be ancient now. Maybe she's already dead and Beatriz and the boys have kept it from me.

Or maybe she's alive, and I will see her for the first time since the trial today.

I can't conceive of not wearing my uniform to such an event. Nothing else I have deserves the respect that this day needs. Surely Beatriz wouldn't expect me to wear anything else. Surely she's already prepared herself and that woman to confront my uniform.

I was buttoning it up when Graciela appeared in the dressing room.

Maybe not today, she said. Maybe not this once. She held a new suit, tailored to my dimensions, looking as much as possible as a uniform without being one. She must have been planning this moment from the day the invitation arrived in the mail.

She should have been the general, my Graciela.

She helped me unbutton the uniform, and eased the suit on to me. I couldn't remember the last time I had worn a suit. I didn't always wear the uniform, as much as Beatriz used to tease me for it back when she still talked to me. But I wore the uniform for all formal occasions, and all work occasions. The casual clothes I wear for golf would not do.

But I could see Mario being delighted if I showed up for graduation in plaid pants.

When I mentioned it to Graciela, though, she was not amused.

Hurry up, old man, she said. She already had on her pearls. She was ready.

Stage

When Mario's name was called, I don't know why I felt aflutter. He didn't carry my name, but the name of that dentist Beatriz married and the name of those people, that woman's family. Still and all, it was my boy, finally my boy, crossing the stage and shaking the hand of the headmaster. A firm handshake, like the ones we used to practice in my study and I'd slip him some chocolate. He was beautiful, clean cut, clean-shaven, an elegant profile like something you'd want to stamp on a coin, nothing like those people at all, like he'd always been meant to be my boy and it had just taken years for everything else to fall away.

He was six when the DNA results were revealed, and Beatriz could have kept Mario and the younger brother, that Fernando, from us forever, but she didn't. It took years for her to come around, the same years I was in prison, and I know about the campaign that Graciela waged to get her back because it was what we talked about when she visited me.

Stopping by wouldn't work. Beatriz wouldn't answer the door. Trying to bump into her in the neighborhood didn't work, because Beatriz's agoraphobia was only getting worse in those years. You could call, and she would pick up, she had to in case it was something about the boys, school or friends or the doctor, but when she heard Graciela's voice on the line, she'd hang up. So Graciela wrote letter after letter.

She wouldn't tell me what was in those letters. They were private, she said. Some memories about Beatriz as a girl. The boys when they were babies.

But I knew that there must have been something to make Beatriz change her mind, something more than nostalgia. Something more than just evidence of Graciela's love.

Graciela must have apologized for my actions, or confessed that she, too, was horrified by my actions, that she couldn't sleep at night because of what I'd done.

She could sleep fine when I came back from prison. Night after night, she slept while I paced around the house. Not over guilt over what I'd done, but trying to figure out how, when every one of my decisions was one I would make again if I was presented with them in a row, I'd reached the point where I'd lost my child and my grandchildren, and my wife was willing to throw me to the wolves in order to get them back.

The only way for Graciela to get me what I most wanted was to betray me most thoroughly.

I am wrecked.

But not Mario. He walks back to his seat, shaking the hands of his friends. Not high fives, or head butts, but a firm shake as if they were lawyers already. He is beautiful. It has all been worth it, all of it.

Then I see her, that woman, sitting next to Beatriz. If she was old before, during the trial, now she's a crone, crumpled into herself, something out of fairy tale.

I stand by all of my decisions except the one to come here today. Or, if I had to come, I should have stayed in uniform. In this suit, I am wearing the uniform of a different man, a man I don't know. How will Mario even find me in the crowd if he should choose to want to look? He'll see his grandmother sitting next to a stranger.

Party

I hadn't been inside Beatriz's apartment in eleven years. She hasn't redecorated. It's the same mishmash of cultural flotsam and jetsam, antique cut-offs from other people's lives. I know she's never accepted anything Graciela offered her from the house. It's hard to find a place to sit that isn't covered by a hideous hippie pillow.

Sit here, Daddy, Beatriz says, moving a pillow and pushing me into a chair.

It's as much as she has said or done for me since I came home from prison. I'd be grateful if I couldn't see that she is trying to keep me from the kitchen, where that woman sits, brooding over the sandwiches and pastries.

Graciela circulates, coming back to refresh my drink. Once, she rubs off the crumbs at the corners of my lips, as if I were her child, or senile. I could walk around the room with her, but I have nothing to say to anybody. The armchair I'm in is lumpy. There is a television across from me, but it's off, and there's a scarf draped across it, as if the television is just a box for display. There are some magazines on the end table, but they aren't for general readership, the kind without pictures and lengthy discussions of matters of culture, things up for debate. The kind Beatriz likes.

I have no idea how my daughter spends her days. She never finished the university. She didn't have any hobbies other than mooning over records and books. Beatriz has told me that she is in therapy for the agoraphobia. We both know she's in therapy for more than that. The agoraphobia is getting better, but maybe not the rest of it, and she's dating again. The bald man wearing a tropical shirt at her elbow seems to be her new beau.

There is the dentist with a woman on his arm who can't be much older than Mario. I want to call him the ex-dentist, a slip of the tongue. He's still a dentist. He's an ex-husband. Graciela has accused me of disliking him, but I liked him well enough as dentist, even recommended him to some of my colleagues. He hugs Mario. He ignores Fernando. Everybody does. He won't graduate for two more years, but even on Fernando's own graduation day, we'll all be thinking about Mario. Fernando is sulking. That woman leaves the pastries to talk to him in the corner of the kitchen. She must be eying me the way I am eying her.

The real party is in the garden. That's where Mario's friends are, and everybody young, even Beatriz and her bald man are drawn to the sun. Graciela wants to be there, too, but she doesn't want to abandon me. She keeps coming in and out, the screen door banging an announcement of her arrival.

Soon, we two will be the only ones left inside the apartment, just me and the old woman. We're both old now. At the time of the trial, she was already old, but I was still a man in my prime, a man in control, a man who filled my uniform. I still played tennis, not just golf.

Prison exhausted me. They treated us well. Politically, the guards were all on our side, and the prisoners on the left on a matter of principle either entirely ignored our existence or treated us how they wished they'd been treated. Not that anything they could do would soften my heart for what had to be done in the years of emergency. Still, the years of being locked up, the fact that when I left the prison I would not be returning to my job and that there was nothing for me to do waiting for me when I got out, turned me old. Maybe I would have turned old in those years anyway. Graciela says that, laughing, but she still is as thin and active as a bird. She doesn't want to be quiet with me. The quieter I am, the more she seems to have a mechanical whir about her.

The dignified thing would be for that woman and me to continue to ignore each other. I would have felt that I had more dignity if I'd worn my uniform instead of this suit. There's something cowardly about not coming to do battle rightly attired. In the suit, I felt like a spy and not a soldier. Graciela wanted me in the suit because Beatriz must have wanted me in the suit. Beatriz wanted me in the suit, I suppose, so she and Mario wouldn't have to constantly explain who I was and why I was here. So it would be Mario's day, not mine.

But Mario is here because of what I did. His very existence is predicated by my actions.

Without me, there might not be a Beatriz, and without Beatriz, no Mario and Fernando. The old woman has to grant me that. Her daughter and her son-in-law were dead before I was involved. They were dead from the moment they picked up their guitars, sang of overthrowing the government, and meant it. Mario and his friends have found more suitable pursuits. Their video games. Their hip-hop.

That woman's daughter never stood a chance. What I did do was save Beatriz. She was such a tiny baby. She fit in my hand. I tucked her into my coat and brought her home to Graciela, who never loved me more. Beatriz was a beautiful baby, and a beautiful girl, and everything would have been fine, I think, if the grandmothers never started protesting in the square. Maybe Beatriz would have finished the university. Maybe she'd still be with her dentist. Maybe she'd be with somebody better than her dentist. Except I still want Mario, so I guess she has to have been with the dentist.

I wasn't in the room when she was born. I had nothing to do with that woman's daughter and how she died.

Yes, if you ask, I was in the building.

When they brought Beatriz to me, I didn't hesitate. She was everything we had ever wanted.

Beatriz means, she who brings joy. Graciela named her. What she was thinking, I don't know. She wasn't a joyful child, she isn't a joyous woman. She brought joy to us, but not to those others. The pregnancy multiplied their pain. Those foolish people. The biological parents, if you insist upon using those words.

The old woman is naïve if she thinks that anybody ever was going to return Beatriz to her. They'd have killed Beatriz first.

The next time Graciela goes back out to the garden, when

we are alone again, I see her creeping over to me on her cane. The kind thing would be to meet her halfway. The cruelest thing would be to walk over to her and show her how much health and strength I still have, that she could not defeat me. She could not erase me from her family. I am a fact. I stay in the chair. I would be neither cruel nor kind. We would meet as equals.

She's pretty for an old woman, a crone, I'll grant her. The intellectuals always stay so thin. She is distinguished as a painting by El Greco. She does not choose to exchange pleasantries. She begins with a volley.

Fernando won't be talking to you again, my General, she says. He's just learning about those years. About the planes. Mario may forgive, he has a forgiving nature, but Fernando won't. He's mine.

You can have Fernando, I say. I didn't want to relinquish him, but I know a lost cause when I see one.

You'll never get Beatriz back, either, she says. You're planning to wait it out, wait for me to die, but she'll never forget. At your funeral, when she kisses your cold cheek, she'll whisper in your ear what I've taught her to. Now you're dead at last, my murderer.

If she hates me so much, why am I here? I stuff a snack in my mouth, something wrapped in bacon, the way everything is now.

She says nothing in response at first, and she knows I'm here because of Mario. Mario, the one she hasn't won over. Mario, who is worth all of the Fernandos in the world.

You're here, my general, so we can look at you and bear witness to what you did. Some of us will forgive, but nobody will forget. You might be wearing a suit, but that uniform is your skin. You're like a snake when you shed it.

From the patio in the garden, Mario and Graciela see us at the same time. Neither of them want a confrontation, Graciela who spends her whole life smoothing the world over, Mario who has found a way to reconcile the sides of his family within himself.

Mario comes over and shakes my hand. I slip him two things: a chocolate and my most honorable medal, the one I want him to have from me in remembrance.

The bald man snaps a photo of us, to Graciela's delight and Beatriz's disapproval. Across the room, the old woman grips Fernando's arm for balance. Everybody is staring, an intake and exhaling of breath in unison, a moment frozen in time with everybody choosing sides. Do not ask me if I dream of the planes. Of course I do. But we do not choose what will be asked of us. It's all happened before. It will all happen again.

THE TRANSYLVANIESS

This research is recorded in the proceedings of the Amnesty International chapter, E.T.H.S., 1987. In a story about student activists, a bomb is going to go off. In a story about a vampire, someone's going to get bitten.

We often wondered about the Transylvaniess. What she ate when not drinking blood, what size her coffin, how broad the wingspan of her bat familiar. What she did after school, because she hadn't signed up for extracurriculars. No one had seen her hanging out at the Burger King parking lot or browsing through records in the back of Second Hand Tunes. We wondered if we would look up and see her Transylvanian family silhouetted against the night sky—even the little one they'd enrolled in kindergarten and the old one who sat on a park bench drinking cold tea—flying off to the pink light of Chicago to feed on the drunks passed out on Rush Street and the homeless sleeping in their cardboard boxes on Lower Wacker Drive.

She had the saddest eyes we'd ever seen. Irises a soft brown, pupils vanishing as if they were designed for night vision, like a cat's. Eyes that had seen too much because the aperture opened too wide. The whites of her eyes were skim-milk blue. There were plush black-blue bags spreading beneath them, because she never slept, what with being a vampire and having to be at school days.

She wasn't like the West Indians, shivering in their tatty cardigans, who swore they'd never be at home here. Yes, her blood ran cold underneath her ghastly porcelain skin, but wasn't she replenishing it nightly? Her eyes drooped at the corners, with an overly defined epicanthic fold that gave her the look of a lizard longing for the sun and made her stand out all the more at the table of Asian immigrants she sat with at lunch.

The Korean girl who'd been here the longest translated. The Transylvaniess would whisper something through her fangy teeth and the Korean would shout it at us until she thought we understood.

"She say, she can't make history project after school. She must to go home."

"She say, she don't like potato chips. They hurt her teeth. Thanks anyway."

"She say, she can't swim. So she can't be on your water polo team in gym class."

"She say, Transylvania is too a real country."

The Transylvaniess shuffled along in her bulky Eastern European shoes, her back bent due to the weight of her voluminous pack, her sad eyes on the floor as if she thought she might trip. Or that someone might trip her. Foreigners were like permanent freshman. We were sympathetic because we were once freshmen, too, but because we knew the only cure for us was to become older, we knew the only cure for them was to stop being foreign.

They had her mainstreamed only in gym. She wouldn't suit up. Illinois mandated four years of daily gym. Maybe it was different in Transylvania, but this was Illinois. The only other class Illinois valued as much was English. There were second-year seniors whose schedule consisted entirely of English and gym. The Transylvaniess allowed herself to be herded into the locker room, but while we changed, while we scoured ourselves with lotion to prevent the horror of ashy legs and shellacked our hair back in place in front of the hazy mirror after we'd pulled the gym uniform shirt over our heads, she leaned against the mirror and watched us, her lizard eyes unblinking. Her lank hair was plastered to her pale forehead. Her dowdy brown corduroy dress clung to her skinny frame. We knew it wasn't coming off, that we would never see what vampires went in for when choosing underwear.

We all knew how not to look for too long, not at the girls with enormous breasts or the ones in various stages of anorexia. Or the ones with polished, shrunken skin on their legs from childhood scalding accidents, or bruises the size of a boy's fist. Cigarette burns on arms of kids who didn't smoke. Or hickey necklaces, each one a dark, lustrous pearl of capillaries, or girls whose formerly flat stomachs bulged once they were revealed in bras and panties instead of the baggy sweats they'd been choosing lately.

She followed us out into the gym. Because she was so thin, her corduroy dress, which on any of us would have squeaked, didn't. There was nothing for the fabric to rub against. The dress covered her knees, so we didn't know how bony they might be. Her ankles were covered by wool socks that ran to meet the dress' hem, leaving only a hint of a patch of that blanched skin. While we choreographed dances to Janet Jackson's *Rhythm Nation* album, or ran dribbling drills, or practiced volleyball serves until our wrists ached and we begged Ms. Shaw to let us start a game, the Transylvaniess stood in the corner and watched us, her arms folded across the corduroy. She never sat down, the way we did when we didn't suit up, crossing our legs beneath us or sticking them out in front until Ms. Shaw shouted we were just asking for accidents. The Transylvaniess never walked laps around the gym, the way girls who had their periods did for credit.

Blood made us anxious. It was an era of great worry over the exchange of bodily fluids. We watched her watch us. She was in street clothes. It was permitted, demanded even. It was like the Transylvaniess was on a permanent period, a permanent state of blood brimming out of control, blood lust at her fingertips.

When the bell rang, the Transylvaniess didn't get on the 202, 203, or 204. The buses were only a quarter with a student ID, so it couldn't have been that she didn't have the money. Unless her family only had gold coins stamped with profiles of medieval princes? She didn't walk home with the Korean. The Transylvaniess walked alone, all the way from the high school's Gothic hulking structure on Dodge Avenue to a shabbily elegant 1920s apartment building off Main Street, past Ridge Avenue.

The apartment building had turrets and peaks and bay windows; we didn't think it was a coincidence that both buildings the Transylvaniess spent her time in looked like castles. Evanston was full of things built to look like something they weren't, built to look older, and we wondered if the Transylvanians chose Evanston because at least it looked old, or because the sham lives they were required to lead as vampires went easier in a town designed to deceive.

We knew that the apartments inside the fake castle were cramped, the biggest unit only two bedrooms and the bedrooms just wide enough for a bed and dresser if you didn't mind having to sit on the bed to pull open the drawers, with windows onto a narrow courtyard that never saw sun. The Transylvanians were living in one of those apartments, all six of them. No wonder they had to get out at night.

How did she move outside during the day? Carefully, her parka hood pulled out as if it were the prow of a ship, her socks pulled up to cover the last patches of skin, ratty woolen mittens no matter what the weather. The Transylvaniess never stopped to admire lawn ornaments or get a snack at a corner store. She didn't stop at lights, either. She looked for cars once and then darted across the street, sometimes catching her clumsy shoes against the curb. We clocked her taking forty-five minutes door to door. She vanished into her building. We waited for her to return, holding the little one's hand. The little one skipped in place while they waited to cross the street.

The little one was almost pretty, the same sad eyes peering out of a pointy face, and the awkward teeth were charming in someone still working on her baby teeth. The Transylvaniess smiled down at her. We'd never seen her smile before, and it was terrible. Her eyes closed up; her fangs were revealed.

They crossed the street into the park to meet the old one who waited for them all day on the bench, wrapped in a blanket and sipping tea from a thermos. She wouldn't share her bench with anyone else. If someone else was there first, she stood next to the bench first sighing, then grumbling in Transylvanian and baring her remaining teeth until she drove everyone off.

They sat together, kicking their heels against the dug-in dirt under the bench, staring at the gnarled elms lining the park. The old one pulled out a packet of European digestible biscuits from her torn trenchcoat pocket, and they chewed through the contents. The old one spat whenever teenagers walked by. She didn't like other old people, either. Babies in strollers caused a strange cooing in her throat; it might have been more of a croaking. It was impossible to tell if she liked babies or hated them most of all.

We waited for the Transylvaniess to push the little one on

a swing, climb up with her to the ship's mast or castle's turret, at least start a wood chip war, but they sat as placidly as the old one did. They roosted there, whispering to each other in their nasal, staccato language, blinking their mournful eyes, red noses running. Once Evanston's old-fashioned street lamps flickered on all at once all over town, they stood up. They shook the crumbs of biscuits off their laps and ground them into the dirt with their heels. Crossing the street against the traffic light, they disappeared into their building.

We tried, but there was no angle to get a good view into their apartment, even from the buildings across the street. They kept their shades drawn and the lights largely off, as if they had sophisticated vision, infrared maybe. Either that, or those bony legs must be covered in bumps as they ran into their oversized Transylvanian furniture. We didn't know whether they shipped it from Transylvania or bought it at the Salvation Army, but we had informants who watched them move it in. It was the kind of furniture that could have secret compartments. For vampire coffins, for hoarding the musty earth of Transylvania that would restore them as they slept.

If they slept. These Transylvanian vampires seemed to have adapted so that the rays of the sun did not fry them instantly, for the Transylvaniess walked to and from school, the old one sat in the park, the young one waited in full sun for her school bus, and they all sat in the park together until darkness fell. Were the rules different for the young and old? The parents and the older brother left the house mornings when it was still dark, and returned at night in darkness. What would they do when Daylight Savings Time ended?

•

We recruited the Transylvaniess for our E.T.H.S. chapter of Amnesty International. There was dissent. Luisa, born under

Allende and smuggled out of Chile under Pinochet, was uncomfortable writing Urgent Action aerogrammes next to a vampire. But we already had Pieter, our white South African, native Afrikaans speaker. Reilly, our IRA supporter, was all for political redemption, and thought we were ready for a Transylvaniess. Sometimes we resented Luisa and Reilly. Some of us thought we had stories as good as theirs worth telling, maybe not better than Luisa's, but certainly better than Reilly's. Plus, Luisa was a baby in 1973. What she knew, she knew from listening to the stories of others. We were good listeners, too.

During meetings, our faculty advisor Mr. Piper sat in the back grading papers, looking up when Reilly or Luisa said something outrageous. His college experiences volunteering for Freedom Summer had radicalized him, but he also had gone to college on a football scholarship. There was a part of him that couldn't understand why we ditched pep rallies to browse at Second Hand Tunes. "You could have school spirit and world spirit," he told us.

We couldn't figure out how the pep rallies were supposed to be us acting locally, as they reminded us more than anything else of a stadium full of Fascists, Leni Riefenstahl at the camera. The fight song was, "E.T.H.S., We will fight for you, for the right to do, everything for you," and that wasn't a right we wanted to fight to win.

When the Korean and the Transylvaniess peeked around the door, Reilly ushered them in. Chan, our Cambodian killing fields refugee, soft-spoken, tiny from years of malnutrition, a dark mark on her throat from years of playing championship violin, passed them aerogrammes and lent them Hello Kitty pens. "I really need these back," she said. After her Cambodian childhood, Chan was especially fond of private property. The Transylvaniess turned the pen in her claw hands.

Luisa called the meeting to order, banging her fist against the desk. There was a touch of Castro about her, solidity to her movements, a tightening of her jaw. She brushed her dark braid off her shoulder and tugged at the red scarf around her neck. Pieter slouched in his chair, reviewing atrocities committed by Nicaraguan death squads. Pieter wasn't albino, but there was something about him that made us think that maybe he should have been. He was thin, with floppy limbs like a rag doll that made him lurch about awkwardly. His hair was urine yellow, his face and arms so full of freckles he was red, not white.

Chan said politely to the Transylvaniess, "Perhaps you could brief us on human rights in Eastern Europe?" Chan was already responding to the Urgent Actions, her frilly handwriting flowing across the page. Chan and Luisa competed to see who could write more letters, but many weeks Pieter, indifferent to them as he burrowed into his desk, indifferent to what city he was in, what country, wrote the most. Mr. Piper knew not to commend him, knew that Pieter didn't want to be commended but punished, maybe by Reilly, his only friend, maybe by Luisa in some vaguely sexual way, a Kafka fantasy of a girl dressed up in army fatigues barking commands at him while he wrote letters until his fingers bled.

If we thought the Transylvaniess would answer our questions simply and smoothly, we underestimated her canny nature, her clever paranoia, the wiles of monsters and immigrants. The Korean bounced in her chair. The Transylvaniess scowled. The Hello Kitty pen was leaking blue ink. Her fingers seemed traced in surplus veins. When she leaned over to whisper something to the Korean, we caught a flash of her dead tooth, a gray moldering next to her right fang usually hidden by the sneer of her upper lip.

The Korean said, "She say, maybe something more specific?"

Luisa tried, "You could talk about Transylvanian dissidents? Transylvanian prisons?"

"She say, food is rationed. Electricity, too. It's always cold. It's like everyone is dissident, because everyone is punished." We imagined a nation of citizens huddled in their cold, dark apartments, waiting for vampire visitations, waiting to feast on their neighbors, waiting for their neighbors to feast on them. The Transylvaniess fluttered her sad eyes at us.

The Latvian twins stared at each other, arching their blond eyebrows in their telepathic language. They were fraternal twins, but they looked alike anyway, both sporting a Prince Valiant bob and Pixies T-shirts, the girl flat-chested, the boy with generous hips. The girl twin asked, "How did you get out?"

The Transylvaniess shifted on her chair. The corduroy squeaked. "Uncle in Chicago."

The boy twin insisted, "Your family must have had connections. Paid something. Nobody gets out for free."

"Luck," the Transylvaniess said.

The boy twin pushed, "Nobody gets out by luck. You must have done something."

"Luck!" shouted the Transylvaniess, her fangs revealed.

"Hey. Hey, now." Mr. Piper waved from the back of the room. He had the gentleness of a big man who'd been fighting the intimidating impression of his size his whole life. Nobody, ever, had really messed with Mr. Piper. We all were suspicious of his sympathy.

"People at least have expectations of you," the Latvian girl said sulkily, her hair in her eyes as she tugged at split ends.

"Of Transylvania. Nobody knows anything about Latvia."

Luisa said, "Come on. It's hard enough being the new kid without having special problems."

"Special problems?" the Transylvaniess asked. "Special? What do you want me to say? That I've come to suck your blood? It's what you believe?" She met our eyes, one by one, surveying her crowd, her prey. We stared back at her. We did believe it, but no one wanted to say it. Not even Reilly. She smiled at us scornfully.

"Hey, everybody," said Mr. Piper, but before he could finish the bomb in the Haymarket diorama blew up, scattering plastic men waiting to hear the anarchists speak, a plume of pink smoke rising. In the next shoebox over, the Hull-House Devil Baby, a plastic trinket from a King's cake, rolled to freedom from its toothpick crib.

"It was an accident, Mr. Piper, I swear," said Reilly. "It wasn't ever supposed to go off. It was a dud."

Luisa said, "Jesus, Reilly, what were you thinking?" She put her arm around Chan to stop her from shaking.

"Reilly, a word?" Mr. Piper opened the door and bowed to Reilly to go first, that overly polite gesture of teachers at their angriest and most sarcastic.

But it wasn't Reilly who set it off. It was Pieter. Chan saw him do it, and the Latvians. He had matches in his bag from the No Exit Cafe. The Transylvaniess and Pieter sat in silent camaraderie. We think she knew Pieter had done it for her, to get her attention, get us to stop talking. We never tired of listening to ourselves. She nodded in his direction, but that could have been a Transylvanian way of saying hello. Pieter's face was entirely a blotchy red. He ran his hands through his thatchy, awful hair. Only a vampire could love him.

Reilly wouldn't talk about what Mr. Piper said, but he was

happy to discuss the next turn of events: the bizarre double date of Reilly, the Korean, Pieter, and the Transylvaniess. When the Korean and the Transylvaniess exited E.T.H.S. arm in arm, leaning to the side due to the weight of their backpacks, Pieter trailing behind them because he was shy but determined to stay in the orbit of the Transylvaniess, who had a capacity for violence above and beyond anything Luisa could dish out, Reilly was there with his beat-up Rabbit. He offered them a ride home, but he also offered them a ride into the city. "Don't you just want to get out of here?"

The Korean and the Transylvaniess wanted to call home from the payphones, but Reilly wouldn't let them. "Wouldn't they say no? Don't you want to say yes?" Pieter didn't have anybody to call.

Reilly drove them into Chicago, past the gray monuments of Calvary Cemetery on the left and the gray waves of the lake on the right. Past the 400 Theater, with its midnight showing of Rocky Horror. "We should take *you*," said Reilly. "Our own sweet little transvestite from Transylvania." The Transylvaniess grunted. Past the senior citizen towers on Sheridan, where seniors desperately waited at lights to cross with their walkers.

Inside the Rabbit, they listened to Reilly's mixed tape. The Replacements: We'll Inherit the Earth. The Smiths: There Is a Light That Never Goes Out. Joy Division: Love Will Tear Us Apart. The Beastie Boys: Brass Monkey. The Clash: Lost in the Supermarket. The Pogues: Streets of Sorrow/Birmingham Six. Eric B and Rakim: Paid in Full. The Pixies: Where Is My Mind. The Korean bopped her head to the music. The Transylvaniess sucked her teeth together.

On to Lake Shore Drive, where the Korean said she felt like she was flying. Her hair got into Reilly's eyes and he thought he was going to have pull over. Past the water giving the illusion that you could sail out of Chicago, that we weren't stuck here, land-locked: a lie like the antique features of Evanston. None of us were going anywhere. We'd gotten here from a great distance. To the wall of skyscrapers at the Oak Street Beach, the spot on the Drive where it feels as if you're going to crash into the city head on and it would be magnificent.

They exited the Drive at Jackson to cut over to Buckingham Fountain. They parked illegally. Reilly led them, the girls together, Pieter still trailing behind, as if he hadn't been invited, as if he were a spy. The Fountain was Reilly's make-out point. Most romantic guys would go up to the Bahá'í Temple in Wilmette, or drive through the winding ravines of the richest North Shore suburbs, and there was always the Burger King parking lot, but Reilly always said nothing was as impressive as a city, and if he couldn't take her to Dublin, Chicago would do.

The Transylvaniess breathed deeply as she and the Korean stood at the Fountain's base. Reilly had never seen her so relaxed. Maybe the ornamental architecture reminded her of Transylvania. Pieter stood off to the side, kicking at the little pink pebbles.

It was dusk. Reilly talked the Korean into walking around the Fountain to examine the bronze monsters circling the basin. She agreed, slipping her hand into his. So Reilly, who doesn't kiss and tell, wouldn't tell us what happened then, and wasn't able to tell us what the Transylvaniess and Pieter were up to, although they must have appeared as two thin silhouettes against the violently pink sky, standing by the pink marble fountain as it gushed forth like blood from a severed artery.

When Reilly and the Korean returned to the car, Reilly overheard Pieter murmuring, "Such extravagant waste," and the Transylvaniess agreeing, "Such a squandering."

On the way back, Reilly and the Korean talked about music. He explained the lyrics to the songs on the mixed tape. The Korean regularly got lost in supermarkets. The lights in Chicago never do go out. "Your Ireland," she whispered during the Pogues. They didn't hear anything from the backseat. When Reilly turned around, he saw the Transylvaniess, carsick, her head craned toward the open window, and Pieter asleep with his head in her lap.

•

Pieter and the Transylvaniess were now a couple. They were the kind of couple that we found most nauseating, couples with dingy hair and pimpled faces, always too fat, too skinny, too tall, too short, and mismatched so that two fat ones, two tall ones never seemed to find each other. The kind who leaned into each other at lockers and chewed on each other's maws until they internalized every last vestige of lip gloss and chapstick. The kind the superintendent called "cheap and desperate" over the loudspeaker when he chastised them for "romancing in the halls," the kind of couple that the resulting "If you're cheap, I'm desperate" and the "If you're desperate, I'm cheap" T-shirts were made for. We didn't enjoy watching the attractive couples, either, but at least there seemed to be a reason beyond biology, rooted in aesthetics, for their rutting around.

We didn't want to see the pointy nails wrapped around Pieter's blotchy neck. We didn't want to notice that Pieter's hickeys were purple against his red freckles, that the Transylvaniess remained unblemished but that her skin had started to glow as if it was lit. We didn't want to see Pieter pressed against the Transylvaniess' locker as she used her nimble tongue, her fangs sheathed behind the pink, pulsating muscle. We didn't want to see them on the bench, their hands furtively inside each other's coats.

Once Pieter and the Transylvaniess were together, her eyes crinkled up with strange little smiles. Her nose stopped running, although she still dabbed at it with a faded, flowered handkerchief. Her spine seemed to straighten as if Pieter's blood kept her aligned. She didn't watch her clunky shoes when she walked, but looked straight ahead as if she was looking for him. This new happy Transylvaniess was what inspired Ms. Shaw to enforce her participation in physical education.

It didn't matter anymore whether the Transylvaniess had a gym uniform. During the swim unit, everyone was required to wear an E.T.H.S. swimsuit. For the girls: shapeless black suits boiled in vats, elastic that had lost its tension. For the boys: Speedos made of the same material. Loincloths would have been more suitable.

Worse than the suits was waiting in line naked to get them. Stripped beneath the fluorescent lights of the locker room, we shifted our weight from one foot to the other to cover what we could, arms folded across our chests or fingers braided around our genitals depending on what we chose to protect. When we reached the front of the line, we had to tell the shriveled lady at the counter what size we thought we were. She peered at us through the bifocals sliding down her nose. Pitching her voice to echo down the tiled corridor, she would correct us loudly if she chose. She took her pair of substantial tongs and dug out a steaming suit from the pile behind her. She dangled it before us. We had to take it, no matter what condition it was in, no matter what size. Hopping back down the hall, using the suit to cover what we could, knowing that our backsides were open to countless humiliations, we made our way back to our lockers and put the suit on.

The myopic amongst us worked on the theory that if you couldn't see anyone, they couldn't see you. The suit pilled up at the area we least wanted others to notice. We exited the harsh light of the locker room and descended the slippery steps into the atrium with its weird illumination of a constant, early twilight. We were divided into those who could handle the big pool, and those who couldn't. The small pool held swim classes for little kids on weekends, and we knew that it was a pool full of piss. To a certain extent, our swimming ability coordinated with how far west we lived, how far away from the lake, how much money we had.

Transylvania is a land-locked country. The Transylvaniess said she knew how to ski, not how to swim. She refused to wait in line, not even clothed, not even when Ms. Shaw tried to drag her over. She held up her hands beseechingly, as if she didn't understand, but we knew she was pretending. Her English was good now; that was one class she would pass. Ms. Shaw ended up tossing a suit straight over to her locker.

The Transylvaniess was the only one who looked dignified in the suit, maybe because in its bagginess spanned across her slight frame, it didn't look all that different from a shorter version of the corduroy dress. She looked like a Hollywood starlet from the silent era, the black suit, her white skin, her hair plastered to her forehead in curls because of the humidity. She arched one trim ankle toward the pool, gracing the water with her toes, then pulled it back.

Ms. Shaw begged, "Please, show us you can swim!" Ms. Shaw's suit was rainbow-colored, a Ziggy cartoon on one breast. Her frizzy green hair was pulled back in a ponytail that bounced as she swam towards the Transylvaniess. "Please!" The Transylvaniess put her face in the water, leaned in to float, and sank like a stone. Ms. Shaw pulled her out, patting her back as water sputtered out of her. Water rushed into the suit to give her a momentarily voluptuous figure. She was assigned to the piss pool.

Pieter had been assigned to the big pool. In South Africa, he must have had a swimming pool, must have done laps as much as he liked, then sat in the sun flipping through comics while servants brought him tea. Pieter was more at home in the water than on land, cutting through the liquid with vicious kicks. In the pool's glow, his hair softened to a whitish blonde, and his ruddy skin seemed healthy against the shifting blue.

Ms. Shaw was teaching us a synchronized swimming routine that started in the piss pool with rudimentary steps that could be done by someone standing tiptoe in the water. The baby swimmers swung their arms out in the direction of the big pool, hailing the superior swimmers, bowing their heads, tucking their chins in to their necks as the action passed on. In the big pool, in the deep end, Esther Williamses of both sexes, of all races, fanned out in every direction, their bodies elongated, all of them opening up into a flower, their kicking legs petals in the breeze. A chrysanthemum, really, a human chrysanthemum. When Ms. Shaw described it, Pieter blushed and the Transylvaniess' eyes flashed red. We thought they were thinking Buckingham Fountain, water turned into a flower. But probably they were thinking about a far more intimate moment, one we entirely would not like to know about. None of us would be able to see the ultimate flowering of the human chrysanthemum, except for Ms. Shaw, because we would be in the pool, and the flower was designed to be seen bird's-eye view. We thought of the spectacle of pep rallies, of gymnastic displays in totalitarian countries. Ms. Shaw told us someone from the AV club was going to film our final performance.

In a nod to the individualized roles that American spectators preferred, Ms. Shaw was developing a solo. Pieter was the honeybee courting the collective flower. He would dive down in the water, skirting our kicking feet, holding his breath so prodigiously he scared Ms. Shaw. Pieter's most impressive feats were performed far below the water's surface, and for his skill to register with spectators, they needed to happen on top. "Think of the surface as a screen," Ms. Shaw begged. "You're only on camera there." But Pieter wasn't interested in being a star. He dove down to the bottom of the pool and waited Ms. Shaw out, arms crossed, blowing bubbles up to the surface.

The student leader, an all-state swimmer accepted early to Dartmouth, was in charge while Ms. Shaw choreographed in the big pool. He was flirting with the girl who didn't think she belonged in the piss pool. "I can too do a butterfly!" she cooed at the senior leader. "Watch me!" So when the Transylvaniess scraped her toes across the slimy tiles at the bottom of the piss pool, when she slipped and her head went under, when her pale skin started to shimmer blue and her arms, instead of flailing, seemed to rotate in the water with the grace of a bird on the wing, a real inspiration for synchronized swimming if Ms. Shaw had been watching, the senior leader didn't notice.

We did. We screamed, but most of us who could have helped were in the big pool learning to think of ourselves as petals of an immense flower, trying not to kick Pieter in the head or to kick Pieter in the head as he swam through our feet, depending on our tendencies. In his watery lair, Pieter heard the cries for help. He crossed the pool, swimming underwater at a pace that would have made him a recruit for the swim team if he hadn't been so contrary.

Just as the senior leader was about to begin CPR on the Transylvaniess' limp, blue body strewn across the checkered tile edge of the piss pool's shallow end, Pieter pushed the senior leader away. He cradled the Transylvaniess' head in his lap. Pinching her nose back, he began the CPR kiss. It was as if all the breaths he hadn't taken underwater were now being expelled into her, as if he'd been angering Ms. Shaw on purpose because he knew he would have to exchange his breathing for someone else's.

When she revived, she revived all at once. Her eyes shot open as if they were attached to mechanical wires. She started breathing through her nose, puffs of steam that turned to mist in the wet air. Her jaw opened wide as her neck twisted her head to the side, breaking Pieter's kiss. We gasped as her fangs sunk into his neck. While we watched her drink, both of their bodies turned the same pale, fishy color, the Transylvaniess losing her mermaid blue, Pieter losing his blotches, his freckles, until he turned into something as marbled as a Renaissance statue, relaxed in the pose of the Dying Gaul. His forehead was smooth as stone.

Ms. Shaw and the senior leader used all their strength together to pull the Transylvaniess off Pieter. The Transylvaniess snarled, turning her teeth to the senior leader. It took five of us to restrain her. Ms. Shaw had to call for security guards to drag her to the office. The Transylvaniess kept calling for Pieter all the way down the hall, in the loudest, clearest voice we'd ever heard her use, a voice that rang over the bell.

Pieter woke up at the bell, groggily rubbing his eyes and the marks on his neck, a purple bruise encircling two precise incision points. For all we knew, Pieter and the Transylvaniess had been performing this act for weeks in private, and the only difference was that this time they'd had an audience. He said he felt fine. Ms. Shaw insisted the senior leader escort him to the nurse's office. At Evanston Hospital, they bandaged him and kept him overnight. When Reilly visited him, Pieter said he felt fine.

We wanted to know what happened next to the Transylvaniess, and to Pieter, but they slipped out of our surveillance. The Transylvaniess was suspended. Ms. Shaw canceled the filming of the synchronized swimming routine, refocusing the rest of the swim unit on pool safety, CPR, and swimming endurance tests. Pieter didn't come back to school. His parents transferred him to Roycemore, the private school for kids too sensitive for E.T.H.S. Reilly didn't want to be friends with him anymore. Pieter had traded his Afrikaans accent for a fake British one.

The Korean said the Transylvaniess moved to Morton Grove after her suspension. The vampires had always had a garden back in Transylvania, and had been saving up to get out of Evanston and their apartment. The Korean wanted to visit her, but couldn't figure out how to get to Morton Grove by public transportation.

People were always disappearing: shifting custody, doing stints at the Audi Juvenile Home, in and out of Catholic school, staying with relatives in the city, simply dropping out. Our class was a fraction of the size it was when we started as freshmen, back when we'd all been tripped by the upperclassmen together. Unless they'd been with us since kindergarten, we tried not to think about it.

We knew the Transylvaniess a long time ago. During the Cold War. Before Mandela was released. Before Ceausescu was shot on Christmas Day. Before Latvia became independent. When Pinochet was in power in Chile. When the bombs went off in Belfast. Synchronized swimming had just become an Olympic sport. We thought that world was going to last forever. When it didn't, we were surprised, but not the Transylvaniess. She knew nothing lasts. What we didn't know was that she was a sign of things to come.

Only Eastern Europeans stroll the promenade in winter. There we are, cheap fur hats and nylon parkas, arm and arm sliding over the ice. The fancy couples shepherd tiny yapping dogs, sometimes carrying them to keep them from getting lost in snowdrifts, shouting when the dogs' pointy snouts root up something nasty in the snow. Lake Michigan looks like a sea, but it isn't. There isn't a salty air, just a fishy one, although in winter even that tang is long gone. You can't use the lake to get anywhere you want to go.

Nastya Ciorici was one of us. You could spot that from down the beach: her skinny ass under her short coat, her gliding strides, the fact that she didn't wear sneakers even on the warmer, slushy days, but always her black boots with one heel ungluing, flapping in the wind. Close up, there was no doubt of her origins: her limp, light hair framing her pumpkin head, her high, almost Asian cheekbones, her knob of a chin. The final proof: she never smiled at strangers. Indeed, none of us did.

But she was different from us because she was always alone. We went out two by two, as if we were lining up for Noah's Ark to take us back to Constanza, Odessa, St. Petersburg, Split, Gdansk, whatever port would have us. Even the recently arrived found somebody, someone who spoke their language or would pretend to.

Nastya walked alone, even when Diana and I invited her to join us. She smiled grimly, only on the right side of her face where her chicken pox scars were. She knew us from the Granville Arms where we all lived; she couldn't treat us like strangers. She said she had things to think about. When we pressed, she said she simply wasn't in the mood. She marched in the opposite direction, toward the city's boxy towers splitting through the branches of the naked trees, her heel slapping the pavement.

Diana knew a good, cheap shoe repairman right here in Edgewater, a Chinese with a shop below the el, but for spite we decided not to tell Nastya about him. It wasn't very satisfying, because she would never know. Not unless we staged an elaborate scenario where we unraveled our own boots, made sure she saw us in the ruined pairs, and then appeared before her, everything A-okay. Diana wanted to try it, but how would I get the time? I worked seventy hours a week as nanny to Baby Madeline and studied English every chance I got.

The next Sunday, dreary and rainy, we invited ourselves over to Nastya Ciorici's apartment in the Granville Arms. The elevator was down. We had to walk up to the tenth floor. No problem. It reminded us of home. Nastya didn't smile when she let us in. We took off our shoes, but she didn't have extra slippers to offer us. We slid to her kitchen in our stocking feet. "I was working on a paper," she said. "That's due tomorrow."

Diana shrugged. She picked up a glass from the counter and watered Nastya's shriveled philodendron. I sat down at the table and tried to read her paper, but it was in French. Nastya put the kettle on. It was battered, red with white polka dots.

Nastya's apartment was a studio, same as mine, but she divided the kitchen from the bedroom with bookshelves stuffed with creamy Gallimard editions. "You've read all these?" Diana asked, dragging her index finger across the spines. She showed off the dust to me, but Nastya didn't see.

Nastya sighed loudly, a bit too theatrically for my tastes. So she was busy? I only had Sundays off. "The program is rigorous. It's not like Bucharest. You don't just show up for exams. You have to keep up with the readings. Also, I teach two classes of introductory French. The students are stupid."

Nastya spooned out the tea leaves into cracked mugs that looked like they'd been stolen from a university cafeteria. A Romanian university cafeteria, too, not the fancy Northwestern up in Evanston where Nastya went, where they probably drank only espresso in miniature cups imported from Italy.

Diana asked, "You ever have time to read Romanian books? You're a mademoiselle now?"

Nastya sighed again. "The Romanian books are on the other side. Some Russian, too. German. English, on the bottom shelf." She cut up a mealy apple and the dried husk of days-old cake for us. "I'm sorry I'm out of sugar," she told me.

I shrugged. I reached for my mug to warm my hands on it. The Granville Arms was somewhat lacking in heat.

Diana pulled out the folding chair and sat on it gingerly.

"Lemon?" asked Diana.

"No."

"Honey?"

"No."

"Milk?"

"Let me see," Nastya replied. In the drawer next to the sink, she rustled up some dented plastic containers of half-and-half.

"Ah," said Diana. She pulled the tab off with her perfectly manicured crimson nails and poured, each movement as delicate as a princess. Lady Di, Diana's husband Nicu called her. Not the American pronunciation, Lady Die, which of course is sadly what happened to Princess Di. No, the Romanian pronunciation is Lady Dee, delightful and delicious. We watched the cloud of cream sink down into her tea. She blew on it and took a sip. She said, "So your Russian's that good? You read Chekhov in Russian?"

"I went to a Russian lycée in Chisinau. I write better in French and Russian than I do in Romanian." Nastya tapped her fingers against her mug. Her laptop was closed shut on the table at my elbow, but her documents would be in Russian or French. Maybe even her e-mail wasn't in Romanian. Nastya gulped down her tea and stared at her ceiling. There was a watermark flowering above the stove.

Nastya was Moldovan, Bessarabian to be exact, from the other side of the Prut, the side that had been part of the Soviet Union. Some people, like Diana, might hold that against her, but I didn't. I didn't see any signs of Russian mafia in her, that nouveau riche chic, the brassy dyed hair, the short, tight skirts and stilettos of mistresses and whores. Nastya wasn't pushy, like Bessarabians are. She was shy and lonely. She was waiting for us to come to her, instead of demanding our friendship. Her Romanian accent, instead of the usual garbled mess from over the Prut, was lovely. I could hear a hint of the French.

I took a slice of apple to be polite and chewed it leisurely. Diana pried apart the stale cake with the plastic fork Nastya handed her. Diana's nostrils were furled. It was the look her husband Nicu had named "the Lady Di."

"More tea?" asked Nastya.

"Yes, please," responded Diana. She speared the cake bits with the fork tines.

Nastya put the kettle on again. She leaned back on the counter, folding her arms and crossing her legs as she watched us. "I'm sorry I don't have anything else to offer you," she said, taking a deep breath. "When I'm writing, I don't eat, just tea and toast. It helps me focus when I'm on a tight deadline, such as today."

Really, Nastya sounded like Bucharest, like a news announcer, and in fact, that's where she studied before she came to Chicago. Diana was herself from Bucharest, but I was from a village in Oltenia. We talk funny there. We use a past tense that has dropped out everywhere else. It is a nostalgic tense. I was looking for somebody in Chicago from Oltenia, so that I could relax with someone in the language I dreamt in.

"Sundays, you'll walk with us," announced Diana.

Nastya nodded. She was staring at her laptop, bereft. She must be thinking that her laptop had been her only friend, cold computer comfort in Chicago, and now she could spend her time with these two kind girls from home. How quickly one's fate changes.

"We'll stop by at noon." Diana stood up. She used the top page of the paper to scoop up the crumbs on the table.

"May I use the bathroom?" I asked Nastya.

Nastya nodded again, her eyes on Diana washing out the mugs at the sink.

I knew exactly where it was; my unit was a mirror image of Nastya's. I passed the nest of her bed, a futon mattress with a tangle of blankets and pillows. A tabby cat should be sleeping there, a paw tucked over his nose, but the Granville Arms didn't allow pets.

On the windowsill, above the mattress, Nastya had two framed photos and an icon arranged in a triptych. In the center was a color snapshot of a dwarfish baba with Nastya's chin perched on a stool, a squinting Nastya looming behind her, another Nastya in ropy schoolgirl braids, a slight, pale boy Nastya, squeezing her hand. A grape arbor framed them, and the whole photo had an eerie green glow to it from the leaves shot through with light.

The picture on the left was a black and white headshot of Nastya on her first day of school, balancing a gigantic white bow on her hair, her hands folded and her head cocked at attention. She was not smiling. School was serious. Here was the attitude that carried her from the village of Vorniceni to Chisinau to Bucharest to Northwestern.

The icon was the Virgin Mary with the baby Jesus and baby John the Baptist on her lap. John and Jesus had none of the roundness of real infants, but were angry, flat, little men. A tear brushed the Virgin's cheek.

The medicine cabinet was empty except for three lone aspirins in a bottle that had lost its label. On the bathtub's edge, there was a thick brush full of Nastya's thin gold hairs, as if she were trying to build a kitten. The towels on the rack were threadbare. I kicked against a pile of *New Yorker* magazines in the corner, warped by water. Had she been reading them in the bath? Ah, Nastya, an intellectual, an *American* intellectual.

As I washed my hands with her sliver of cheap, astringent soap, I could hear Diana calling, "Come on, Marina." I ducked back into the entryway, tripping on Nastya's boots lined up at the door.

Diana kissed Nastya goodbye on both cheeks while I pulled on my shoes. "I'm sure your paper will be an excellent one," I whispered in Nastya's ear.

Nastya didn't kiss us back, only pecked at the air. She backed away into her apartment, pushing her boots back in place with her slippered foot. "Do come again," she called after us.

We decided Diana's cousin Marcel would be perfect for

Nastya Ciorici. Didn't he have a French name? Plus, he was Romanian-American, so if she married him, she could get a Greencard. He was a real estate agent. Diana was his receptionist, her husband Nicu his contractor. Marcel was over thirty, and on his own, drawn to flashy American girls with blonde hair and oversized purses they treated as pets. If Nastya married Marcel, she could quit teaching the stupid American students, send more money home. She could get a kitten. She could use his fluffy towels that puffed up when you pulled them out of the linen closet. She could eat whatever she wanted from his brushed steel refrigerator.

Diana had introduced me to Marcel immediately after I met her at Truman Community College's free language classes. The first break, we'd smoked a cigarette together and Diana complained about how stupid the rest of the students were. Her English was already pretty good. She particularly disliked the Chinese and the Africans. "If they can't get their fat tongues around English, why did they have to come here?" I was shivering. She lent me her gloves. When I tried to give them back, she insisted I keep them. She had Marcel pick us up from Truman in his BMW with the heated seats.

Because I was only free Sundays, I tagged along to Marcel's open houses. I would run my hands along the marble counters and turn the jet faucets on and off. When I was growing up, we didn't have running water, and when Marcel looked at me, no matter how smart Diana had managed to rig me up, I knew Marcel saw the village behind me: cows coming home, plums in the fruit press for next year's brandy, the gossiping line at the well.

Marcel wanted me to go out Saturday nights, but I said I was too tired. After a week of Baby Madeline clinging to me with her sticky, chubby hands, Madeline's mother upset when Madeline refused to let go of me while I got ready to go home, I needed to be somewhere that was mine. Saturday nights, I wanted to stay in, smoke the cigarettes I couldn't have around Madeline, fall asleep watching something on TV if I could keep the rabbit ears steady.

But Nastya would say yes to dinner. She needed a good meal in her belly. Unfortunately, whenever we knocked on Nastya's door at noon on Sunday, she didn't answer. She must have been at the library, or attending a lecture, maybe tutoring some of the more stupid students.

Once I ran into her at the mailboxes. She smiled at me as she shuffled through her mail, digging for the purple Moldovan stamps. She asked me to join her for a coffee at Metropolis, but when I said I'd call Diana on her cell, Nastya remembered an appointment to meet with colleagues to discuss Flaubert.

On Easter Saturday, we knocked on Nastya Ciorici's door. Sfinta Maria was difficult to reach by public transportation, so it was a real kindness of Diana to think of Nastya and me. We could see light streaming out from underneath Nastya's door. Diana didn't stop banging until Nastya opened it.

"Oh. It's you," said Nastya. She seemed tired, her eyes puffy, her hair disheveled.

Diana clicked a heel on the threshold. She said, "You're coming to Easter vigil. To Sfinta Maria. But we've got to go quickly-quickly; Marcel is waiting for us downstairs."

There was someone behind her sitting in the kitchen, paging through the creamy Gallimards. Nastya said, "We were planning to walk over to the Greek Orthodox church over on Bryn Mawr. St. Andrew's? It's such a beautiful night. Perhaps you would like to join us instead?"

I brushed past Nastya without taking my shoes off,

tracking dust across her carpet. It didn't look like she vacuumed regularly anyway. In the kitchen, I reached for a mug drying on the rack and filled it with tap water, turning to gaze upon Nastya's guest, a courtly little brown gentleman with his nose in her French papers. He hurried to stand up once he saw me.

"This is Absalom," Nastya said in English. "Absalom, these ladies are Marina and Diana. My neighbors in the Granville Arms."

"Pleased to meet you," said Absalom. He was wearing some sort of linen pajamas. The wrinkles had been ironed out. By Nastya? She was touching him, her hand resting on his shoulder. He smiled a tight little smile underneath his pencil mustache. He had the big, blinking round eyes of Ethiopians, eyes that seemed to rattle in his head.

Diana called out, in staccato Romanian, "But you're not Greek. You're Romanian. Or do you speak Greek, too?"

Nastya responded in English, "I guess, maybe because of going to Russian services in Chisinau, Orthodox is Orthodox for me. I don't care what language the priest speaks." She rubbed her hand across Absalom's back.

Absalom took her hands in his. He said, "It's good to be with people from home sometimes."

I could see Diana wincing at the door. Bessarabia wasn't her home. Diana taking up Nastya was a kind of charity.

Nastya hesitated, glancing at me and back at Absalom. "But the service at St. Andrew's?"

"We'll go some other time."

"But it's Easter!"

"There will be other Easters." He walked Nastya to the door and helped her put her coat on, holding out the sleeves. She left the top button unbuttoned. He buttoned it, then rummaged through a drawer for a scarf. As Nastya buckled her boots, I waited for Absalom to find his coat, to cross the threshold with us, but once he wrapped the red silk scarf around Nastya's slender neck, puffing out her fair hair to frame her face, he retreated back to the kitchen to settle into the folding chair and resume his reading.

"Come on, Marina," said Diana, pulling me through the door. As the elevator's cage closed, none of us said anything. We stared straight ahead. Diana kept hitting her heels on the floor.

"Did you get something stuck on them?" I asked her.

"No."

We slid into the back seat, Diana first, me in the middle, then Nastya. Marcel flipped through the satellite radio channels, looking for jazz. Diana, arms folded, breathed heavily through her nose, staring angrily out the window at the storefronts and apartment buildings we passed, as if Chicago would never do, as if she'd like to buy it all up, raze it and build a better Bucharest. Nicu snored in the passenger seat.

Nastya asked me, "What was your favorite thing about Easter when you were little?"

"Oh, the food!" I blurted. "Helping my grandmother prepare it. Smelling it cooking while I slept. And eating until I fell asleep again. What about you?"

"Staying up late," Nastya whispered. "Staying up late with my friends in front of the church, waiting for the bread to be blessed, even though we were too short to see anything. I thought maybe in cities, people stayed up late like that outside all the time, not just on Easter. That we were very cosmopolitan, for that one night."

"What are you two gossiping about?" asked Marcel.

"Don't even bother asking," Diana told him. "It's all too

boring. If you miss Easter at home so much, why don't you both go back?"

"Maybe I will," Nastya said. She stared at Diana fiercely. "Maybe you will?" she asked me.

"I think about it," I admitted. "But what would I do? They need the money I send."

"Once Romania joins the European Union?" Nastya pressed.

"Ah. Well, then."

"Moldova's never going to join the European Union," Nastya said. "Never."

"How do you know that? You're a political scientist, too?" Diana asked. She lit a cigarette, even though she knew Marcel had American ideas against smoking indoors.

Marcel said, "Diana. What's with you today? Come on." Diana rolled down the window to ash. Marcel told Nastya, "Try to be more optimistic. You're in the States now. We know things get better here. All you have to do is drink a Coca Cola! Just kidding. How do you know that Moldova won't join?"

"Marcel, have you ever been to Moldova?"

"No. Of course not."

"I thought so." Nastya folded her arms.

We pulled up to the church, surrounded by little pink houses with tiny yards, grills, birdbaths, statues of the Virgin, and other accessories. "Why, it looks like the suburbs!" said Nastya.

"What's wrong with that?" said Diana. "I'd love to have a house here. I'm not living in the Granville Arms forever."

"Portage Park is still affordable," added Marcel. "I could work some connections, Lady Di, if you want."

We had to park six blocks away. We were too late to get a good position inside Sfinta Maria, even up in the balcony.

Diana dragged Nicu alongside her. Nicu's left foot had gone to sleep in the car, and he was trying to stomp it out, but she wouldn't wait. Marcel escorted Nastya and me, but there wasn't room to walk three abreast. I kept track of them by watching Nastya's red scarf catch on other people's coats.

The priest's voice was scratchy, as if he had a permanent cold, but it wasn't any worse than back home. The choir was better. In my village, anyone who knew the words made up the choir, which meant my grandmother's friends singing loudly and off-key because they'd long since lost some of their hearing and any sense of pitch. Sfinta Maria was admirable in that they'd thrown up such a large church in such a short time, but there was something off about it. The walls were too white. Years of smoke and incense hadn't yellowed them yet. It made the icons flat. They wouldn't, the longer that you stared at them, rise off the walls and float around us, the way they did at home. But the biggest problem was that Sfinta Maria didn't smell old. It didn't smell hallowed. It didn't smell at all, and we didn't, either; all of us, recently arrived or Romanian-Americans, were using copious amounts of deodorant underneath our best clothes.

Diana tugged my arm. "We're not speaking," she said, glaring at Nicu's slouching form. "He's always like this on holidays."

"Like what?"

"A lump. A big, sleepy lump."

"He works hard!"

"So do I, but I wake up for Easter. Or Valentine's Day. Or New Year's. Or…"

"What's with you? Can't you see you're in a church?" hissed a tiny, angry baba grabbing at Diana's elbow.

"Excuse us," I said.

I refused to talk to Diana for the rest of the service, even when she whispered in my ear, "What do you think Marcel and Nastya are talking about? She's not good enough for him. Clearly her standards are low indeed, after what we saw her up to tonight. Consider Marcel again, Marina? I know you said he was like a brother, but maybe it's time to think of him as a very sexy brother. Who you aren't related to. With money. And a car with heated seats!"

The lights dimmed slowly, plunging us into midnight darkness. The candles held by the congregation were lit one by one. I let the hot wax run down my hands and peeled it off slowly. Nicu offered Diana and me each an arm, and we joined the procession walking around the church. The first time around, I could see Marcel and Nastya ahead of us. The second time around, Marcel was walking with a school friend, Nastya's scarf bobbing up near the front of the crowd. The third time around, she was swallowed up completely.

The beefy Portage Park neighbors watched us from their screened-in porches. Marcel said they always complained to the city, but it was only once a year. What was wrong with the Catholics, that they wanted their Easter indoors when the whole point was that it was finally spring and that truly, Christ has risen, *Christos a inviat*? The crowd had grown so large that there was no possibility of us fitting back into the church. We stood near the steps, sheltering our candles with cupped palms.

Diana wanted to wait for the bread to be blessed, but Marcel had an early appointment the next morning. I volunteered to look for Nastya, but Diana pointed out that we'd just have to look for me, too. Nicu and I walked quietly to the car, Diana and Marcel ahead of us chattering about who was coming to Easter dinner.

When Nastya nonchalantly appeared, Diana greeted her, "*Christos a inviat.*"

Nastya answered, "*Adeverat, a inviat,*" truly, he has risen, but without any inflection.

We were silent on the way back to the Granville Arms. Marcel found Coltrane's "A Love Supreme," and that was the finale to our Easter. As we got out in front of our building, Marcel raced out of his seat to circle his car. He kissed Diana on both cheeks, shook Nicu's hand, squeezed mine as I was already moving past him toward the door, Nastya ahead of me. She didn't turn back to say goodbye to Marcel, not even when he called to her that she had dropped her scarf.

He handed it to Diana, who handed it to me. I passed it to Nastya when we stood together boxed into the caged elevator. Nastya murmured thanks and wrapped it through her fingers. We got off at the fifth floor, leaving Nastya to ascend alone.

Was Absalom waiting for her? Had he gone to the Greek Orthodox church alone? Or was he still in the Granville Arms, thumbing through her books, readying tea and toast for her return?

The next Saturday evening, I ran into Nastya Ciorici in line at Devon Market. "You," she said, smiling warily, only on the right side with the chicken pox tracing their constellation across her profile. She did not say, "*Christos a inviat,*" which she should have for forty days after Easter. She shifted awkwardly against her basket.

We walked home together because we were going in the same direction, no point pretending we weren't. The fruit trees were heavy with pink and white blossoms, the Americans wore sandals as they passed us by, but Nastya was still wearing her boots with the loose heel. Nastya's bags were cutting into her wrists, and I offered to carry one of hers. In that moment, as the plastic handle slid from her hand into mine, we became a kind of friends.

The petals from the trees caught in our hair and on the bag's folds. It reminded me of home. "It's spring," I told her.

"Oh, I'm so tired of snow I could cry," she said. "It whistles in my apartment when the wind is up. Does it do that in yours?"

It did. I'd wanted to hope it was my imagination. I nodded.

She asked, "Do you have any plans for the weekend?" Such an American question! Northwestern had taught her well.

Diana had asked me to join her and Nicu and Marcel, with some of their Romanian friends, at Moody's Pub for a drink. I'd said no. But the appeal of Moody's was its outdoor beer garden. It was like being in Europe, drinking out on a terrace and running into all the people you know. "Some people are going to Moody's tonight," I said softly. Nastya had to lean in to hear me. "Nothing special. Just a chance to talk Romanian."

Nastya rested her bags on the curb. "Including Diana?" she asked shrewdly.

"Yes, but not just Diana."

"Including Diana's obnoxious yuppie cousin?"

"Yes. But it might be fun."

"Fun," said Nastya, twisting the word in her mouth. "Fun." She wrapped her bags around her wrist and started to walk again. "Absalom has to work. He's a waiter at the Ethiopian Diamond. Have you ever been there? The food is so interesting. I was going to read tonight."

"Maybe some other time then." I wasn't sure I wanted to go myself. Marcel's friends were all citizens or working on it, constantly calling their immigration lawyers with their cells to complain into voicemail. They were quite pleased with themselves, listing their most recent purchases of espresso machines and laptops and their elaborate travel plans to California and Arizona. The women glanced in their compact mirrors after each sip, pursing their lips to check their long-lasting make-up, and the men were always trying to look down the shirts of the women they hadn't come with. In fact, spending time with them made me realize that Nicu, Diana and Marcel weren't so bad at all.

We'd reached the door of the Granville Arms, but neither one of us went inside. We put the bags down, careful not to lean against the terracotta tile façade. It left a chalky residue on clothes that was hard to get off if you were washing by hand. The building, a bulky Moorish fantasy masking the cramped apartments within, with spiraling columns like minarets and false balconies every other floor, made no sense in Chicago. I'd wondered if immigrants like us were drawn by its incongruity and not just the low rents.

Nastya pointed to Metropolis down the street and said, "That's where Ab and I met. We were both reading French novels. I went over to talk to him. In French. At Northwestern, the students don't like to talk in French unless they're from France. Or Lebanon. I don't know, they're scared of mistakes or their accent or something. But I like to speak French."

I told her, "I like to speak Romanian on the weekends."

She didn't react to it the way she would have if Diana said it. Instead, she calmly picked up her bags again. "Okay. I'll come, for a little while. It's too nice to stay indoors."

Nastya met us later than she'd promised. Unfortunately, Marcel was already drunk, Diana tipsy, Nicu ready to pass out, Marcel's friends frantic on their cells. The ashtray was jammed with butts. Our table was covered in a blue, smoky air. Hovering above us were the new leaves on the trees, shimmering in the moonlight and the artificial blaze of the street lamps. Beyond the trees were the bright tracks of planes wending their way to O'Hare. There was the scent of linden in the air, and I could almost forget where I was.

While Nastya leaned to kiss my cheek, Marcel stole a plastic chair from another table. It scratched at the cement as Nastya squeezed it in between me and Nicu, not me and Diana.

Diana said, "*Christos a inviat.*"

Nastya offered a jaunty little wave as she tried to duck underneath the cloud of smoke coming from Nicu.

"What? They don't say *adeverat, a inviat* anymore in Bessarabia? Or they don't say it at Northwestern? Which is it, Nastya? Do tell us." She gave Nastya the Lady Di.

"Oh, they say it at home. I just don't. I guess I'm not as traditional as you are, Diana."

Nicu beamed at Nastya, showing the silver-capped tooth Diana liked him to hide. "Might I buy you a drink?" he asked.

We ordered another pitcher of sangria. Nastya requested a Moody Blue Burger, rare. Blue cheese oozed over her paper plate, turning it translucent. She scooped the cheese up with her fries. She urged me to have some fries, and Diana, too. Diana took one, pinching it between her fingers, examining it.

Marcel said, "I always think the Moody Blue sounds like a jazz tune."

"Jazz," said Diana. "If I have to hear about jazz tonight, I'll scream."

Nicu asked, "If the Germans founded this part of Chicago, why aren't beer gardens on every corner?"

"There should be. Let's build them," said Marcel. "It will be our next real estate project."

Diana said, "The Poles are everywhere, but they didn't rebuild the cellar bars of Krakow."

Marcel said sadly, shaking his head, "Everybody wants to drink American once they get here. All that crappy piss-water Budweiser. Watching sports on their big TVs."

"But never football," said Nicu. "Real football." He stretched, drooping one arm around Nastya's chair. She leaned forward.

While Marcel and Nicu argued about football, and Diana gossiped with the other wives, Nastya told me she'd never wanted to come to the States. "I wanted to be a bus ride away. A bus ride from hell, but a bus ride just the same. France would have been perfect, but the French know French. I should have chosen Germany, even if the funding wasn't as good. I should have realized I'd be stranded *here*. Until my research year in France. After my preliminary exams. I'm counting the days. When was the last time you were home?"

"I haven't been home. Every time I start pricing tickets, somebody needs a surgery. Or my grandmother's goat dies. When I won the Greencard lottery, I felt unlucky even though everyone envied me. I'd signed up with my ex-boyfriend on a dare. At home, I taught the second form. My parents are teachers, too. But my English will never be good enough to teach here. Diana says to try something I would have never gotten to do at home. Become some kind of businesswoman. But all I want to do is what I did before."

I don't know how much of our confessions Diana overheard, but she began to peal with bright and tinny laughter. "Everyone should have your problems, Marina. What I wouldn't give to be free of Nicu and find a better match for myself here. I mean, look at him." Nicu was flipping fries through Marcel's salt-and-pepper-shaker goal, keeping score on a napkin with blobs of ketchup and mustard.

"And you? Nastya who wants her bus ride back home so badly? You're getting a degree from a famous university, and they're paying for it. All you have to do is show up. Instead of dating an American, you pick yourself an immigrant, a black one at that. Would it be possible to more willfully dash your chances than you already have? Why can't both of you spend more time thinking about what you *could* do?" Diana's lips puckered up as she talked, revealing the crannies her lipstick hadn't been able to reach. "You disgust me, both of you."

Nastya protested, "I *am* thinking about what I can do. Ab is the best thing that's happened to me since I came to Chicago."

"Your best thing," asked Diana, "is Ab? The little man in your apartment?"

I tugged at the shirtsleeve of Diana's peasant blouse, newly fashionable, one she'd purchased at Marshall Field's, decidedly not from home. "Diana!" I said. "Coptics are practically Orthodox." I could hear the whine in my voice, the same as when I asked my mother to explain to me why my grandmother needed a new goat when she could buy goat milk from her neighbors instead. As Baby Madeline's voice did when she begged me to stay over.

Diana lit a cigarette from Nicu's pack. Nastya's attention was already elsewhere, her eyes on her watch. Absalom must be done with his shift by now. Diana uttered smoothly, "My goodness, Nastya. What would your mother say? Why didn't you just stay in Chisinau and marry one of the Africans studying at the Agricultural Institute? You didn't need to come all the way to Chicago to find a black." She rubbed out her cigarette.

Nicu mumbled, "They can be your waiter, your taxi driver, but not your boyfriend." He shook his head solemnly.

"Come on, guys," said Marcel. "This is America. You go to school with all kinds, work with all kinds. You have to"—he switched to English midstream—"deal. Deal, Lady Di. Don't you remember Princess Diana kissing and hugging all those people with AIDS? And without legs?"

"Look. Nobody's very happy about *him* being with a white woman. Let alone from a country they've never heard of. He's from a vast and ancient culture, and we're just peasants," said Nastya. "That's right, Diana. I said *peasants*."

"I'm from Bucharest!" she cried. Her eyes and nostrils narrowed. She wasn't regal. She'd moved on to feral, like the Bucharest street dogs with their red eyes.

Nastya stood up to go. "He's from Addis! He was studying to be a doctor. *And he speaks French.*"

"A monkey speaking French in his little monkey suit. You're going to smell like one of them, Nastya, and your children will, too."

"Like we're some great prize!" I protested. Nastya stared at me, her eyes wrinkling behind the shelf of her high cheekbones.

"But you are," said Nicu, bewildered. "Prizes. You're lovely, all of you."

In the corner of the garden near the gate, there was a gathering of Ethiopians. Absalom stood among them, greeting them one by one, but he kept looking back into the garden for Nastya. She waved and went off to him, her heel slapping, but he insisted on being led back to our table so he could greet us. He nodded to everyone and bowed slightly to Diana and me.

Marcel and Nicu froze their game, fries in gluey piles. Diana wouldn't look at Ab, as if he were too short for her to ultimately make eye contact. Marcel's friends shifted in their plastic chairs, worried about the black at their table. Was he panhandling? Would he say something horribly vile to them in his sophisticated slang? Would they be shamed in front of their wives if they didn't take some kind of definitive, irretrievable action?

Absalom focused his huge eyes on me. "Hello, Marina, Nastya's new friend," said Absalom musingly, chewing a little on the tip of his mustache. "Marina. An old name meaning *of the sea*. The mermaid amongst us."

I smiled wide at him, as if I were trying to stop Baby Madeline from crying. Nastya didn't care. She was already tugging at his arm, dragging him away from Diana's contempt, but from me, too. She stared Diana down, her chin jutted out, her cheekbones so sharp you could cut yourself on them.

"Nastya's name," Marcel said in English, "is just nasty." He giggled, appraising her from the ancient boots to her blonde hair, real blonde hair without a hint of darkness at the roots, her red chicken pox scars. "I mean that in the best possible way. Like in a rap song."

With that, Nastya and Absalom left our lives forever. Nastya was practically racing for the gate, but Absalom made them stop at the Ethiopian table, where I imagine they had to endure a similar set of reactions from people Absalom knew, because they didn't stay at that table any longer than they had at ours, and Nastya banged the gate as they left so loudly we could hear it echo in our corner.

I didn't run after them. I didn't follow Nastya and Absalom out into Chicago and away from Moody's Little Romania. I didn't tell Diana off, but I didn't make nice with her, either, ask her whether she'd gotten the peasant blouse on sale. I sat there sipping my sangria until all that was left was the sad, drunken fruit hugging the bottom of the glass. I tried to imagine a sea breeze from the lake, but there wasn't anything but the cloying lindens.

When Marcel offered me a ride home, I took it, even though he was drunk. When he wanted to come up, I let him. I didn't feel like being alone. He was quick and efficient and fell asleep instantly. Afterwards, I didn't like Marcel any better, although I didn't like him less, either. In Romania, I might have known someone like him. A friend of my pushy cousins in the city, perhaps, someone I'd see on holidays and then forget again. Certainly no one I'd sleep with, or someone who would want to sleep with me.

I sat on the edge of my bathtub, wondering where Nastya and Absalom had gone. A party for people like them? An all-night cafe for French-speakers? A walk on the beach, ducking into shadows to avoid the hovering cop cars?

I crawled back to bed, angling my spine and pulling in my feet to make sure not to touch Marcel. In the morning, he was gone. He'd left a note asking me to meet him at an open house in Uptown, that we needed to talk, but I didn't go. I knew what Americans meant when they said they needed to talk. I'd twisted my rabbit ears enough to glean that kind of information from my television.

•

The promenade is crowded now that it's warm. It's not just the Eastern Europeans anymore, but everyone. I don't mind walking by myself. I don't walk with Diana. I duck her calls. I don't answer when she pounds on my door. It's strange, but I miss Nicu more than her. Marcel, of course, never called, not that I cared much. Nastya was worth the bunch of them.

On the promenade, there are others walking alone, and I can pretend I belong to a clump of mothers pushing their jogging strollers with the triangular wheels, to the gossiping girls kicking their feet on the graffitied boulders at the water's edge, to the magnificently muscled Labrador running past me on the path, his leash dragging behind him. If I had roller blades, or a bike, I'd be getting exercise. If I had sneakers, I could pretend to jog.

I keep thinking of what Absalom said to me, if I'm some kind of mermaid. Diana always could smell the fishiness on me, how much I wanted to go home. I might not get my land legs. I might stay here, at the edge of something instead of in it. At the edge of the water, you can fall off and be lost forever. When you can't see the lake on foggy days, it isn't water but an abyss. You could walk out there and be nowhere, into a damp and peaceful cold.

Once in the crowd at the promenade, I saw Nastya Ciorici. She wore a sun-dress patterned in cherries, the kind you find in a second-hand shop but can never get its stains out, and plastic flip flops a size too big.

She stopped to admire the view of the city at the promontory. As she scanned the path ahead of her, shielding her eyes from the sun and frowning, I thought she was looking straight at me, but then I realized she hadn't seen me at all.

CHILDREN IN THE TIME OF DUST

Once it was dirt. It was in the ground, it was the ground, it stayed at our feet. Now we call it Dust. It's in our hair, our eyes, our lungs, coating the house in film, whistling at the door for us to let it in. It lives in the whorls of our fingertips. It can't be washed away, not with soap or water, no matter how hard we scrub.

Every day we compiled a list of new metaphors for the Dust. It's like a curtain, a wall, a scrim, a screen, a death. I couldn't remember before the Dust, but my sister could. She had two years on me. She was four when the Dust came. We weren't sure which one of us was better at the Dust metaphors, because of what she could remember, because of what I couldn't. What do you remember before the Dust? I asked. She told me, You could see the world and touch it, press it, without a barrier between it and you. Everything was realer then.

It's the world, I said. That's what changed, the world isn't the same. It's the Dust, she said. If we could clean the Dust, the world would be back. We just have to scrape at it.

You're both right, and neither of you, said our mother.

It was the Dust Bowl, and we ate it. That was a cruel metaphor. There was nothing to eat that the Dust wouldn't get into, so that everything had the chalky taste of Dust. Soon, there wasn't anything to eat at all. The Dust suffocated the plants, a vine, a snake, a squeezer. The garden withered. The Dust choked the hens. They laid Dust and not eggs, and then nothing, not even when we brought them inside with us to roost in the kitchen in crates. We couldn't keep the Dust out, not even with quilts and patches for quilts tucked into the cracks and crannies of the house, at doors and windows. Not when we swept all day. We're Cinderellas, said my sister. That was ash and cinders, I told her. Not Dust.

We were children, girls, one bigger, one smaller. We slept in the same bed at night, curling in toward each other. In the day, we played out in the Dust, kerchiefs wrapped over our mouths. We played bandit. There wasn't anything to steal but our mother's old shoebox of stray buttons. And Dust, if you wanted to collect it in rusty tin cans and mason jars. We went to bed early because it wasn't worth it to try to light lamps against the Dust. In the morning, we drew grimy pictures on the deposits across their windowpane.

When I got sick with the Dust pneumonia, they knew it would happen. It was only a matter of time. The little ones went first, and the old ones. Our grandfather went, and we'd expected our grandmother to go before I did. My father, when he left for the road, said goodbye to my grandmother and me like it was for forever, squeezing us close, wishing it was different. He didn't have enough money to take us with him. He needed to get a job first and send for us. We weren't sure we were going to see him again, either. He pecked my mother and my sister on the cheek and dashed for the door, ready to drive the Model-T before the Dust picked up again.

My mother stopped telling people my age when she was asked, willing me to grow older, willing me to grow out of the Dust. I lay on the bed, coughing Dust out of my lungs into dingy handkerchiefs, counting and sorting the buttons. There was a red one I wanted to keep, rubbing it between my fingers, rubbing the Dust off it. I wanted the red dress that would match that button. It was so red that even coated in Dust, the ruby would still shine through, the way that in paintings, blood looks all the more red when next to black. I hid the red button under my pillow. When nobody noticed it was gone, I slid it into the pillowcase itself. I could feel it, hard like a bone, under my ear as I slept, listening for my pulse to know I was still alive, listening for the Dust grating down the pane.

It was my sister's favorite, too, and the very next day after I hid it was when she took sick, when she couldn't find it in the shoebox, when she crawled around the corners and swept under the sofa, when she fretted because where could it go missing? Our home was small, two rooms downstairs, two rooms up. The Dust got it, she said, the Dust ate it. She started to cough. They laid her down next to me, my grandmother wetting her brow with a twisted rag. It turned black with the fever coming off her, and the Dust. That night, when everyone else was asleep, my sister's fretful breathing like static on the radio, I pushed the button under her pillow instead, but it was too late. The ruby button had exchanged my health for hers, and she, the girl who remembered before the Dust, was the one who died.

The tiny coffin, not much bigger than the crates for chickens. They'd had to use the box built for me, with some boards added to extend it. She only had a few inches on me. We'd wanted an open coffin because she was so pretty and we wanted to see her one last time, but in the end, my mother told the undertaker, keep my baby out of the Dust and close that box. I pushed the ruby button through the slats. Where did you find it? my mother asked. Oh, never mind, at least the Dust didn't get it.

The sky was bright the day of the funeral, so bright that the other towns in the county, the ones that didn't have funerals, had picnics. You could see the sky and it was blue, not gray-blue, but blue, like my sister's eyes, and the clouds weren't black-gray, but like clouds of chicken feathers, like the storybooks they tried to teach me to read from at the school, but that I didn't believe in because the stories weren't about Dust. It was a gift to bury our girl, my mother said, but then it wasn't. That day was the worst Dust storm we ever had.

We stood in the churchyard. The preacher was done, and they'd shoveled the Dust over the coffin, but to leave meant it was all done, that my sister was done, and nobody wanted to be the first to go. I saw it on the horizon, and tugged my mother's hand. She shushed me, and I tried to be quiet the way she wanted, but before I could compose myself to be good, everyone saw it and I didn't have to pretend anymore.

The black cloud rose up on the day of the funeral, the blackness of midnight descending upon us at noon, a cloud taller than the church and wider than the stretch of Main Street shops, a cloud that could more than engulf the town. We ran inside just before it hit. In the church, as we huddled on the pews, my grandmother said, Judgment Day, and nobody said, look on the bright side, the sunny side of life, life would be so sweet on the sunny side of the street. Like the Woody Guthrie song, we thought, So long, it's been good to know you. When the preacher cracked open the doors and pushed us out into daylight the next morning, it was as bright as the flames of hell. I hid under my mother's skirts. My grandmother cried without wiping the tears off her wrinkled face. They left a trail they carved out of the Dust.

My sister was my best friend and she was dead. At home, my grandmother had taken to her bed and all my mother would do was sweep. I needed her to tell me how to live once there wasn't Dust anymore, but maybe she needed me to tell her how to live in the Dust. All the babies were gone now, in our town, and most of the children younger than five. When I walked back and forth to school, on the days it was open, to sit and read with the other children, people rubbed my shoulders for good luck.

The day we buried my grandmother between my grand-father and my sister—we were running out of spots for the grave—was the day my father came back in the Model-T. When he couldn't find us at home, he drove to the church-yard. He wouldn't let my mother pack up the house or sweep one last time. We took the teakettle, the frying pan, the last chicken, and my grandmother's patchwork quilt. My mother asked me if I wanted to bring the buttons to play with in the back seat, but I told her I was too old for toys. I was six.

We drove out of the Dust and into the desert. What a relief it was. To be out of the Dust. The desert shimmered in soft, sunset colors, pinks and oranges, and when there was dust, it was that color, too, not our Dust but a pink, dusty crumble that was drier than anything. When we stopped at gas stations, I let it run through my fingers, like sand through an hour-glass. The attendants at the station kept warning my father about running out of water and gasoline, but he said our car was powered on Dust.

When we got to the edge of Los Angeles, and saw the oranges growing on the fields, like sun in trees, like you could grow sun, we cried and the desert air dried our tears for us. We drove closer to the cheap motor lodge where we had a room for a night until the cold-water flat my father had rented for us in Angel's Flight was available. To see that city, glass buildings shining green in the sun, was to have made it to Oz, and to ride the cable car at Angel's Flight was like flying. I'm a country girl at heart, my mother said, but I said I was never going back to Kansas.

When they asked me at school about Kansas, I wouldn't say a thing. When they said I was an Okie, I agreed. I'd rather be from Oklahoma, anywhere but the truth. They're so pink and innocent, like toys for babies, they who haven't lived through the Dust.

When *The Wizard of Oz* came out, when I was ten, I wouldn't go to see it. I wouldn't spend my nickels, not even to hear Judy Garland sing. You made me love you, and she did. I loved her. But I didn't want to see Kansas again. Even when my father wanted to take me as a treat, I didn't want to go. They made me go, my father and mother holding my hands, me between them without room for the ghost of my sister, the ghosts of my grandparents trailing behind, a treat before the school year started, me in my new plaid skirt, the white light of Los Angeles, the nodding palm trees, into the dark of the cinema and the movie I never want to see again, even though I watch it every year on television and will for the rest of my life.

It's too close to Dust. It's not just the black and white grainy world of Kansas, which looked right to me, when I thought of my first years of life I couldn't remember any color other than the red button and my sister's blue eyes, the faded patches of my grandmother's quilt, but also Oz, which was terrifying in its Technicolor. It still revealed a world gone wrong.

Kansas, where if you fall into the pen, the pigs will eat you. Who had a pig left by 1939? Why was Dorothy living with her aunt and uncle? Did the Dust take her people? Why didn't she have any brothers and sisters? How could Henry and Em pay for farmhands? Had they been exploiting others? Wasn't that left for Miss Gulch? Toto, that sooty puppy like personified Dust.

Then Oz. The town of stinted children. The yellow brick road like the desert highway we rode on. The poppies choked by the Dust. Your horse is a different color because Dust changes you. In the book, the Emerald City is only green because everyone wears green glasses. I've got Dust glasses and I see everything that way. Winged monkeys flying like a storm of dust across the prairie. The wizard, like our powerless preacher on Black Sunday. The dead witches, killed by a house, by water, like our destroyed grandmothers.

We can't go home again, and Oz isn't home. It's silly to try and make it so. The Dust is coming for them, too, those who dwell in Oz. The shining city built in a desert—it's calling out for Dust to come and claim it.

OLD MAIDS

My first love story didn't end well but I suppose it could have ended worse. That summer I wasn't a student anymore, but hadn't become a social worker yet either. I was visiting Anya that summer, Anya, who I loved better than anyone. Anya's grandmother told us, my first night in the village of Grinauti Raia, "The sky's blue like an evil eye charm up here. Here girls find husbands if they try."

She didn't grin at us with her toothless mouth, or assure us that we had a chance the way my own grandmother would have. She stared angrily at our tight black pants. Once we received our scholarships to attend Romania's oldest university in Iasi, the first things we country Moldovans learned were to wear the pants and take up smoking. The scholarships were supposed to be a gesture of friendship from the big Romanian-speaking country to its junior brother, former Soviet Moldova, but Anya and I couldn't help thinking it was for the Romanians to have someone to feel superior to when the Hungarians and Bulgarians looked down on them.

Blinking with her eyes of Grinauti Raia-blue, Anya's grandmother plucked the dead chicken splayed in her ample lap by feel alone. She said, "Romanians talk too fast. You can't tell when they're lying, but you know they're going to. At least you didn't bring home one of them. You'll have to work twice as hard. You're old maids now."

Anya was pacing across the kitchen while I watched uneasily. In the candlelight, I tried to see Anya's features in her grandmother's collapsing face. I knew Anya's face better than my own. Those Grinauti Raia eyes, that cobalt blue with the same intensity as the black eyes of gypsy girls. Peaked eyebrows, cheekbones edged high as if daring to cover the eyes, pimples at the bridge of the nose, smudges below her eyes from too many late nights. My own face in mirrors surprised me, always so clearly not Anya's. My blinking eyes like dingy bathwater, pudgy cheeks and lumpen chin, docile where I wanted to be fierce.

Anya swooped down and grabbed the chicken from her grandmother. She wrenched off feathers that floated across to me, hovering below my nose until I sneezed. The grandmother's one-eyed dog jumped after the feathers as they fell. Anya said, "I told you, I don't need a man."

"Sweep up the feathers, or you'll need a man—to protect you from me." She took back her chicken and slapped Anya's backside.

We didn't talk in my family like Anya's did. I looked at my hands to hide my discomfort. My nails were ragged from chewing them at the exams the week before. I swallowed the homemade wine the grandmother offered me.

Late that night, as we slid under the chilly sheets of the spare bed, Anya whispered, "Don't mind her."

"She's always like that?"

"She's waiting to die. All she does is pick weeds off my grandfather's grave and fight with the neighbors." She kissed my forehead. "Good night, sleepy Viorica."

As she rolled over, she lazily draped one arm over me. The arm was heavy settling around my waist. It was a weight I always welcomed. At the dormitory, all the Moldovan girls slept two by two because our stipends wouldn't pay for individual beds, but the truth was we needed the extra warmth in winter anyway. Anya and I had been bedmates for years. Soon it would all come to an end. As I breathed, the tiny hairs on her arm rippled. A mosquito buzzed in my ears, but I stayed still.

I couldn't bear to think about us being apart. I'd be an old maid if it meant we could be old maids together. At the university in our psychology courses, we'd read case studies about deviant women who desired each other. When I told Anya it sounded pleasant to live your life with a girlfriend, she laughed and said, "Don't worry, Viorica. We'll find you someone." I was beginning to realize that someone might not be her. I didn't think having a man would make me feel any less lonely.

·

In the morning, we picked cherries for the grandmother. She directed us from the shade of the grape arbor, the one-eyed dog panting at her feet. We stood on rickety wooden ladders, our heads encircled by the branches. The trees in the garden grew both the velvety sweet cherries and the glassy red sour ones. They slipped in and out of my hands. The undersides of the leaves were shot through with sunlight, and the sky was Grinauti Raia blue.

We scratched at mosquito bites, at the sweat running down our necks. First, we sang Pioneer songs from our childhood, comrades on picnics, raise high the red scarf! Then wedding songs, crying brides who didn't want to leave their mothers behind no matter how handsome the groom was, how tall with shoulders how wide.

Stray hairs of Anya's snuck out from under her kerchief. Her cheeks puffed in and out as she pulled off cherries at the top of the tree. "Of course you don't like heights," she said. My braids banged against my back as I reached for the lower branches. Anya grabbed at my hair, hissing, "I'm such a bad boy, aren't I?" until I had to tie the braids together to keep them out of her reach.

Anya said, "Hey, there's this local boy Evgeny Dobrescu. Except for the fact that he's ugly and can't dance, he might be perfect for you. Scratch my ankles, Viorica?"

"Your ankles are a bloody mess."

"Should I let Evgeny scratch them, then?"

"Yes, if he's anything like Sorin, or Cezar. For a student, you didn't study much."

"For a student, during what should be the best days of any girl's life, you were busy studying, little Miss Viorica." She spat cherry stones at me. They grazed the back of my head and fell to the ground.

I asked her, "Do you like red or dark best?"

"Always the one I'm eating right now. Sour for you, of course?"

"Always."

At the university, I had a reputation for being melancholy. I made up stories about sad love affairs to tell Anya. How he tried to hold my hand in church on Easter, how he died from pneumonia one horrible winter. In turn, Anya told me everything about Sorin and Cezar. I hated them, their beefy frames, their beady eyes, the money they had to spend on her. How could the jug I filled with wildflowers compare to their roses?

"Since you're already suffering, I wish you would scratch at my ankles. And rub my stomach, too. I've eaten too many cherries again." With her usual exploding grace, she jumped down and over to the outhouse. I followed, bringing down first my right foot to each rung, then my left foot to the same rung, careful to keep my place until I was on the ground again.

"Anya, I need to use it, too."

"Stop whining," she said. She banged open the door and left. I went in. The outhouse had gaping knotholes between the boards and an old history textbook in the corner for toilet paper. Even with the holes, the privacy was greater than at the university dormitory with the girls rushing in and out. There, the running water toilets stopped up more than half the time, and the water was off often anyway. I supposed soon I would be nostalgic even for that: the stink of my student days.

I wished I could learn to take less of what was offered me, to learn to eat only sour cherries and like it as my own grandmother had urged. As practice for how hard my life could be, she said. When I closed my eyes, I could see what the cherry trees must look like in April, the white blossoms dipped in pink against the metallic blue of Grinauti Raia. I imagined Anya as a child dancing underneath the branches, her grandmother clapping for her, petals dropping down on her as she spun, clinging to her upturned face and arms as if she were sprouting feathers, dancing faster, faster, with all the athletic power of Anya now.

When I came out, Anya dragged me back. "We thought we were going to have to call the police in after you, Viorica." I climbed back up the ladder and tried to focus on each cherry. The redness or darkness, the length of its stem, the curves and hollows of each one.

"Temptation is a sin," said the grandmother. "Eat less, pick more. Don't scratch."

In the evening we rode the bicycle with its broken brakes out to the lake where Anya's old classmates met to play cards and smoke. Anya steered and I grabbed hold of her waist. Our legs trailed in the dust to slow us down on the hill. Barking, the one-eyed dog chased us out to the full length of his chain. The gates in the village had just been painted blue again, and the bright new paint against the dulled boards of the fences made the road seem to shimmer as we passed.

The lake was small and choked with the plastic debris of picnics. Anya introduced me as "my classmate from Iasi." I wished she had called me her friend. She pushed me playfully, knocking me into the tall boy at my left. "Viorica, meet Evgeny Dobrescu." Evgeny muttered hello.

When it was clear Evgeny was done talking, and that the one word uttered had taken effort, Anya added, "He studies law in Bucharest." So I knew he must have received a scholarship like us. He stared off into the murky lake that refused to catch the sky's color.

He was awkward, gangly, arms dangling at his side, nowhere to put his thin, agitated hands, so tall I couldn't see up into his face without tilting my head high. Eyes of deep-set Grinauti Raia blue, burrowing in up above his nose, wide forehead running away from the eyes to meet thin hair. He walked away to smoke with the boys on the dock, with his hands in his pockets and his arms squashed to his sides.

The girls played whist, then poker for cigarettes and sticks of gum, losing the cards sometimes in the breeze. Anya ran and caught them before they blew into the water. She won more hands than the rest of us put together. They said, "She's always been that way. More like a boy. But you must know that, over in Iasi."

We tried to describe Iasi to them, the monasteries ringing the hills all around the city, the botanical gardens growing every rose of the world, the late night discos at La Scala, students packed elbow to elbow drinking Romania's cheapest beers. How in the spring the smell from the linden trees would waft down into the valleys and take hold. What we wouldn't describe was how some professors wouldn't call on us in class because we were girls, and not just girls but Moldovan girls. What it felt like to be teased about our Moldovan accents, what it was like knowing that Iasi was steeped in history but it wasn't ours, that we were guests.

Anya hugged the girl next to her, then wandered off to wade in the shallow water with another. "Go sit with Evgeny," she commanded. I sat down next to him on the dock, kicking my feet above the water, willing my sandals not to fall off.

"So, the law, then."

"Yes, the law."

"Do you like it?"

"No."

"Do you like Bucharest?"

"No." As he sat on the dock, he held his knees up to his chest.

I told him, "When you do that, sit like that, you look like you're trying to fold yourself into an envelope and mail yourself back to Bucharest. You don't like Grinauti Raia either?" He turned red and walked away from me.

I had meant it as a joke. Someone in Iasi might have laughed. Anya laughed when I repeated it to her on our way home, walking the bike through the dark village. The one-eyed dog was quiet when we unhooked the gate, sleeping with his head tucked between his paws.

·

Anya bossed me around as we walked to the village club for the Sunday night disco, our hair teased high, tripping down the road in our platform shoes. "In all of Grinauti Raia, Evgeny Dobrescu is the only boy without a girlfriend who's tall enough to dance with you," she told me. "Not that you're particularly tall, but the unattached boys are particularly short. And it will be worse down south at your work post. They'll be only grandfathers or schoolboys to take you out."

The club was nothing special, techno, scruffy floor, surly

DJs who wouldn't play requests and fought amongst themselves over whose turn it was to spin. The lights were too bright, bare bulbs dangling from a ripped-up sconce on the ceiling. Anya whispered, "They'll turn the lights off for the last dance. Make sure you're dancing with Evgeny."

We danced in a circle with Anya's friends. Every ballad, there was Evgeny, looming over me. He was wearing a shiny brown jacket that crinkled as he moved. He didn't take the jacket off no matter how hot it got inside.

In the bathroom, Anya's friends sharing lipsticks and cigarettes, Anya said she could tell that he was falling in love with me. If he was, I couldn't tell. The university boys in Iasi had held on as if the closer they got, the more likely we would be to sleep with them. Sometimes I gave in a little to have something to tell Anya because she always had something to tell me.

As the DJ turned out the lights, Anya moved on to the dance floor, spinning herself around until her partner caught up with her. As my eyes adjusted to the darkness, I could see the dark shadowy forms of people kissing throughout the hall. Evgeny and his jacket were waiting. I put my head on Evgeny's shoulder. It squeaked.

"That's better," he said, and leaned his chin on the top of my head. "See what can happen when we get along?"

•

I woke up to use the outhouse late that night. The air was still, the way it is before dawn on a blisteringly hot day. The one-eyed dog was up, nipping at my heels. Anya's grandmother grabbed my arm as I came back in. She slapped a fifth of vodka into my free hand and said, "Hey girlie, have a drink. Come on. No, don't call Anya; just you and me." The dog sat just outside the door, his eye squeezed shut.

The vodka stung my throat. The grandmother pushed me into the chair next to her and settled herself down.

"What will you do when you leave here?" A fly landed on her cheek. Next to the black iridescence of the fly, her skin was faded and worn.

"I'm going to be a caseworker down south in Cahul." I reached over to brush the fly away. She didn't seem to notice.

"There's no money in that. You'll need a man."

"Why do we need men if I can make my own money?"

"You don't. Need them, that is. They're more work than children. Look, I prefer the dog." He woke up and panted at her beside the door.

"So you do want Anya to marry? Instead of just getting her a dog?"

"What else will she do? Have you come up with something better?" She opened the door and rubbed the dog's ears. His eye rolled back with pleasure. "You do know she's going to marry that Romanian fool Cezar? The one who's always calling her up on the neighbor's phone?"

Anya hadn't told me. I thought she liked Sorin better and didn't like either one of them very much. She laughed when I said they were cloned from some poor unfortunate original. I told the grandmother, "But you don't like Romanian boys; you don't trust them."

"I don't trust any of them. But if you didn't catch yourself a man in Romania, you better get busy in Moldova." The fly landed on the hand that stroked the dog, and this time she waved it off, and me, too. "Go," she said.

I climbed back into the bed with Anya, poking her to get her to roll over. She did, and then rolled back to me. The only way to share the narrow bed was to sleep curved around her. She always slept in the center. I used to say I didn't mind, because at least she didn't pull the covers like some of the other girls in the dormitory, or have terrible morning breath like the borderline bronchial cases. Anya's breath smelled sweetly of potatoes and dill. Anya and Cezar would be sharing a bed. Cezar would find a way to move her over.

•

Evgeny was leaving for Bucharest after the last disco of the summer. He asked me if I would miss him. We were in line for Mirinda sodas when Metallica's "And Nothing Else Matters" started playing. I thought it sounded too gloomy to be a ballad, but Evgeny said, "We have to dance."

"I'd prefer a Mirinda." I shrugged and watched Anya out of the corner of my eye. Her friends were dragging her outside for a smoke.

"What I should do is ask you the opposite of what I want, and then you'd probably do it."

Anya was holding hands with one of the boys. They didn't ask me to come or nod in my direction as the door banged behind them. I said, "If I asked you to stop dancing with me, would you do it?"

The people behind us in line bumped us forward. Evgeny's chin hit my ear. He gripped my elbows and whispered, "No. I'm in love with you." He pushed me to the corner, careful not to catch the wall's clumping plaster on our best clothes.

I said, "I'm not nice enough to you for you to even like me, let alone love me."

He told me, "I like that you make fun of me. When you told me you thought I looked like I was folding myself into an envelope? You looked at me like you were considering me for something."

"And you liked that?" I said.

Evgeny's brown sleeve shimmered in the light as he handed

me my bottle. The bubbles from the lemon Mirinda flew to my nose; the couples separated just before the techno began again and the lights went back on, insects fizzling in the clubroom's bare bulbs. Anya and her friends were not back yet.

"Yes, I like it," he said, moving toward the door and pulling it open.

I followed him outside to look for Anya. We walked over to a lonely band of poplars, ineffectual chaperones who couldn't turn to see what the bad children were doing outside the disco.

"I don't want you to kiss me," I told him.

So he did. He pulled me close, then kissed me hard, our mouths smashed together. I had my eyes closed so I could imagine someone else, anyone less real than Evgeny whose stiff jacket smelled of too much cologne, who was holding me tighter than anyone in Iasi ever did, whose hands were unbuttoning my blouse and then roaming under the flowery bra Anya had selected for me. He squeezed my breasts like the grandmother choosing fruit. His mouth tasted of cigarettes, which seemed to be more of the essence of Evgeny than the fakery of the cologne. When he tried to pull me down to the ground, I stopped him. We sat together in the dusty grass, but I wouldn't let him kiss me anymore.

"Evgeny, why do you love me?" I asked him. He was still holding on to my hand, leaning back against a tree, his eyes closed.

"You're different. Unusual, even."

"Like Anya."

"Anya! Anya's nothing. You're nothing like Anya. When you grow up, I'll be waiting." He dropped my hand and with his long fingers, brushed the dust off the brown jacket. He stood up and left me behind with an over-elaborate bow.

•

I didn't tell Anya about Evgeny or ask her about Cezar at first. I wanted to, on the walk home, and later, while we had wine with the grandmother, more than usual because the grandmother said her head hurt. She wouldn't drink alone, so we finished off the jug. I wanted to tell Anya about Evgeny after the grandmother went to bed. Anya and I ate a bowl of cherries and spat the pits out, trying to hit the one-eyed dog on the head. I wanted to when we took turns at the outhouse, waiting under a star-scattered sky.

I waited until we pulled on our nightshirts, pulled down the sheet, climbed into bed, turned out the lights. "Evgeny's in love with me."

Anya poked me in the arm in triumph. "I knew it! So?"

"He told me at the disco, when you were out by the lake."

"And?" She undid my braids and fluffed my hair about my ears. She hadn't done that in a long time, since the winter before at its coldest, when we had been huddled alone in our bed under wool blankets. The other girls had gone back to their homes to wait for the heat to come on. We'd stayed to study for the exams in the library from the time it opened until it closed. We couldn't afford the train tickets back to Moldova. Back in the dorm, we made a tent out of the blankets of the other girls and read case studies out loud to each other by candlelight. Before bed, we would undo each other's braids. When Anya combed out my hair, she'd pull. If I squealed, she'd kiss the back of my head and the comb itself and start over.

"Your grandmother thinks I'm running out of time."

"What does she know? She's ancient. I say do what you want, Viorica. You can have as many and as few boys as you like."

She kissed me good night, brushing her lips against mine. It was the same simple, barest of kisses, the kind we used for all of our greetings and partings, the same kind I used with the other girls in the dormitory, with my grandmother, with Evgeny. I thought I could taste the wine in the corners of her mouth. My tongue darted out to touch them, almost inadvertently, I swear, as if it were my badly behaved one-eyed dog. She let me part her lips, kept her face turned toward mine, and kissed me back, her tongue moving bossily, with the force and determination that Anya, of course, would have. I closed my eyes and touched my tongue to the roof of her mouth, to the sharp edges of her teeth. I stroked her hair and let it run through my fingers.

She closed her teeth over her tongue, then her lips, and shifted away from me. The sheet bunched up around her tanned legs. She shook her head and said, "You're not a bad kisser, you know. Evgeny will love it, or whichever boy you choose."

"I wish you were a boy," I whispered. My hands moved, now, to touch the soft pads underneath her eyes which always looked tired, as if she never slept, although I knew better than anyone how she slept the sleep as deeply as an overtired child at the end of each day.

"Viorica, what a sweet boy you'd be. I'd marry you in a minute." She yawned. As I looked at the cavern of the mouth that I had just kissed, and watched those blue eyes flicker open and close above the dark half moons where my fingers had just pressed, I knew that she did love me, she loved me best, but that this kiss would be the only one between us. We would remember it forever, but we would never talk about it, and even in our memories she might blame it on the wine.

"You're going to marry Cezar." I traced her cheekbone with my finger.

"Who told you that? My grandmother? Nothing's decided yet. Nothing, Anya, nothing at all! You know I would have told you. He might not even be placed in Bucharest. And I told him I won't live with my mother-in-law, not ever. I'd rather he come here to Grinauti Raia, as awful as that would be, than live in a crowded apartment in Iasi. Here we could breathe a little." She hugged her knees to her chest. I don't think I'd ever seen her more guarded.

I reached for her hand. "Why didn't you tell me?"

"I guess I thought you'd be jealous." She squeezed my hand hard.

I swallowed and said, "Jealous of Cezar."

"Of me, of course. I thought you might be jealous but it's different now that you have Evgeny. Maybe we'll all be in Bucharest together! Besides, now that we're done with university we won't be together all the time, anyway. You knew we weren't going to be old maids forever." She dropped my hand. She turned away from me to look out the window and into the night.

I whispered, "I knew."

"Bedtime," she said. She stretched out, pulled the sheet up under her chin, and tossed an arm over me casually. In that moment, I couldn't make the switch, to exchange one pair of Grinauti Raia eyes for another. Anya for Evgeny. To leave the love of my girlhood and cling to the love they would let me keep. I don't know what evil eye has looked upon me and made me like this, still when I should move, faithful when it is time to change.

Anya would marry Cezar, have children, bring them back to Grinauti Raia to pick cherries and swim in the lake. Anya who knew me better than anyone would spend her life with someone else. I was deviant. It was deviant to want to be with

the person you loved most and to not want to be with someone you just met, deviant to be uninterested in that stupid
attraction between men and women, the sudden, random,
lazy love Evgeny offered. I moved out from under Anya's arm
and tried to sleep, curled up in the corner of the bed, our
bodies just barely touching beneath the sheet.

•

Evgeny left for Bucharest. I didn't say good-bye. I didn't want
to give myself the chance to say yes to him, to fall into the
trance that Cezar had placed Anya in. I followed Evgeny's
bus a little bit out of town. The gates were dusty blue now,
August dull. The bus had to swerve to avoid the one-eyed
dog. There were pieces of paper caught in the poplar trees by
the lake. Evgeny's cheek was pressed up against the smudged
glass, I think, the brown jacket rolled up for a pillow. Or
maybe it was the face of another young man leaving Grinauti
Raia. Or leaving another village, for the bus started up at the
Ukrainian border and would wind its way down south.

At the end of the summer, I took that bus myself. I began
my life here, in this town. I take care of married women with
terrible husbands. I share a studio apartment with another
caseworker—orphans are her specialty. There is gossip about
us, but the men know we know too many secrets so we are
left in peace.

Sometimes I dream about Anya. She's dancing under
cherry blossoms under that Grinauti Raia blue sky. Her hair
lifts to her ears as she spins faster and faster. I'm waiting for
her, up in the tree. The tree is heavy with cherries, so some-
how it must be spring and summer all at once, flowers and
harvest together. I drop cherry pits on her head and wonder
if she'll notice. She doesn't look up.

WORLD'S OLDEST LIVING MUSICIAN

Ten kilometers outside of Iasi on the Pascani road, they swerved in and out of the narrow lane, their Dacia bounced by potholes. Drivers from the city going to other cities raced to pass them from behind. Village traffic in front: ancient buses jammed with people, goats pushing their heads out windows. The buses stopped at every hollow, and the carts drawn by decrepit horses had no desire to pull over into the mud to let them pass.

The violinist was at the wheel, and she loved to drive, the more complicated roads the better. She was tall, folded into the Dacia as if it were a clown car, but she didn't mind. Her half-drawn, sleepy eyes, which made her appear as if she were listening to secret music on a private frequency, masked the nervous energy pouring out of her fingers. She honked to get the goats bleating. She forced carts into the mud.

Her current partner in more ways than one, the folklorist, fiddled with the radio dial, searching for anything that wasn't *manole*, the hybrid Gypsy pop form he detested, not that Romanian pop would be any better. He was a man who liked old things. He liked his music and fashion to come from before the war. Romanians didn't have to ask, which war? They knew he meant World War II as soon as they saw him in his shabby suit and fedora, his wire-framed glasses perched on his upturned nose. Sometimes he carried a pipe. He was impish and slight. He bent down as he asked questions to win the hearts of children and the most shriveled-up, aged villagers. He and the violinist would become part of folklore themselves, the first foreigners sighted by more villagers than he could count.

They stopped for coffee at a roadside cafe. She demanded Turkish coffees, strong and hot. He asked for cigarettes. She incessantly tapped the pack against their plastic table. The other customers were drunk, wavering where they stood. They stared at posters of naked women wearing fur hats and wrapped in fur coats they opened to display their own fur.

The cafe was a fine place to hatch a conspiracy, and the ethnomusicologists felt like they were part of one. They were in the heart of Moldova. They could have been in Transylvania: mountain views, Sacher torte in patisseries, Austro-Hungarian influence. Alas, Transylvania had already been picked over by ethnomusicologists since the 1920s on. When they'd pulled up to those mountain villages, the locals were bored. Sadly, musicians were bored in Moldova, too. Under Ceausescu, his folklorists moved in, as aggressive in their own way as foreigners. Their nationalist concerts still aired on RTV1: fifty screaming women, fifty shrill violins.

The folklorist leaned forward. "What are we looking for? That hasn't been found?" he asked, nudging her with his pointy elbow.

She chanted, "What do we want? World's Oldest Living Musician! When do we want it? Now!"

As he cheered, the contents of his pocket spilled out onto his lap and to the sticky floor. He'd crammed it with scenic postcards of beaches and historic downtowns, snapshots from Brownie cameras once hoisted by amateur photographers, the kind of ephemera cast off by ruthless, unsentimental heirs found in antique shops between Soviet-era textbooks and plastic costume jewelry. A postcard of skinny children on a Black Sea beach, their suits bunching up in rolls as they did jumping jacks, landed on the violinist's toe. She flipped it over.

"Of course, you'd look to see what they wrote. Have you no sense of privacy?"

"You're the one who bought them," she said. "What were you going to do? Put on a new stamp and mail them again?"

He wiped his glasses on a monogrammed handkerchief. None of the embroidered letters matched any of his own initials. He folded the handkerchief around the postcard stack and left the cafe in a huff. Water from dripping icicles hit him on the head on his way out. Everywhere, ice was coursing through dirt to make more mud. In the car, he gave up on the radio to play last week's catch on the tape recorder hooked up to the Dacia's lighter. The violin's faint warbling sounded like a warning: stay out of my village, don't record me. See how I can barely make a noise? Listen to my scratchings? You're paying me for this? I spit in your soup!

"He wasn't old *enough*," she complained. "I knew more repertoire than he did."

"The people of Mamaliga de Jos are said to be very long-living." He patted her knee.

"Not while I'm driving!" she squealed, swerving through a flock of muddy sheep.

"There it is. Down in the valley."

It wasn't much of a valley, just a hollow, a depression formed by mounds, bumps, slopes, not real hills. There was a stream trickling down to the hollow, and one hundred houses scattered like toy blocks. The Orthodox church with its gleaming cross wasn't on the hills, or in the center of the hollow, but off to the edge of town, where the village receded into the mist. In the light, the peasant houses glowed cornmush yellow, the cross, too, as if the village was a fairy-tale town made of mamaliga rising out of the mud. They skidded down the muddy slope into the village. The houses were painted soft yellow, muted orange, and lime green, streaked by wind and rain, with sagging foundations. After winter's reduction of the senses to four, the village as it melted was beginning to smell like a barnyard again.

Barefoot children pushing each other into the mud stopped to chase the Dacia. The children were dark, clay-brown like the pots fired in this region, and this rich color was the physical proof for the current theory that the troupes of professional Roma musicians in contemporary Romania were only a few steps removed, by way of medieval Gypsy serfs in their chains, from Indian troubadours singing the Ramayana from town to town, bangles on their ankles rattling as they plucked their ancient instruments.

The scrawny mutts chained up to gates and henhouses growled out a melody as they drove through the maze of narrow lanes into the heart of Mamaliga de Jos' Gypsy quarter. The violinist stuck her head out the window and trilled, "Good day, my children. We're looking for Andrusha's house. Leader of Taraf de Nebuni?"

The boys stopped in their tracks, their feet sinking a little further into the mud. At the edge of town, the church bells pealed noon. The folklorist stepped out of the car gingerly. From his vest pocket, he began pulling out reserves of chewing gum.

"Don't blow the gum budget," the violinist warned.

He held gum out to the boys in a fan of pieces, and they took them solemnly. The boldest one said, "Andrusha's house is down the road to the right. But you can't drive through."

The violinist opened the trunk for her violin and the battered valise that held the recording equipment. As she slammed the lid down, her eyes met those of a row of little girls, their dark eyes unblinking, wiping the snot running down their cheeks with their chubby fists as they sniffed at her.

Andrusha was waiting for them at his gate. Broad shouldered and stocky, chest hair peeking out of his coat, hair leaking out of his ears, he crushed the folklorist to his breast. "My brother! At last you've come!"

He took the violinist's hand to kiss it. He stopped and stared, puzzled by her frayed mittens. She tugged them off and jammed them into her pockets. She flopped her right hand in front of Andrusha, who took it gratefully. "I kiss your hand," he said, bowing slightly.

"Oh, Andrusha," she gushed, "I never thought we'd make it. It would be so much easier if your cell phone worked up here!"

Andrusha tossed the valise up onto the immense tiled soba that dominated the room. His tiny wife, who they first confused for one of the children, tucked a wool blanket around the violin case. Her earrings glinted gold. Nothing else in the room was bright. A single bare bulb hung from the ceiling; the windowpanes were glazed over with soot. A row of quinces hugged the windowsill. There were handmade woolen rugs on the whitewashed walls, draped over the soba, covering the sagging bed, on the stools framing the table, everywhere but the floor. The rugs were done in patterns of gaudy pink, crimson, and aquamarine flowers against a black background. Exactly the kind the folklorist hated: traditional patterns, chemical dyes.

"Children, call for my Taraf. My wife, fetch a little something from the cellar for our gadje guests," commanded Andrusha. The children shuffled out slowly until Andrusha clapped his furry hands.

"It's left to me to pour the wine, if you will be the ones who drink it." He took up from his table a ceramic jug painted with the same impossible flowers and poured wine into a tumbler.

The violinist demurred. "My fingers have to be sharp, Andrusha, to keep up with your Taraf." She pushed it back across the table.

"Nonsense! Wine's fuel for fingers."

"Is it *vin de casa?*" asked the folklorist.

"But of course. You're going to tell me that the good wine of Mamaliga de Jos is too powerful to let you push the bulky buttons on that machine of yours?"

"How old are the barrels you use to age the wine?"

"How old? What a strange little man you are."

"And how," added the violinist.

"From my grandfather's day. Maybe older. This wine, if we could ship it to France, if we had modern bottling equipment, we'd all be rich."

"Noroc," toasted the folklorist.

Andrusha poured again and carried it over to the violinist. He cajoled, "Between us musicians. How can you not drink my *vin de casa?*"

The violinist held the glass daintily, pressed between her thumb and forefinger. She tossed her head back, her hair settling around her like the haloes in Orthodox icons.

Andrusha toasted, *"La multi ani!"* Andrusha's wife arrived with sheep's cheese and cold mamaliga, pickled cabbage salad, and wrinkled grapes. The cheese reeked of the barnyard from which it came, and the mamaliga was as slippery as a fish.

Andrusha's dog throttled himself at the throat with the full length of his chain barking in warning. "Did someone call for Taraf de Nebuni?" a baritone bayed at the door. Twenty gentlemen entered the room, dressed in shimmering polyester suits of plum, emerald, ruby, and olive, porkpies perched gallantly on their heads, muddy dress shoes on their feet. Burnished brass instruments, accordions in embroidered cases, slinky violins were tucked under every other arm. They were uniformly portly men, with bellies that proclaimed their presence a step ahead of them, but none of them was as monumental as Andrusha himself. Behind them, the children, hands behind their backs.

Andrusha leapt up, pulling the violinist to her feet. "Nebuna, you'll play with Taraf de Nebuni. How can you refuse me in my own house?"

"Impossible," she said. Before the violin was nestled between her shoulder and chin, the Taraf was off. Brass instruments trumpeted out a fanfare, propelling a wild syncopation while violins soared above, each group daring the other to go faster.

When the violinist began to play, her notes hung over the others. She used less vibrato, she was hitting the melody, not playing in its corners. Watching Andrusha—his eyes closed tight as his bow ripped across his violin, sweat dripping on his forehead from his thick hair, his stance constantly adjusting—she saw herself on the unpaved road into Mamaliga de Jos, walking barefoot through the mud, getting closer and closer to a village that shone like gold. Inhaling and exhaling to the downbeat, tapping her toe as the road bent up to meet her, her eyes half-closed to the meeting of her secret music and Taraf de Nebuni's, she began to play within the piece instead of through it.

It was a *sirba* in the northern style that the folklorist had heard a thousand times. He wasn't impressed. Too much Bollywood in the screeching of the brass, too much Turkish pop pushing the accordion along, thoroughly corrupted. There was nothing left of his fragile world between the wars, no glimmer of klezmer and jazz and Hungarian classical music and the gypsy oral traditions. He didn't bother to balance the contrast between bass and treble, to build a filter to block out the children shuffling their feet up on the soba. It wasn't a recording he'd want to hear again. There wasn't a gray hair on a single head of these musicians.

The violinist kept up with the Taraf. The musicians she regularly played with in Bucharest were amateurs compared to the Nebuni. The room seemed to close in on them as if they were in danger of becoming rolled up in the rugs, the soba's tiles crashing down on their heads. The music teased out the smell of quinces, stilled the barking of dogs. The children whirred around the table, stuffing the fattest grapes into their mouths. The folklorist swung little girls round and round until they hit themselves in the head with their own braids. One got gum in her braid and wept in the corner. Her sobs echoed as the sirba finally and abruptly stopped.

Spent, the Taraf slouched against the rug-covered walls while Andrusha's wife poured wine. The violinist asked breathlessly, "So where's the oldest musician? The one you were telling me about? Who played with your grandfather?"

Andrusha shrugged. "Oldest? I thought you were joking about 'oldest.' Who isn't interested in the best? Taraf de Nebuni, we're the best. The absolute best outside of Bucharest. Oldest? Who've they played for, the old ones, but other villages just like this one? They don't know how to play for anyone but themselves. We've played in festivals in Bulgaria and Poland. *We've been to France.*"

The folklorist folded his arms. He said, "Andrusha, have you been wasting our time? Have you had us come all the way up to Mamaliga de Jos to hear Taraf de Nebuni again? Because we've already heard you play in Bucharest. Twice.

And you're not old. You don't even play in the old style!" He pulled out the tape and tossed it on the table.

The Taraf de Nebuni arrayed themselves behind Andrusha, glaring at the folklorist.

"You are the best," said the violinist. "I can barely keep up with you. I don't deserve yet to play with you, and maybe I never will. We're looking for the oldest musician, because we're trying to understand *how* you became the best."

Andrusha's wife said, "What's with you, gadje?" Her hands were on her hips, her tiny frame taking up as much space as possible, like a housecat trying to scare off a rival. The members of Taraf de Nebuni nudged each other in the gut. The children on the soba giggled.

She asked scornfully, "Why do you think the Moshul is still able to play? And if he could play, at his age, why do you think he would play for you?"

"How old is this Moshul?" interrupted the folklorist.

"Old enough," said Andrusha.

"He fought in the Great War," Andrusha's wife shouted, stamping her tiny foot, her black eyes flashing. The folklorist was delighted by her. "He is the Moshul to us all."

"So you really want to see the Moshul?" Andrusha asked the violinist.

"Oh, yes. Andrusha, you know what he could teach us because you've been taught by him." The violinist ran her fingers through the hollows of her violin as she talked, as if the Moshul could teach her how to play the very holes themselves.

"Go to the house of the Moshul then," said Andrusha's wife. She shooed the children off the soba, slid the stools underneath the table, wrapped the mamaliga and cheese in a threadbare towel, and turned the tumbler upside down.

"Will he speak to us? Andrusha, can you introduce us?" pleaded the violinist.

"What ever makes you think the Moshul will even be awake?" asked Andrusha's wife.

"I'll take you to the Moshul, if that's what you want."

They walked out into the dimming afternoon light, Andrusha's wife slamming the door behind them. The Taraf started up a march. Panting, smacking their now tasteless gum, the children trailed afterwards. The violinist squeezed the folklorist's hand. She knocked on the door before Andrusha could. She beamed at the wrinkled man who leisurely opened it, letting three toddlers squeeze in through the crack. He patted each one on the head as they darted in.

"We're so pleased to meet you," she said, reaching out her mittened hand.

"That's not the Moshul," Andrusha said, tugging at her mittens so that the man who was not the Moshul could kiss her hand. "That's the Moshul's grandson."

The Moshul's grandson wouldn't let the Taraf de Nebuni in. "The Moshul is sleeping. Andrusha, send your crazy boys home." They wouldn't. They waited in the yard, playing for the children. The Moshul's grandson peeked out at the Taraf from behind a dingy lace curtain.

There were rugs on these walls, too, in natural colors, the brightest a blood red. Above the rugs, someone had stenciled a border picking up the rugs' geometric flowers, but the stencils were fading into the wall, as if the whitewash was swallowing them whole. Spider webs dangled from the eaves and the corners of the soba. By the window, old North Korean calendars with pin-up girls smiling in their bulky traditional costumes had been glued directly to the wall, the lumpy glue giving the girls wrinkles to match the Moshul's grandson.

There were piles of carrots, beets, and potatoes in the corner. Nobody had bothered to put them in a barrel, a bucket, a bowl. The toddlers kicked at the potato pyramid until they got one to roll along the gritty floor. "Naughty children," the Moshul's grandson murmured.

His words disturbed a lump on the bed's sagging mattress, covered in coats that slid to the floor as the wizened form of an ancient child sat up rubbing his eyes. Before the violinist could say anything, Andrusha said, "That's not the Moshul."

"Who, then?"

"That's the son of the Moshul."

"Is the Moshul even here?" she cried.

"Don't worry, my *nebuna*," said Andrusha. He pointed to the mound of twisted blankets on the soba. "This, this is our Moshul."

"Andrusha, who are these people?" said the Moshul's son, yawning.

"American ethnomusicologists from Bucharest."

"Again! These people hound you, my child, but why have you brought them here?"

"They want to hear the Moshul play."

"He hasn't played in fifty years!"

"It's over," said the Moshul's grandson, stirring the pot on the soba. He could barely reach it, even on his toes. "He played for my father, and he played for me, but he won't play for his great-grandson or his great-grandson's fancy friends."

The Moshul's grandson dragged the table to the bed and Andrusha jumped to help him. The folklorist tried to help, but they wouldn't let him. Andrusha brought down the pot from the soba, and the Moshul's grandson poured thin soup into bowls. Andrusha pulled up stools. They warily watched the potatoes and carrots float through the beet-purple broth.

"Eat, eat!" ordered the Moshul's grandson.

The church bells pealed, the vibrations traveling across the hollow. Even through the filmy windows, they could see darkness falling. The Taraf stopped playing, and the noises of the children scuffling and prattling ceased. In the quiet of the Moshul's house, in the growing gloom in the soba's corner, the mound of blankets stirred.

"That's the Moshul," Andrusha said in case they had forgotten.

A desiccated head poked up from the blankets. "Andrusha, my child," it whimpered imperiously. The Moshul's head was dotted in liver spots as dense as a leopard's coat. His eyes, cheeks, and lips had shrunken in, hugging his skull, so that the only remaining feature was his imperious nose that cast shadows against the Korean calendar girls as he turned his head about this way and that.

A bony finger beckoned. Andrusha ran to the Moshul's side. The Moshul bent down from the soba to whisper in Andrusha's ear.

"Eat, eat," said the Moshul's grandson. He poured new soup into empty bowls. He pinched the nose of the Moshul's son, forcing his mouth open for more.

The Moshul announced shrilly, "I, I, am the Moshul." He bowed his head and settled back into the blankets.

The ethnomusicologists stared, unable to believe their luck. They'd interviewed musicians as old as the Moshul's grandson, and had their best success with the dwindling generation of the Moshul's son, but they'd never been in the presence of someone as old as the Moshul himself.

"Speak up! Speak up, I say. I can't hear you." The sunken eyes blinked. He kept his mighty nose tilted up towards the ceiling. His ears were flattened to his skull. To be reduced to a nose in a smelly village like Mamaliga de Jos! What a fate for a musician. What a fate for anyone.

The folklorist asked, in his dulcet, most ingratiating tone, a tone largely lost in Romania sometime before the second World War, the tone that made old men croon lullabies for him and ladies explain the oldest, dirtiest jokes, "May we record your answers to our questions?"

The nose wavered. "Ha! If you dare."

The violinist couldn't wait for the folklorist to finish his syrupy set-up. She blurted out, "How many *doinas* do you know? How many *horas*?"

"Many."

"How many?" she pressed, ignoring the burping of the Moshul's son, the Moshul's grandson's sighs.

"None."

"Did you play with Moldovans? Jews? Hungarians?"

"I played alone."

"Alone?" the folklorist asked. Those years had to have been a time of hybrid musical communities, of possibilities for folk culture that were neither the Western lonely brilliant artists nor the monolithic, mindless group art of communist ersatz folklorica. The Moshul wasn't saying what he was supposed to say.

The Moshul's bony finger came out again to admonish them, the shadow slashing across the calendar girls. "I played with anyone who was there. Gadjo, yid, Russian, stranger— we didn't care. We got paid. There was wine. Villages could have drowned in it. Women when we wanted them." He closed his eyes tightly.

The violinist stood below the soba, pleading, "What was your first tune?"

"I won't tell." The nose smugly held itself higher in the air.

"Maybe you could play it for us?" coaxed the folklorist, fiddling with his machine to make sure that the Moshul's voice would register.

"*Nu*," he said. "*Nu, nu, nu, nu.*" His voice, even as he tried to be fierce, held as much force as the chirping of crickets. There was something more plaintive about *nu* than *no*, an opening up of the throat instead of a rounded, abrupt *o*. *Nu* was a violin that broke the violinist's heart.

"*Nu*. Niciodata," he hissed at Andrusha, who backed away into the arms of the Moshul's grandson. Was the Moshul trying to say that not only would he not play, he had never played, that he was a fraud, that he'd usurped the title of World's Oldest Musician from some other, older Moshul? Who could question him? Who else remembered songs from before the Great War?

The folklorist flipped through his snapshots until he found one of a village wedding. A young gypsy stood in the center of the square, poised between the moment of tucking the violin beneath his chin and beginning to draw his bow across the strings. Although younger than the other musicians, and possibly the only gypsy in the band, he was dressed in a woolly shepherd's hat, embroidered shirt, and felt boots laced up to his knees. Above his fine Roman nose, his dark eyes were wary and glared dead on at the camera. He'd seen the photographer, and wouldn't draw the bow. He'd stay in this moment in between, just for spite, to keep himself from being recorded in a moment in which his dignity was not arranged to his liking but this stranger's.

"Is that you?" asked the folklorist. The fire in the soba hissed and crackled. The Moshul held up his skeletal hand out over the soba to ward him off. The folklorist held the postcard up closer to the Moshul's glassy eyes.

The Moshul's talons gripped his arm and pinched, knocking the picture to the floor. The folklorist darted to scoop it up and brush it off. The Moshul shook his head frantically, his nose bobbing up and down. "*Nu. Nu. Nu.*"

"Could it have been you?" the folklorist demanded, as if he were a detective in a city police station instead of an ethnomusicologist in a peasant's shack in the middle of nowhere after nightfall.

"Is it possible? *Nu!* I tell you *nu.*"

"Isn't there anything you can tell us?" the violinist begged. She stood in front of the Moshul, her legs apart in the stance that made her appear at her smallest, most vulnerable, her palms open.

"No," he said. "I'm done."

She stepped up to him, her hands gripping the soba's ledge.

The Moshul leaned his head over the soba and whispered into her ear, "There's nothing here, little girl. Nothing for you. Music? It's gone. Nothing here but death and decay and an old man stuffed with dirty, dirty thoughts. Girl, you reek of sex. They've never sent a woman before. Tell them to do so again. Tell them even younger. And naked. And plumper."

"Andrusha, get them out of here!" cried the Moshul's grandson, wringing his hands. "Can't you see it's late? You've tired the Moshul out, and Tata, too. Who will have to pay when they're cranky and naughty, staying up late and asking for sugar in their tea? Me!"

Andrusha led the violinist by the hand out of the house of the Moshul. The folklorist, and then the Taraf and the children, dawdled behind them, the only sounds they made their feet slipping into the mud. Andrusha said, "I never wanted to take you there."

The citrus-colored houses of Mamaliga de Jos were silvered

in moonlight. They now looked cheap, made of tin, a reverse Potemkin Village designed to display poverty instead of wealth, as if inside the houses were treasures the villagers didn't want anyone else to have, treasures they guarded the way the Moshul hoarded his music.

The engine sputtered when the violinist turned the key in the ignition. The Taraf pushed the Dacia out of the thickest mud only for it to settle again. The tuba player's jumper cables had no effect.

"You must stay tonight," said Andrusha. "My wife will prepare a feast."

So they would have to stay in Mamaliga de Jos forever. The ethnomusicologists would settle down with each other, the folklorist's head resting on the violinist's shoulder until his fedora fell off, crushed in the cranny between them. Someday, they themselves would be the oldest musicians in the village.

"We've got to get out of here or I am going to freak out," said the violinist.

"Leave the Dacia?" asked the folklorist.

"It can't be more than two kilometers back to the main road."

The violinist grabbed her violin. The folklorist followed, his valise banging against his legs. The children took them to the stand of oaks at the village's edge.

"Aren't you going to take our picture?" asked the boldest boy.

"It's too dark, my dear," said the folklorist. "Next time."

The children jumped up and down and waved not just from their wrists, but elbows.

He'd come back for the Dacia with a city auto mechanic. He'd bring a calendar to bribe the Moshul's grandson. He'd show the Moshul his postcards and snapshots, his collection of photographs of gypsies and Jews probably lost in the camps. They sold them in Transylvanian antique shops, jacking up the prices for the children of Holocaust survivors going on to Sighet. He was incapable of abandoning the possibility of talking to the last citizen of his lost world.

"The Moshul's beyond senile to a whole new category," he said.

"That just makes you like him more. Do you think that once you get that old, even music goes?"

"All you have to do is look at me to know I think that everything lasts." He grazed her earlobe with an airy kiss.

As they trudged uphill through the hall of trees, they heard music through the leaves and branches, through the mist. It was the brass of Taraf de Nebuni, drumming them out of town. In the woods, the notes floating off unbound into the night sky before the next note could be registered by human ears, the music itself sounded haunted. It was impossible to tell if it was an invitation to return or an announcement of exile.

"Someone killed the violins," he commented.

"Someone killed the *violinists*."

"Stuck-up bastards, violinists. I'll take brass any day."

They stood at the fork of the road to Mamaliga de Jos, the violinist's thumb in her mitten out as high as she could extend it. He danced around her, kicking up tufts of mud and grass wherever he landed. He kept it up, long after they could hear the last lingering coda from the Taraf de Nebuni.

UNDERGROUND PASTRY

Opening

It's a storefront that has gone through multiple incarnations, the kind that lets you date the era as easily as the calendar. We haven't been in the City long after spending last year on the planet Versa apprenticing, and we walked around looking for a neighborhood that might work: plenty of foot traffic, but cheap enough rent. We've found an apartment in a far cheaper neighborhood, two elevated ribbon stops away, but we'll only sleep there, and some nights, we won't make it back to sleep. We'll count time watching the pod launches through the skylight, to Versa, to Yorn, to Leleonia, and further, planets we've never been to. But we have all their cookbooks.

We've put up the sign in the window promising Bedapian pastry and we watch people count down the days until we open, stopping to peek in on their way to and from the ribbon mornings, evenings. They watch us painting the shelves, stripping down the walls, making everything barer, sparser, plainer, but the effect is less weirdly elegant than making the shop look poorer than before. Maybe it would work in another neighborhood, somewhere that the contrast between clutter and junk is more than organized, catered, curated clutter.

Oculata's Pastries, the sign says in Bedapian, in Bedapian script, in apricot paint with white trim, like the cheap creamsicles you can buy in the converted amusement park along the old wharf as you sit and watch the pod launches, but our customers insist on calling it the Bedapian bakery, even though it isn't a bakery, technically. Bedapian: specific, not just the planet of Versa, but the country of Bedap. My family is Versan, although I grew up in the City. We aren't Bedapian, but I've been studying Bedapian cookery every summer for as long as I can remember, apprenticing with cousins of cousins, and reading old cookbooks all winter. The medieval ones of the lost cooking arts out of the nunneries are the best ones, even if all the measurements have to be converted from the old Bedapian systems to City metric.

I have a Bedapian name because my grandmother liked it. It means *eye*, and I have a name pastry, an oval with a furry apricot in the middle for an iris, a conenut mashed in for a pupil.

My husband isn't Bedapian, either, and not Versan at all, a City boy through and through, but he's a Bedapian wannabe. (For the purpose of this Device Diary, my first Device Diary Entry on behalf of Oculata's Pastries, I'll call him Oculus. It's not his name, but now he wants me to call him Oculus all the time. He's turning into a character.) He dresses Bedapian, like a Bedapian teenager anywhere, the tight trousers, the sandals with striped yellow socks, T-shirts in Bedapian script with lyrics from vintage Bedapian bands with tiny holes the Bedapian moths had pricked through. He's ridiculous, but so committed.

No Bread

Together, we offer the promise, the crunch, the texture, and taste of authenticity. We don't make bread, as the three other bakers up and down the street keep whispering when we became popular, when the lines went out the door even in winter. *They don't make bread. How can you call yourself a bakery without bread?*

But we don't call ourselves a bakery. It's pastries. We're a patisserie. It's not bread, the staff of life. It's pastries, the ridiculous luxury that requires sugar, medieval wealth to colonial wealth to postcolonial wealth. People with so much money that they can pay others to spend hours in the kitchen, let alone buy the sugar in the first place. Bread is life. Pastry is art.

Savories, Specifically, Churches

When we moved to the neighborhood, we found out it was full of pregnant ladies and new parents strolling infants about as if they were something precious. Like a Bedapian T-shirt ringed in moth holes under glass. (Oculus' image, not mine!)

All the mothers craved were the small savory Bedapian pastries that looked like peasant churches with steeples made from slivered nuts. They had fatty ground lambkin meat inside, and cone nuts, and dried furry apricot chunks, and were covered in sea salt that looked like small stones and made the churches glow in the light. Oculus kept asking me why the way they looked mattered. Would the babies be religious? Would the babies grow up to become Bedapian nuns?

The best, most complicated Bedapian pastries were perfected in nunneries, the nuns working to delight the nobility they'd so recently left. (Most of them were third or fourth daughters, practically abandoned at the convent gates and baking for the older siblings who forsook them.) These pastries they wrought require hours even when done by many delicate hands, the meditation of many dainty souls.

I wasn't sure the furry apricot jam stained-glass mattered

to making eaters religious, in the church pastries, I mean, since they would be instantly eaten, but the more I thought about the churches, I couldn't separate the image of the little churches in a row in the case or nestled together in a box tied up with string, as if any village would ever have more than one, from the taste itself, of the butter and fat and salt and the layers and layers of pastry melting on the tongue. If I have a religion, it's the religion of the tongue and not the eye.

Except for the pregnant ladies, the savories didn't sell, and the church pastries weren't supposed to be eaten year-round, but just during the Holy Month. At first, I didn't mind making and selling them out of season, but soon, it felt decadent, and then, it felt wrong.

No More Savories

The pregnant ladies were most indignant about the reduction of savories, and with all their complaints, it was easier to cut out savories altogether, not just the churches, but all of them. I type this DDE to explain what Oculata's Pastries will and will not be doing.

It appears that the City has voted no on savories. Every savory that sat uneaten in the case was a savory that could have found a home.

If you don't want something delicious and healthy and exactly what Versans eat in Bedapian cafes and kitchens, what's worked on Versa for millennia, what can I say? The City doesn't deserve it. You don't deserve it.

If you only want the sweet, you'll get the sweet. Oh, city, expect to drown in syrup. I'll glaze you whole. Even the Pods trying to launch at the port will be held by my sugary stickiness. Only the ones bound for Versa, and savories, will have the strength to escape my sweet gravity.

Dessert Isn't a Daily Occurrence

What Oculata's Pastries will not do: the saccharine, either artificial sugars or the metaphorical saccharine, the cloying and ingratiating.

Dear Citizens of the City: your tastebuds have been destroyed. One day on Versa would kill you. One hour in Bedap would kill you. Good God, if you went to Yorn, the peppery air would kill you while you still sat at the controls of your Pod. You have to retrain yourselves to taste: salty, bitter, sour, umami. Sweet only lives in contrast to the others. Sweet is a weird glucose reward, a sign of the hopes of survival, not survival itself. Sweet is killing you. The sugar you crave is squeezing your heart. Your veins and arteries have been filled with sugar water.

The City wants you that way, glazed over and dumbed. They'd put sugar in the water if they could. Maybe they have, all of us hooked up into an IV of sugar, so we can go to our airless office jobs and type on our Devices, and go home to our windowless apartments and type some more on our Devices. Or work in the warehouses stacking the containers that arrived in the port from the offworld Pods, or unpacking the containers to message them throughout the City. Whatever we're doing, waiting for the jobs that await us offworld, when our real lives will start, out of the steel, cement and glass that box us in now, our whole life feeling like we're moving through it trapped in a car on a ribbon. We can see, but we can't touch, we can smell, but we can't eat.

That's not how they live on Versa. In Bedap, the sun

shines on your skin, and it's gentle, and there's a breeze, and the radioactive level is low enough that you don't need a screen. It's sun on skin. You can touch the bark of the cone trees. You can climb them. Bedapians don't, once they're not children, but they don't mind adults from the City doing so, as long as you don't mind them laughing at you a little. You can pick the furry apricots. You can chase lambkins around a meadow.

Who's not eating the sugar in the City? The illegal aliens in the City's kitchens, that's who. They want salt, bitter, sour, umami, never sweet. The search for sweet killed their planets. The City's drive for luxury is what drove the aliens off their worlds, back to the squeezed heart of a planet we call home, dreaming of another.

Oculus keeps telling me to stop typing, that he'll take away my Device, that I still believe that any publicity is good publicity but that can't be true anymore because the customers who still come in are hostile and wary now, resentfully asking for their sugar drug. They won't look him in the eye or ask him what his Bedapian T-shirt says. The Device Diary is broadcast over and over, but the percentage of new customers plummets.

You want dessert. But I don't want you to want dessert.

I want you to need dessert, the way you need art, the way you need air, and I want you to pay me accordingly. I want you to save all month for it, the way I save so I can take a Pod to Versa in the summer. I want you to be intensely aware of time and money with each bite you take. Dessert is time itself. You are eating the hours I spend in the kitchen. You are eating the hours I spent apprenticing in Bedap, the hours I spent on Versa in my grandmother's kitchen. You are eating the time of my life. What price could I ask of you for a pastry?

No price is high enough, but I'll take a tithe of your salary, thank you. Come again.

Uses of Children in Order to Accumulate Cookies You Don't Deserve

This Device Diary Entry is about the custom of bringing in your children in order to have an extra, free cookie added to your order.

You know the cookies I'm talking about. The ones in the jar next to the Device we use for registering the buying and selling. The cookies shaped like lambkins, with a furry apricot sour glaze.

Those cookies are my childhood, and they are not for you. You cannot buy them. They are for your children.

If you walk outside my shop and eat the lambkin cookie where I can see you, and stop and pull a candied sugarroot from your purse to give your crying child, crying because you stole the cookie from their chubby little fist, you're stealing from me. That cookie will stick in your throat and scratch it, as if the lambkin had a spine, if that spine will stab at your innards until it will come out in green shit.

These cookies are for your children, and your children alone. They are not to offer you even a bite. If you must, you can smell them, but first you must stoop down to the level of the child to sniff.

Did I tell your children, I'll eat you up? Yes, I did, the little lambkins.

Don't ask me why candied sugarroot is cheaper than my pastry, at a ratio of a dozen to one. If you actually prefer the taste of a candied sugarroot, you or your screaming child, there are certainly many more places you can go to buy it than Bedapian pastry, and aren't you lucky. If you don't prefer it, and you do prefer Bedapian pastry, what does it say about you that you would rather have the cheap treat whenever you want it than wait for luxury that could transport you all the way to the planet Versa as you eat?

There's no such thing as the difference between expensive pastry, pastry as luxury and cheap, quotidian pastry. Pastry is luxury. Cheap pastry is crap dressed up to look like pastry. Cheap pastry is paid for in your blood, by your blood, by the death of your heart, by your children. Cheap pastry is pastry at its dearest.

What Oculus Does

Some of you regular customers have queried this Device Diary, and asked in the shop itself, what does Oculus do?

I stand by my oft-stated claim, it takes two to tango, baby, but I am also willing to share this information with my audience, my congregation, my flock.

Oculus is the ingredient procurer, scouring City markets for our ingredients. We will not buy in the supermarkets of the City. That's something made in factories, not anything for food, let alone art. Oculus meets wholesalers. Oculus wants us to start catering. Oculus is genial and everybody likes him. If Oculus did the Device Diary, he'd manage to be an evangelist of pastry, he cares as much as I do, but he'd work in less fire and brimstone. He isn't a pastry activist. He's an enthusiast.

And he's a prep cook. He's my apprentice. With more practice, he'll be as good as me. After hours, we take turns shooting cream into each other's mouths.

Sex Rumors

I meant that last entry to be taken literarily. We have a funnel that we use to shoot cream into each other's mouths during baking. Yes, we always sterilize before we use it on pastries meant for customers to consume. Yes, it is nothing short of transcendent.

But since the last DDE, there have been so many queries that I feel compelled to respond. The rumors of sex happening after hours at the bakery are true. I fail to understand why it would bother anybody. Isn't this a neighborhood where people moved to have children? How do these people get their children? Is each one funneled from a test tube into waiting wombs in the City Hospital?

I will try not to point out that Oculus and I do not have children because we have chosen to provide you with pastry, and we cannot, at this point, have both: a pastry career and a child.

Sometimes Oculus says, fuck it, let's go back to Bedap and work as shepherds and have all the kids we want. He does not always appreciate my artistic temperament.

Yes, Oculus and I regularly have sex in the kitchen walk-in refrigeration unit. It is sound-proof, and cold, and everything, I assure you, remains sealed in its sanitized containers.

Nothing sexual has happened to the lambkin cookies you give your children. Nothing sexual has happened to the eyes and the furry pudding you buy yourselves.

Or has it? What do you think the nuns were up to, in their convent? Delicate, experienced hands, so good at kneading and poking? There's a reason why Bedapian slang calls broth-els, convents. And that's not even to mention what the nuns were doing to each other. It was lonely, and cold, and they were teenagers trying to keep warm. What they did to each other's bodies is not so removed from what my pastry does to you, as it travels through your system, a Pod mooring in your port. Are you trembling with memories?

Silence of the Shop

Outside of the Holy Month, we are only breaking even. We are now living in the kitchen, sleeping in sacks in the back. We didn't have an expectation of doing better, not in the first year. We knew most bakeries and restaurants fail. But when the glowing reviews were typed and broadcast, when Bedapian grandmothers cried when they tasted our food and had to be hoisted to rest for a minute on the stools at the counter, we'd hoped we wouldn't be volunteering our art. Forever.

That people would care enough to pay for it.

Unfortunately, there seem to be customers for whom the experience of a single eye is enough. They can hold it in their memories, the taste evoking an era, a world, a bubble of taste, and not need another to keep the effect coming.

Our best customers are the ones who keep needing the hit, who need flavors more and more intense, in order to feel what they first felt. Pastry is a manipulation of time. My time and yours. My time as I make it, pulling at the dough until it is fine as silk, pulling it until the moment just before it shreds. My hours of manipulating ingredients so that you can manipulate your memories: as my pastry enters your mouth, there are one of two thoughts. This tastes like something amazing I have had before *or* this tastes like nothing I've ever had before. Or, best of all, this tastes like something I had before and loved and *also* like something completely new. Either way, a chronology of taste is set off in you, of the past and what you will have in the future, and most intensely, what you are having right now, in the moment, as you chew and swallow. Right now, this entry is pastry. The only way around it is to let it enter you.

Rumors of Drugs

No, in spite of my last entry, there is nothing actually physically addictive in the pastries. Oculus and I aren't dealing drugs in the back of the kitchen. Morphine powder isn't in the pastries. No, we don't grind poppies into dust and bake them into the flour. Yes, the pastries are addictive. Yes, you need them the way our lungs need air.

Yes, these rumors have meant that we are under constant surveillance by the City's Board of Health. Yes, the sleep sacks in the kitchen have caused some consternation. We now sleep outside, in the alley, under the stars, watching the pulses of light as the Pods launch. We wake up to the rumble of the ribbon, ready to serve hot, boiled beverages and eyes to the first customers of the day, our addicts, our acolytes, our friends.

Oh, customers who have stuck with us throughout our trial, by the City, by the tastemakers, by the Citizens, we thank you and love you. Don't worry. My last DDE will broadcast the receipt for eyes. We will not leave you hanging, even if the apricot-lettered sign no longer hangs upon the door and there's nothing but junk left in the shop.

Maybe pastry wasn't meant for business. Maybe the model at the convent, of nuns making the pastries out of religious devotion and out of jealousy for their noble older brothers and sisters, of high and low purpose but with no exchange of cash, no exchange of anything but a sack to sleep in and food to eat and maybe bodily fluids, is the one that should remain.

Maybe instead of being an artist, I should think of myself as a priestess.

Or maybe pastry, for me, was at its best when I was apprenticed in Bedap, always a student, again, working for a place to sleep and enough food to eat so that I could stay on my two feet to finish the pastry.

I'm taking my pastry out of circulation, out of the cases, out of the shop. To find them, search the banks of your memories, close your eyes, and eat. The best way to be a pastry activist is to force your acolytes to eat pastry in the most active, intense way, and that does not involve the grinding gears of commerce.

Receipt for Eyes

Flour ground from the Bedapian wheat kernel measured out by feel, enough to fill two fists of angelic nun hands.

An equal amount from conenut flour, ground in a mortar and pestle.

Pinch of sea salt (only that dried from Versan seas will do.)

Sugar derived not from cane, but the heart of the purple root vegetable called the swan's penis, grown only in the south of Bedap. If you haven't been able to find swan's mandrake flour in the market, you can distill it yourself and let it crystallize in the sun. You need as much as your flour weighs. Balance them on the scale until a tiny tightrope artist could walk it, or visualize an ant.

Mix the dry ingredients together, until they form sand.

Eggs (Ideally, you have inspected the hens in advance. They must be the kind of hens a rooster would find attractive.)

Water (Not City water, but since most of what you find in the market is City water with a fancy label, City water is acceptable *if* it is first saturated with basil, then drained.)

Separate the eggs and whisk the whites into a froth. They'll be your waves.

Next, add the sea to the seashore, stirring the wet ingredients into the dry. Fold the egg whites into the batter. They should remain separate and distinct.

Taking a spoonful of batter, roll ovals with your fingers, pinching the ends to make the shape of the eyes. Place them on a buttered sheet of tin.

One furry apricot, dried and quartered (It should make you think impure thoughts).

One conenut, slivered as tiny as you want your pupil to be: surprised or drenched in sunlight.

Assembled, it should look like an eye is staring up at you, never blinking.

Cover the sheet with eyes, but don't crowd them. Give them a view.

Bake until you can't stand it.

Set to cool in a window where the view never fails to defeat you.

Goodbye, or as they say in Bedap, Until We Meet Again

The shop is shuttered now, the sign down. Maybe we've packed our bags for Versa. Maybe we've slunk off in the night to a new neighborhood. Maybe we're stealthily baking pastries on the sly.

You think you've defeated us, City, but pastry will not be defeated. Pastry doesn't need you, but you need it. You need cells of pastry, pastry converts, pastry fellow travelers, pastry activism.

The pastry has gone underground.

Acknowledgments

Thanks so much to the team at Brighthorse Books for their editorial sensibilities and for publishing this book. Part of this collection was written while I was a fellow at the Virginia Center for the Creative Arts. I appreciate the time, space, and companionship. I am grateful for the support I received from the University of Iowa and the University of Illinois at Chicago, which gave me time to write. I am grateful for the professors who worked with me over the years, who made me want to write. I thank my faithful readers Scott McFarland, Mirela Ramona Tanta, Eugene Wildman, Caitlin Creevy Wootton, and especially the ever vigilant Rajesh Parameswaran, who made these stories better. I thank my parents, for telling me stories. My brother and sister, for being my first audience. My children, for letting me fall into the world of story all over again with them. And James Pate, for traveling with me from the wilds of Romania, to the Emerald City of Chicago, and on to the wilds of West Virginia, and for being my favorite storyteller.

About the Author

CARRIE MESSENGER grew up in Evanston, Illinois She is a graduate of Yale University who served as a Peace Corps Volunteer from 1994-1996 in Straseni, Moldova. She is a graduate of the Iowa Writers Workshop. In addition to publishing short stories and translations, Messenger's nonfiction has appeared in *Harpur Palate, Ecotone*, and *Barrelhouse*. She is also an associate fiction editor for the literary magazine *West Branch*. She lives with her family in Shepherdstown, WV, and teaches at Shepherd University. *In the Amber Chamber* won the 2017 Brighthorse Prize for Short Fiction.

www.ingramcontent.com/pod-product-compliance
Lightning Source LLC
Chambersburg PA
CBHW050343190726
48284CB00007BB/2126

9 781944 467135